£2.50

Our Freedoms

Our Freedoms

Essays and Stories from India's Best Writers

Edited by
Nilanjana S. Roy

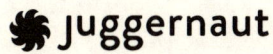

JUGGERNAUT BOOKS
C-I-128, First Floor, Sangam Vihar, Near Holi Chowk,
New Delhi 110080, India

First published by Juggernaut Books 2021

Anthology copyright © Juggernaut Books 2021
Foreword copyright © Nilanjana S. Roy 2021
Copyright for the individual pieces vests with the respective authors
Page 287 is an extension of the copyright page

10 9 8 7 6 5 4 3 2 1

P-ISBN: 9789353451455
E-ISBN: 9789353451462

All rights reserved. No part of this publication may be reproduced, transmitted, or stored in a retrieval system in any form or by any means without the written permission of the publisher.

Typeset in Adobe Caslon Pro by R. Ajith Kumar, Noida

Printed at Thomson Press India Ltd

To our freedom fighters, then and now

Contents

	Foreword *Nilanjana S. Roy*	xi
1.	Beauty and the Beast *Snigdha Poonam*	1
2.	Freedom and the Indian Constitution *Gautam Bhatia*	19
3.	Bread, Cement, Cactus *Annie Zaidi*	26
4.	Crossing Over *Perumal Murugan* *Translated by N. Kalyan Raman*	40
5.	The Freedom Exchange *Yashica Dutt*	50
6.	Krantijeevi Tarangini *Vivek Shanbhag* *Translated by Deepa Ganesh*	62
7.	An Evening Walk; Question and Answer; These Days; Falcon *Akhil Katyal*	86

Contents

8. The Women on the Wall — 92
   Raghu Karnad
9. Why I Choose Hope — 106
   Rana Ayyub
10. Agendas — 115
    Roshan Ali
11. I Have Faith in My People: Dr Usha Mehta and the Congress Underground Radio — 135
    Aanchal Malhotra
12. Emergency and Freedom — 151
    Salil Tripathi
13. Exile in the Age of Modi — 168
    Aatish Taseer
14. Vaishnava Jana to Kone Kahiye? Reclaiming Gujarati Identity from the Haters — 177
    Suketu Mehta
15. The Actual Shafi Shauq — 192
    Amit Chaudhuri
16. Arachnophilia — 203
    Amitabha Bagchi
17. Freedom and the Idea of India — 213
    Romila Thapar
18. Freedom in a Different Key: The Bhuinyas of Bihar — 224
    Gyan Prakash
19. Hasdeo Arand: Mine Is the Voice — 236
    Karthika Naïr

Contents

20.	Raga Swaraj *T.M. Krishna*	238
21.	Fear and Belonging: Fraternity in the Time of COVID-19 *Menaka Guruswamy*	245
22.	Grief and the Freedom of Forgiving *Priyanka Dubey*	259
23.	Afterword: A Brief History of Freedom *Pratap Bhanu Mehta*	269
24.	Ghazal: India's Season of Dissent *Karthika Naïr*	285

Copyright Acknowledgements   287
A Note on the Contributors   288

Foreword

Nilanjana S. Roy

One night in the biting cold of the winter of 2019, huddled in a fog so dense with pollution and the last drifting traces of tear gas that they could barely see one another, a group of students and women shared their dreams. They were out in the cold to defend two ideas, one sewn to the other: of belonging to a place and a country, and of a promise made at the time of the country's independence, a wishful promise of azadi, an elusive but always possible state of freedom.

This was not at the famous protest in Delhi's Shaheen Bagh, but in another part of the city. That winter, the discriminatory provisions of the Citizenship (Amendment) Act and the National Register of Citizens law, sharp as a knife aimed at the collective throat of the country's Muslims, had sparked some of the largest mass protests across the country. The women who led this all-night sit-in faced reprisals from state forces that were all the more brutal and unrestrained because of the lack of media attention. A few knew each other, but most were strangers, coming together in solidarity to protest the new citizenship law.

In the national capital, the events of the past few weeks had been tumultuous, one protest springing up after another, police crackdowns following in their wake. The streets swelled with songs and slogans; in the aftermath of clashes or police beatings, the pavements were sometimes streaked with bloodstains.

Many had placed their lives and bodies on the line to stay up all night, to talk and read, to share their fears and hopes for themselves and for the future of India. Sleep was one of the several casualties of that winter. Few had a peaceful night's rest, even when they took a break at home.

Most nights, people discussed the Constitution and citizenship, or sought news from the many parts of the country, from Kashmir to Assam and Uttar Pradesh, where news of severe repressions, of beatings, torture, mass imprisonment, disappearances, seeped through the few cracks in a wall of silence.

One evening, the impromptu adda was halted so that everybody could help a young mother pick tiny splinters of glass and plastic fragments out of her baby's tiny feet. The mother and child had been caught unawares when the programme – the singing of patriotic and revolutionary songs, the reading of the Preamble to the Constitution in Hindi and Urdu, some guest speakers talking of Dr B.R. Ambedkar and pluralism – was disrupted by goons from a nameless political party. (It had a name, but nobody at this gathering wanted to say it aloud.)

On other nights, the discussion veered to the slender but growing possibility of building solidarities across barriers of religion, class and caste, clasping hands despite the many divisions cemented into Indian lives. Often, people spoke of the waves of hate directed by national television channels at different groups of selected victims: liberals, academics, independent-minded universities, Muslims, Christians, other minorities, creative artists and writers, or anyone who questioned the ruling establishment.

It was past midnight when Zahreen,* a lively twenty-one-year-old who hoped to set up her own biotech company some day, said, 'Tell me what you dream about in this time,' and one by one, the group started to share.

Razia, the fifty-year-old mother of three, dreamed every night that the windows of her house were smashed, and that someone she couldn't see was breaking their front door down with an axe. Vipin, a seventeen-year-old medical student, said he dreamed of a suffocating cloud that first choked him, then spread across the country.

One young girl had the same recurring nightmare: she and her friend fled, running through empty streets, clutching one another's hands, but gradually she lost hold of her friend's

---

* All names changed to protect the identity of protesters

hand, and she could not find her way back to her again. Someone dreamed of searching through a discarded suitcase for lost papers, someone that he returned home to find that everyone he loved had mysteriously disappeared, their shopping bags and tins of baby milk knocked to the floor.

Zahreen herself sometimes woke up at night convinced that she had heard a loud explosion and that a great monster was roaming silently in the alleys of her neighbourhood. The last one to share was Khadija, seventy-two, who was well known for her ability to produce a seemingly endless supply of biscuits and chocolates from the folds of her burqa.

'Every night since this began,' she said, 'I have dreamed the same dream. They go to [Ferozeshah] Kotla and other places, and they drag out the djinns of Delhi, all of them, one by one, catching their smoke and fire in gunnysacks. The sacks wriggle on the ground as the djinns try to break free, but they are held fast, and then bruises come out on the sides of the sacks, you can see them. Then they are bundled into one of their vans, and then – oh, it depends. Sometimes the sacks are shot and sometimes they are thrown into the river, but by the end of it, all the djinns are gone.'

The group was silent and the air felt frozen, dank with pollution and fear.

'Wait,' said Khadija. 'Many nights, my dream doesn't finish here. Whatever is done to the djinns, their forms break apart into smoke and blood, and fill the air and the water and the earth. And slowly, everyone who lives on the earth

Foreword

and breathes this air and drinks that water, they also sicken, everyone suffering from the same plague. That's it, that's my dream.'

Ten days later, a wave of violence, instigated by incendiary speeches made by members of the ruling party who faced no serious legal consequences then or later, devastated several mohallas in north-east Delhi. Some called these the Delhi riots; others called them pogroms.

And a month later, in March 2020, the pandemic reached India, freezing everything in place for a while. That summer, the air felt heavy, still, unfree.

~

In 1946, a year before India wrested independence from the British, paying a blood price for freedom with Partition's jagged lines of severance, the film *Humjoli* was screened in theatres across the country.

Noor Jehan sang, '*Ye desh ye desh humara pyara / Hindustan jahan se nyara / leke rahenge hum azadi / woh din aane wala hai / woh din aane wala hai / leke rahenge hum azadi . . .*' In partial translation: this beloved country of ours, we will not stop until we've taken our freedom, that day will come.

Many years later, the azadi chant would return to India via a Pakistani feminist song that went in part, 'My sisters want their freedom'. In the late 1980s Kamla Bhasin created her own feminist version, where women sought freedom from all that held them back. 'My sisters want freedom, my daughter wants freedom, every woman's slogan is freedom. From endless violence, azadi, from helpless silence, azadi, from patriarchy, azadi, from hierarchy, azadi, for breathing freely, azadi, for moving freely, azadi . . .'

That word, and that chant, winds in and out of history's alleys, used in anti-caste movements, in women's marches, but also in all kinds of protests – sometimes, more controversially, pressed into service by separatists.

But on the streets of Delhi, the version that rang out was closer to Noor Jehan's lines in the song. It shone with love and with the determination to make something of the founding promises, to create a country based on healing the wounds of the past, not on creating new divisions and stirring up ancient grievances.

> We'll take back that freedom,
> Freedom from attempts to create differences between us,
> Freedom from hate and violence,
> What do we want? Freedom.
> We'll wrest it back, our freedom.
> It's our right, freedom.
> That beloved freedom,
> Shout it loudly: freedom.

The *Modern Review* records the moments of India's independence in its August 1947 issue – at least 200,000

Foreword

people swarmed around the Council House to celebrate the instant when Lord Mountbatten addressed the Sovereign Constituent Assembly, and the national flag was unfurled over the dome, the crowds cheering as the tricolour fluttered in the air. At midnight, the Indian Constituent Assembly passed a resolution assuming power for the governance of India. When Dr Rajendra Prasad read out the pledge, the formalities were followed by the blowing of conch shells and cries of 'Mahatma Gandhi ki jai!' before Jawaharlal Nehru rose to make his historic speech.

But by September the *Review* was recording the grim realities before the nation: the food crisis, the reports from both sides of the border of the beginning of the carnage that accompanied Partition, the trains pulling into Lahore and Amritsar with their silent, grisly cargo of the slaughtered.

It can be comforting to read unfiltered accounts of your country's past: they cut through the myths that surround any nation's founding. Independence came after centuries of uprisings and rebellions against the British; it was hard-wrested.

Late one night at India Gate, I listened to a young generation recite the promises in the Preamble, their eyes lit with hope and fervour: 'We, the People, give to ourselves this Constitution...'

Liberty, equality, fraternity were supposed to be gifts. I took those words for granted through most of my adult life, assuming that the country would always have the first, would continue to strive for the second and would never completely abandon the third.

And here we are, with all three of these extraordinary, moving promises made by the country's founders to their people in jeopardy at this juncture in the nation's history. How daring their dreams seem now – and how much trust they placed in the generations ahead, the leaders who held power over their country's fate, and were free to ignore these three essential, fragile founding values.

~

Another song of freedom, from Jharkhand:

> Sidhu, why are you bathed in blood
> Kanhu, why do you cry 'hul hul'?
> For our people we have bathed in blood
> For the trader-thieves have robbed us
> Of our land . . .

The first rebellions against the British were led by the Santhals and the Bhils, the Kols and the Mundas, as anthropologists like Dr Alpa Shah and others have recorded. The first stirrings of a desire for independence, the first banners of revolt against the Raj, were not driven by a love of a nation that did not then exist, but by a deep love and claim over the land. In the country's collective memory today, these waves of resistance have almost been erased, though these are where the seeds of freedom first took root. But in every tribe that sent its warriors up against an empire mightier and more resourceful than they could have imagined, these are living memories, preserved in song and thought. The idea of 'hul', roughly translatable as 'victory to revolution', as a just struggle against oppression has stayed alive for three centuries.

One of the biggest uprisings against the East India Company was the Santhal Hul of 1855. In 1824 the British demarcated the Santhal Pargana, calling it the Damin-i-Koh; then, as now, those who worked the land, listened to the breathing of its forests, worshipped the spirits who preserved the rivers and the earth's bounty lost their rights to the most precious part of their universe.

By 1855 the Santhals had been dispossessed, cruel taxes forced upon them. Four brothers – Sidhu, Kanhu, Chand and Bhairav – and their two sisters – Phulo and Jhano – of the Murmu clan staged a fierce, one-month war against the Raj and its agents. Sidhu and Kanhu were captured and hanged from a tree on 26 July, in Bhognadih, ratted out to the British by one of their own; Chand and Bhairav were murdered in Bahraich. This rebellion, one of many across the provinces of British India, took the lives of over 15,000 tribespeople, and entire villages were put to the torch. In some versions, it is sung that the sisters Phulo and Jhano rode into a British encampment and cut down twenty-one British soldiers before they too were killed.

Sometimes it feels as though all countries keep dismembering their own histories, forgetting and erasing too much. And perhaps none of them, from India to the United States of America or Turkey or Brazil, can move forward until they have remembered all that is pushed aside in favour of a dominant version.

Freedom is not simple. To claim it, you must know what came before. Every so often, the powerful forget this. A regime, a political movement, a strongman can briefly or not so briefly create a history shaped to their satisfaction, and that history can be dominant, for a while. But what really happened cannot be changed; the lives that people lived, the causes they believed in, what they fought for, what they yearned for, have a reality to them, and it keeps breaking through. Sometimes dormant for decades, the past can surface in the most unexpected ways.

~

Our Freedoms, this collection of essays, short stories, poems and personal memoir, was suggested to me by Chiki Sarkar, Juggernaut's publisher, as a way of exploring what this particular moment in India might hold for the future. We asked a range of writers, across generations and genres, some basic but increasingly urgent questions: What did freedom mean to them? With political and other freedoms steadily shrinking in India, what might the promises made by the nation's founders mean to Indians today?

Foreword

Their answers have an immediacy and urgency. The range of their responses, some written into the heat of this moment, some contemplative and thoughtful, are surprising and sometimes heartening. Though this does not attempt to be a serious academic exercise, I hope *Our Freedoms* might persuade other editors, writers and scholars to collect their own set of dialogues and reactions.

As an anthology, this does not attempt to be a direct response to the protests or their aftermath – from Aligarh to Delhi, students and their leaders have been arrested and jailed under the strangling provisions of an anti-terror law that denied them the basic right to bail or an immediate trial. But the winter of 2019, and the events that led up to it, left their mark on many writers from Raghu Karnad and Rana Ayyub to Snigdha Poonam and the poet Akhil Katyal, though their accounts are also reminders of other conflagrations of communal violence from Independence to this decade.

Vivek Shanbhag, Karthika Naïr, Roshan Ali, Amit Chaudhuri and Amitabha Bagchi elected to send in short stories and unsettling poems, some surreal, some hyper-real. In short essays by Aanchal Malhotra, Salil Tripathi, Suketu Mehta, moments of resistance – underground radio stations, the Emergency, another bend in the river of Gujarati history – are explored, voices reaching out from their time to our own.

Annie Zaidi's powerful essay, 'Bread, Cement, Cactus', is a reminder that to claim belonging is an act of freedom, independent of what the state or rulers might do; Rana

Ayyub explains why and how she chooses hope, in the face of a barrage of constant hatred directed against Muslims, especially those who fearlessly speak out. From his state of involuntary exile, Aatish Taseer writes of Modi's India and his own relationship with the country. Many writers chose to explore freedom through the old, deep fault lines of caste and gender and the betrayal of many promises of liberation made to both, from Yashica Dutt in her searing personal essay, 'The Freedom Exchange', to Perumal Murugan examining how caste controls every public space, and T.M. Krishna running up and down the scales of Raga Swaraj. Priyanka Dubey writes eloquently of terrible injustices, of every woman's personal freedom struggle, and the need to forgive.

In three magisterial essays, Romila Thapar re-examines the idea of India – always under threat, sometimes robust; Gyan Prakash asks what freedom would mean for the Bhuinya bonded labourers of Bihar, unless it also includes dismantling inequality; and Pratap Bhanu Mehta attempts a history of freedom itself, from philosophy to politics. And Menaka Guruswamy and Gautam Bhatia return to the Constitution, from different angles, both caught by the dream of fraternity, imperfectly realized or roughly shoved aside, but still carrying a thread of hope.

~

Foreword

It took many years to understand that the opposite of freedom is not incarceration: it is slavery. The politics of hatred have triumphed, in our country as in many parts of the once-free world. As an emotion, hatred can feel liberating – it frees people from the constraints of having to work at love for the stranger, kindness towards those not your kin, fraternity to those whose ways are not yours. It is hard work, imagining and creating a country in which every citizen might truly feel or claim their many, complex, essential freedoms and identities.

But hatred is slavery. It traps first haters and then entire countries, shrivelling their souls as they lose their guiding angels, their djinns of benevolence, and shoving them into a narrow cage. You can either build a Republic of Inclusion or a Republic of Exclusion. To do the first is far more difficult. It requires empathy, the ability to see that the needs of those with very different lives from yours are as important as your own, and humility, the ability to see beyond the privileges of being 'upper' caste or a member of a majority religion or community, of being wealthy or owning land or having access to education.

A Republic of Inclusion demands that you exercise both your imagination and your compassion. It is so much easier to exclude, to say that this one or that one does not belong, and to set little fires everywhere, forgetting the hopes, the dreams and the promises the founders of this country made to the people. It is a great deal easier to destroy freedoms than to create and share them.

Nilanjana S. Roy

The future for India often seems grim. But among the ads for Filaria, Oatine Snow cream, Calso-Phosphorin for Tuberculosis and Swadeshi Floral Essence that show up in the pages of the *Modern Review* for August 1947, there is one by the makers of Rhino Genzies that I cut out and kept.

A genzie (spelled genjee in some versions) is the humblest of garments – a light cotton vest, called a banian in Hindi. 'Whatever may be your religion and nationality,' the ad says persuasively, 'and status of life, surely you would prefer our Rhino Brand Genzies.' Perhaps freedom should be offered like that – the most everyday of commodities, available to all, regardless of their caste, creed or status, to be worn as you go about your business.

Many thanks to the contributors, who dealt with rounds of edits with remarkable patience, to our miraculous editor Jaishree Ram Mohan, our typesetter Ajith Kumar and our proofreader Shyama Warner, who kept this anthology from breaking its already overflowing bounds, and whose sharp eyes and warm hearts helped to see *Our Freedoms* through to the finish line.

1

Beauty and the Beast

Snigdha Poonam

In the riots, Noor* told me, she lost her vanity. Vanity? I asked to make sure I had heard it all right. 'My vanity box. It was worth more than one lakh [rupees].' It must have been, considering its contents. 'Two foundation tubes, three concealers, ten to fifteen lipsticks . . . I only used the top brands: Mac, Kryolan, Colourbar, Huda beauty . . .'

Noor lost much more than the vanity box. Between 23 and 27 February 2020, Hindu–Muslim riots ravaged large parts of north-east Delhi. During the burning and destruction, her beauty parlour in Bhajanpura market was looted. 'Everything was gone, from shampoos to blow dryers. They were probably more thieves than terrorists.'

---

* Names of the riot victims have been changed to protect their identities.

Luckily she wasn't in the market the day the parlour was targeted (25 February). 'I finished work at 6 p.m. on Saturday, having made six hundred to seven hundred rupees that day.' Then she left for her mother's house in Shahdara, taking the Sunday off but leaving her assistant to see through the weekend. When she heard about the rampage, her first reaction was relief: 'I had finished most of the bridal [makeup] assignments for the season.' Except the one she had booked for Tuesday. But in Bhajanpura, everything was cancelled, including beauty parlour dates.

Noor got into the business when she bought her first parlour in 2017. 'I worked there for a couple years, saved up, and bought it from my boss.' But a few months later, the Municipal Corporation of Delhi started sealing unauthorized basement establishments. 'Mine was locked up too.'

I asked her why even bother owning a parlour when, with her talent, she could get a job at any. She answered in one word: Tashan. I had never heard the word before moving to Delhi ten years ago. It translates best to 'daring', of a reckless kind that only applies to people born in this city. 'There was talk in the family and locality about me going to work even though my husband brings in enough money. But I wanted my own.'

In 2018 she set up a new parlour in Bhajanpura market, a short scooty ride from her house, renting a room and a reception area. Ladies came in hordes after she put up the board outside: Beauty Life. 'I had quality clients. Working women with beauty budgets.' A facial alone cost them between

1000 and 2500 rupees. 'Five hundred if they brought their own kit.'

By 2020 she was earning up to 60,000 rupees a month from shaping eyebrows, colouring hair and grooming brides. She didn't take all of it home. 'Part of the cash I kept in a shop drawer, hidden from my husband. If I had put it in a bank, it would have become household income.' But a secret bundle of notes can't survive a riot.

Noor returned to her parlour the following week and surveyed the wreckage in fury. Everything that could be taken was gone. She picked up the shredded posters and took stock. The water filter and hot plate were gone, but the waxing bed and shampoo chair remained. 'The only things still here are those fixed to their spots. Not one beauty product remained.' A small crowd had gathered around her. Glaring at the locals who she knew had been in the mob, she cursed their wives aloud with eternal plainness. 'May they never find an occasion again to paint their faces.'

That curse came true in a way. Four weeks after the riots, the prime minister announced a national lockdown because of the novel coronavirus pandemic. As salons and parlours shut down, men were forced to grow out their beards and women embraced hairy upper lips and greying hair. Ordered inside their homes, people had little to do, so they made bad jokes.

The bulk of India's lockdown humour sprang from the presumed horrors of women cut off from their monthly rituals of bleaching, waxing, threading and colouring. Fearing that words alone wouldn't be enough, the meme makers also gave us pictures of hairy legs and wild eyebrows.

Noor wasn't laughing at the jokes. After the riots, she stopped fussing over her appearance. She had never cared for makeup anyway; in her own expert estimation, she didn't need it. Her face glowed naturally, and she knew how to play up her features. 'A dash of kajal and a swipe of red lipstick.'

In her pre-riot photos, she is always well turned out: high ponytail, dangling earrings, snug jeans and cute tops. 'Look at me now. I look like a *gharelu mahila*. A housewife. An auntie.' She was wearing a salwar-kurta with the dupatta draped over her head. She could easily give herself a facial at home, but she wouldn't. 'The glow won't come no matter what I do to my face. It will come only when I go back to work.'

～

I first met Noor at a Hindu temple some weeks after the riots. She was part of a neighbourhood team that cooked large quantities of food on the temple premises to feed those displaced by the violence. The atmosphere was still fraught. No one slept at night. The men kept watch in shifts and the women huddled in the homes that were still standing. The temple priest remained in shock. 'The Hindus and Muslims in this colony have always been on good terms,' he told me. This isn't the first time I have heard this statement from the locals while reporting on a riot. It's easier to explain violence between neighbours as an aberration than acknowledge deep-rooted divisions.

On Sunday, 23 February, Noor received a phone call at her mother's house from her husband, Aamir. '*Mahaul kharab ho raha hai*,' he said. The atmosphere is becoming tense. She shrugged it off. By the end of that day parts of north-east Delhi were on fire, but their own locality was largely spared.

The damage stood a few stations away on the Delhi Metro. 'In places where people were provoked,' Aamir told me. On Sunday, a politician from the Bharatiya Janata Party (BJP) had addressed a crowd of party supporters in Jafrabad and asked them to 'hit the streets'. This wasn't his first call to violence. In December 2019, while campaigning for the BJP in the elections to the Delhi assembly, he had issued the command to 'shoot the traitors'. He wasn't the only BJP leader to use that poll slogan. The party lost the February 2020 elections nevertheless, winning 8 seats against 62 for the Aam Aadmi Party (AAP). Many saw the riots as the Hindu nationalist BJP's revenge against the Muslim voters.

On Sunday evening, shots were fired in Karawal Nagar, Maujpur Chowk, Babarpur and Chand Bagh. On Monday the trouble moved closer home. 'By 10.30 a.m., the riots had reached us. One by one, I kept getting calls about this happening, that happening.' That afternoon, Noor's assistant rang up from the parlour. 'She said clashes had broken out in the market. People were closing their shops. I told her to lock up and rush home.' By 2.30 p.m., the shutters were coming down but the rage was building up.

'That night, I heard a shop in the same gali as my parlour had been burnt down. Aamir told me to turn off my phone. I couldn't do that.' On Tuesday morning, ten people were reported killed in the riots. 'This madness must end immediately,' tweeted Delhi's chief minister. But it wasn't going to any time soon.

Tuesday evening, Noor's phone rang again. It was the woman who owned the shop across the lane from her parlour. 'She said a mob had gathered outside Beauty Life. They were trying to break in. I called up my landlord. He said, "I can't hold them off for long. You send someone from home to collect the valuables." I said, "How can I send someone knowing they could be killed?"' Minutes later, the mob was inside the parlour. 'They first tried to break the lock, but it was too big, so they broke the door.' By Tuesday night, even the petrol pump nearby was burnt down. The next morning, Bhajanpura was reported to be one of the worst-hit neighbourhoods.

~

At our second meeting, Noor drove me around the market on her scooty. She had picked me up on the main road. We made a U-turn from a dargah that had been burnt to ashes by a petrol bomb. A month had passed since the riots and many of the shops were reopening. As we zig-zagged our way through, she pointed to the shops that were still shut. The tailor's shop had been looted, the butcher's burnt and the bangle seller's vandalized.

'How could the mob know which shop belonged to a Hindu and which one to a Muslim? Some shops were half-Hindu- and half-Muslim-owned. Only Muslim portions were looted. Those shops weren't burnt.' Noor's parlour too escaped the ashes. 'They would have set it on fire if not for the fact that it is separated from two Hindu-owned shops by wooden partitions.'

'Everything was fine here until the elections. Then the polarization began,' Aamir told me later. Early in February, Bhajanpura's market association had put up a hoarding declaring its support for the controversial Citizenship (Amendment) Act (CAA). The BJP government's constitutional amendment granted citizenship to Hindus, Sikhs, Parsis, Jains, Buddhists and Christians from Pakistan, Bangladesh and Afghanistan who took refuge in India in or before December 2014. Everyone but Muslims. Those who opposed the act were labelled traitors. Easy to identify and fit to be shot.

By Wednesday morning, curfew was extended across north-east Delhi, but even that didn't stop the madness. When it ended on Friday, fifty-three people had died, 581 were injured, ninety-seven of them with gunshot wounds, and countless houses and shops had been destroyed.

Noor stopped her scooty outside the parlour. She had yet

to clean up the mess. It was that time of the week when her long-time agent dropped in with the newest bridal kits in the market. She showed up right on time. Noor asked her if she didn't know about what had happened. The agent said she had no idea they had come for parlours as well. She first commiserated and then offered credit. Noor asked her to come again in a week.

~

Next month, Noor received in her bank account 25,000 rupees in donations from people trying to help the riot-affected get back on their feet. It was enough cash to buy the basics and get back to business. We set out for a wholesale market in north-west Delhi the same day – Noor and her daughter, Aaliya, on the scooty and Aamir and I on his motorbike – all of us wearing masks bought in last-minute panic.

The market was deserted except for the shops selling beauty products, where parlour owners were stocking up at war scale. Noor and Aaliya were carrying a list of all things lost, one they knew by heart. Their dilemma: which items to buy with the limited budget – moisturizer or primer? Summer base or monsoon base? Highlighter brush or blending brush? They settled on a whole bridal kit.

The bridal kit is more magic wand than makeup collection. The expectations are extreme. The bride enters a parlour looking like a girl and leaves a goddess. Over the next hour,

I watched as the trio, the husband as knowing as his wife and daughter, picked eye-shadow palettes to suit summer, winter and monsoon trends, foundations that can survive sweat, tears and selfies, fake lashes as tall as a bridegroom's turban.

This was my first time at a shop for professional makeup and I felt I should buy something. I decided on a foundation. Everybody around me sprang to attention – mother, father and daughter on this side of the counter and the shopkeeper on that – all eyes on my face.

My bare forehead would not suffice. They demanded I pull down the mask and I had to obey. All of them went quiet in the way biologists do looking into a microscope. They arrived at a simultaneous conclusion: blemishes. I went back home with a tube of Kryolan No. 22. Noor reopened her beauty parlour.

∼

Twenty-four hours later, the prime minister appeared on national television without any notice and ordered a long lockdown. Beauty Life went dead once again. After six weeks, the country began to 'unlock' in phases. First trains and buses resumed operations, then shops and offices, and later temples and mosques. In every state and city, people were eager to know when parlours and salons would open, but the governments kept saying, not now. Shopping websites reported a surge in sales of personal grooming products.

Every day, I received press releases highlighting the items flying off the virtual shelves – shaving creams, electric razors, waxing strips, facial kits... But not everyone could afford to adjust to the pandemic. As the months passed, Noor's family used up every bit of their savings until they went broke. 'I have received four calls since the lockdown ended from old clients – I am talking at least 3000–4000 rupees' work – but none of them wants to come home for the service. I understand that.' Beauty, she said, is best dealt in at a parlour.

In early May, Noor told me her family would have to borrow money to buy the next week's groceries. Some of the riot victims were joining the long queues at the Delhi government's free ration kiosks for wage labourers rendered jobless by the virus, but it takes courage to act poor if one was comfortably middle class just the other day. Noor said she couldn't bear the thought. She was waiting for her rightful compensation from the state for her losses in the riots. So too were thousands of others who had listed every single item looted, burnt or destroyed against its estimated value in the government-issued forms distributed after the riots. Noor's own estimate came up to Rs 3 lakh, but three months after she submitted her form at the local police station, no one knew how far that file has reached.

At the end of May, I began looking for clues. I filed a questionnaire under the Right to Information [RTI] Act, emailed the chief minister's office (CMO), called up the Member of the Legislative Assembly (MLA) from Noor's locality and sent WhatsApp messages to the subdivisional magistrate (SDM) in charge of the paperwork. Over the following months, I kept adding more names and acronyms to what became a weekly routine of find-the-file. I received more excuses than answers.

The SDM said there were problems with her paperwork. The CMO said the Delhi government was setting a new timeline. The MLA kept saying he would update me as soon as he had any information. My RTI query was forwarded to the 'concerned authority'. That turned out to be the SDM, who was sounding more and more annoyed with me. He said I did not understand official processes.

'The file has to move through multiple departments. It's a long route. At every step there are multiple people who need to approve everything.' He said I did not understand his situation. As an administrator, his life hadn't been easy lately. 'First riots, then elections, then corona. I am working eighteen to twenty hours every day.' I told him he didn't understand Noor's situation. He said he couldn't focus on one woman when hundreds of files lay piled up on his desk.

∼

When Noor first entered her beauty parlour after the riots, what shocked her wasn't the loot alone. Besides the stock posters of beautiful models, the walls used to display photographs of Noor standing next to the brides she had made up herself. 'They had been torn up too, but only my face was cut out.' The remaining parts of the photographs stayed glued to their spots, resembling a gallery exhibition of deserted brides.

Someone hated her; maybe all of them did. 'Some people in the market begrudged my success.' I asked her why. *'Main dabang hoke rehti thi.'* Dabang, again, is a word not an ordinary person would use to describe herself. It means the kind of person who would have tashan. A man would be feared if he were dabang, a woman punished. A Muslim businesswoman acting dabang in a Hindu-dominated market would be an obvious target in a riot.

Noor wasn't conceding defeat yet. 'The market association is now saying they won't rent shops to Muslims, but there is no way I am moving out.' At the end of June, even as the virus continued to cause mayhem, beauty parlours were permitted to reopen. On 30 June, Noor opened hers. The posters were glued back together, chairs repaired, wiring fixed, and a new name board commissioned. 'We had a lot of empty cosmetic boxes lying around. We lined up those across the shelves. Who would know if they contained anything or not.'

Then she updated her status on WhatsApp and Facebook, announcing Beauty Life open. The clients didn't come rushing in, though. Regardless, she went to work every day, opening the parlour at 10 a.m. and closing it at 6 p.m. 'Occasionally someone drops in for an upper lip or eyebrow threading.' She blamed patriarchy.

'The men are going everywhere but not allowing their wives to step out. What better excuse than the virus!' I had to agree. The pandemic was more a prison for women than men, and few things spelt freedom louder than going to a beauty parlour.

Only one bride showed up in all of July. Noor and Aaliya marshalled their whole arsenal. It took two hours. The result, I could tell over a video call, was electrifying. I asked the bride if she was pleased. She fluttered her false eyelashes.

Not a lot of weddings were happening in the area. 'After the riots, the weddings are being organized during the day instead of at night,' Noor said. The makeup for a day wedding is light and easy – a bride needn't even go to a parlour. Given the circumstances, Noor was thinking of plan B: women's underwear. Hair and makeup can wait until the world is back to normal, but no woman can do without underwear.

'I know a wholesaler from whom I can buy the stock to display at the parlour. All I need is one lakh rupees to invest.' She was waiting for the compensation, but so far I had failed to trace it down. At the end of July, reacting to a petition, the Delhi government informed the Delhi High Court that it had received 3041 applications for riot compensation of which only 1526 had been approved thus far.

The process was hit by the pandemic. The forms that were filed at the police stations could not be submitted at the SDM offices and those that were submitted could not be verified. As of 29 July, fewer than one-third of the applicants had been compensated. In every riot-hit colony, everyone knew the names of those fortunate few. Noor too kept the score: 'Zaheer and sons: 5 lakh received. Damage was 1 crore. The steel grid shop got 1.25 lakh . . .' She mentioned at one point a beauty parlour owner, another Muslim woman, whose bank account had been credited. A single bank transfer from the government was able to make hundreds of people anxious, impatient and, in some cases, even jealous.

To the state, however, not all riot victims are the same. Some variables are unfair but obvious, such as a victim's religion, others more technical. For example, 5 lakh rupees was to be handed out in the case of 'complete damages' to a property and 2.5 lakh rupees for 'substantial damages'. In the case of looting, the value of every item reported missing would have to be 'officially ascertained'.

In Noor's case, the officials were yet to verify the worth of every hair remover and lipstick looted from the property. The government told the court its officers couldn't carry out that work in the lockdown. I wondered what it would entail. I still had so much to learn. A lawyer working on compensation cases explained why some victims got only a fraction of what they deserved. 'It's complicated. Take the example of this bike repair shop. Because things were removed from the shop and burnt outside, it wasn't considered the same as the shop being burnt. The owner got only five thousand rupees.'

The more questions I asked, the less hopeful I felt. My own life was deteriorating at a steady pace since the virus struck. I felt trapped at home, work hardly inspired me and everyone around me was falling sick. At some point, I tested positive for the virus and fell into deep despair. I became uninterested in everything including my skin and hair.

One day I swept my long hair down my face and chopped it close to the skin. One day when I was feeling brave, I sent Noor a photo of my new look. By then my hair was growing out wildly, each strand poking in a different direction. She was shocked, and laughed until she cried.

~

We finally met again in September. By then, she had exhausted every official channel. The MLA didn't take her calls, the SDM had blocked her number and the party worker in charge of the compensation committee ignored her messages. She couldn't get over the irony. Before the February elections in Delhi, urged by the local unit, Noor had registered as a member of the Aam Aadmi Party to help canvass votes for its MLA candidate in her locality. No one in her family cared for politics, but people listened to them in the area.

The AAP won the seat, and the BJP lost the election. But riot-victims like Noor got the worst end of the deal: punished by one party and abandoned by the other. She took out her party membership card from her purse and gave it a long look. 'It would have been better if I had joined the BJP.' We were sitting in the waiting room of the Delhi Public Grievance

Commission, where bureaucrats are supposed to help citizens hold to account any officer of the government, including the chief minister. Perfect on paper, its biggest problem is that the people who would need it the most are the least likely to know it exists. On its website, one can track the public grievances dealt with to date. The last compensation complaint settled relates to Delhi's anti-Sikh riots of 1984. It was filed in 2010.

A sarkari office is a strange place for an occasional visitor: you can never be sure what room to enter and which person to address. Now imagine a sarkari office in which everyone is wearing a mask. We begin the rounds between the departments with detours to the photocopier. There should be a word for when you keep being directed from one office to the next until someone sends you back to where you started from, and the person who set off the circus now looks at you as if you are wasting his time again when you should have handed in your file the first time. We find our 'concerned authority' somehow.

The officer looks at Noor's complaint and tells her she isn't surprised. 'You are lucky you are not in jail,' she says. Noor hasn't followed the news in months. If she had, she would have known only Muslims are being charged with rioting as the investigations proceed. Addressing me, the officer says that being a progressive officer she too grieves over the state of affairs. This is the second person in a week who has introduced herself as 'progressive' to me – the first was a lawyer.

They could say that freely knowing I was a member of

their threatened tribe. I nod in comradely fashion. She says she will do the best she can. We write a final application. Signing it, Noor only puts down her first name. She tells me she has dropped her last: Khan. It didn't matter before the riots. 'No one saw me as a Muslim. I had more Hindu than Muslim clients.'

But things have changed. According to official investigation reports, most rioters who struck north-east Delhi were outsiders and hired goons. Many locals disagree. 'No one from outside came to loot my parlour. That much I know,' Noor said. Having learnt that business isn't above religion, she would rather keep hers under the radar. We leave the building with our fingers crossed.

~

Days pass, then weeks. Everything seems to be coming back to normal – workers are going to factories, fitness enthusiasts to gyms, friends to bars – except for the virus, which is knocking down thousands of people every day. By October, I hardly know anyone who hasn't caught it yet, a roll call that features my mother, sister and sister-in-law. I have given up on good news. On 13 October, Noor calls me up ecstatically to say she has received a bank transfer from the government – of Rs 2.5 lakh. We shriek in relief.

When I call her again a few days later, she has just wrapped up a facial at the fancied-up Beauty Life. In the tiny video frame, I can see her relaxing in a chair while Aaliya is giving a client a pedicure. Another 'season' is upon them, beginning with Diwali and stretching to New Year's Eve. The year being almost at its end, the women want to make up for all the lost months. 'The virus has added so much work. We have to wash every towel by hand, sanitize every surface, put on the PPE.' I realize I haven't seen her this happy before. She is talking non-stop while smiling from ear to ear. Then she takes a closer look at me on her screen. My hair needs intervention. I am summoned to Beauty Life.

2

Freedom and the Indian Constitution

Gautam Bhatia

The Preamble to the Indian Constitution speaks of liberty: liberty of thought, expression, belief, faith and worship. Scattered throughout the Constitution's fundamental rights chapter we find the rights to freedom, to freedom of religion and to personal liberty. And if a constitution outlines a vision for society — a blueprint of what society *could* be — then the society that the Indian Constitution imagines is a society founded on freedom.

There are those who find this objectionable. They argue that this overemphasis on freedom is the result of colonized thinking. Indian society, they say, has always been founded on different values: on the primacy of family and society, and on a chain of duties and responsibilities. The Constitution, they say, is a Western import upon a people fundamentally at odds with its prescriptions. We have all heard these sentiments – or elements of them – expressed everywhere, including in the pages of the *New York Times* by its India correspondent, and sometimes even by judges of the Supreme Court.

It is tempting on some occasions to agree with this point of view. Watching the gulf between the promises of the Constitution and the realities around us, it is easy to fall into the trap of believing that freedom is not something organic to the Indian soil, that it is something that has never really been valued by Indians, and to give in to the belief that those who advocate for freedom are a rootless, cosmopolitan 'fringe', out of touch with the realities of Indian social life.

This belief, however, has no basis in reality. It obscures a diverse and plural history, a history in which women and men framed, articulated and grappled with a vocabulary of freedom that was forged out of the many injustices and wrongs that plagued (and continue to plague) our society. These historical traditions go back many centuries, but here let us limit ourselves to our colonial history. As early as the 1810s, Raja Rammohan Roy argued eloquently for the freedom of speech and of the process, locating it within ideas of representative government. Such was Roy's influence that, in faraway Spain, the 1812 Constitution of Cadiz – drafted by reformers – was dedicated to him ('to the liberalism of the noble, wise, and virtuous Brahmo Ram Mohan Roy').

Freedom and the Indian Constitution

In his time, Roy was attacked for being a deracinated not-quite-Indian, an attack that is quite familiar to us today. But his words and his writings would echo throughout Indian colonial history. Indian nationalists used the language of freedom to express – and then critique – their subjection by the British regime. From the late 1890s, Indians drafted constitutional documents where freedom was given pride of place. As the liberation struggle took shape in the early 1920s, Congress presidents C.R. Das and Motilal Nehru delivered presidential speeches setting out the importance of civil liberties to social life and to the public sphere. The freedom of speech and expression was defended by no less a figure than Gandhi (and who would accuse *him* of being a deracinated Indian?): Gandhi (famously) condemned the sedition law while on trial and (less famously) penned a stirring defence of the freedom of speech in the pages of *Young India*, making the now-familiar argument that short of inciting violence, the only remedy for speech was counter-speech.

What united these individuals across more than a century was the basic understanding that wherever there was concentrated power, the individual was under threat and at the risk of effacement. The Indian Constitution was born encoding that simple wisdom: that no matter how benign or well intentioned those who held the reins of power might be, and no matter how convinced they might be that their actions *were* for the benefit of Indians, freedom was too important – and too precious – to be left only in their hands.

But it would be a mistake to imagine that the vocabulary of freedom came into being only in the context of Indians' struggle against an authoritarian state. It was always understood that the state was not the sole locus of power and oppression. The vocabulary of freedom, thus, was excavated and put to use in what we now call the 'private sphere'. In the late nineteenth century, this was spearheaded by women such as Pandita Ramabai, Rukhmabai (who fought a long legal battle against being forced to live with a husband whom she had not consented to marry), Tarabai Shinde and others. In letters, epistles, memoirs and other genres of writing, these women subjected the life of the family and the home to searing critique, in the language of equality and freedom. The constraints that family structures placed upon women, their loss of liberty and comparisons of their situation to that of slavery – all this and more was the subject of public debate, bringing the langue of freedom into a space that, for centuries, had been defended upon the very basis that it reflected the *natural* inequality and subjection that existed in the world.

It was this sustained movement that ensured that, at least in formal terms, the Constitution granted freedom on equal terms to women and men. Unlike in many other countries, where the right to vote began by being limited to property-owning white men, and was won by women only after many decades of struggle, the Indian Constitution granted universal adult franchise in one sweep. Not only that, an attempt to tag on specific limiting provisions in the Constitution was expressly rejected. For example, in the Constituent Assembly, an attempt was made to specify that certain forms of work may be inherently unsuitable 'on account of sex'. The attempt failed comprehensively.

While women were making the argument for freedom in the private and public spheres, so was the movement against caste oppression. Many centuries ago, the poet Ravidas had dreamt of the ideal city of Begumpura, where all citizens had the *freedom* to 'walk where they may'. In Begumpura, Ravidas imagined a city that was not broken up into ghettoes and enclaves, where everyone had equal freedom to go where they wished. Unsurprisingly, from the 1890s, the earliest petitions to the British authorities against caste oppression framed their case in the language of the freedom of movement, pointing out how access to common roads was barred to the Dalits. Two decades later, B.R. Ambedkar's movement was defined by its call to equality and to freedom – freedom *from* the strictures and dominance of caste power. In his numerous testimonies to various commissions, for example, Ambedkar stressed upon the prevalence of social boycott in Indian society (a practice that exists to this day) and pointed out how the freedom of individuals – to walk on roads, to live where they may, to draw water from the village well, to engage in the economic and social life of the community – was perpetually hostage to the arbitrary power of that very community. Once again, the Constitution reflected that simple truth in its abolition of untouchability, of forced labour and of discrimination in access to shops, wells and places of public resort.

The idea of freedom, therefore, shaped some of the most important social movements during our colonial history, in the years and decades leading up to political independence, and to the framing of the Constitution. The Constitution, indeed, embodies the best of those traditions in the language that it uses. This idea of freedom, as we have seen, was not simply an abstract one. It was grounded within the reality of Indian social life – not just in the public sphere, but also in structures and institutions such as the family and community. For this reason, in Indian political and social thought, the idea of freedom was always linked with that of equality and of fraternity. In his speech in the Constituent Assembly, Ambedkar explained that liberty, equality and fraternity constituted a 'trinity'. None of them would be meaningful without the other two: liberty to ensure that the individual was not erased by concentrated power, equality to address the systemic and institutional barriers that had undermined the liberty of so many for so long and fraternity to ensure that liberty and equality existed not simply in the relationship between state and individual, but also percolated deep *into* society, into those spaces that had so long been defined by their absence.

At the end of the day, a constitution is, of course, a document – nothing more. It is neither self-enforcing nor self-executing. If freedom is not *practised* in society – in our structures and our institutions – the Constitution's promises will remain promises only. But even in such times, words matter: they matter because they reflect an alternative vision of society, and tell us that the reality need not be a permanent one. If an alternative can be imagined – with words – then it is an alternative that can be created. And also – as I have tried to show in this essay – these words anchor us to our past, to the traditions of freedom and equality that we are heir to. They tell us that we are not alone. They give us a treasure trove of resources to draw upon, and the knowledge that in far more difficult circumstances, Indians (like us) drew upon the language of freedom to shape a different world. And above all else, they tell us that – in the words of the Kenyan poet Christopher Okigbo – the quest for freedom has always been a 'thirsting for sunlight': that freedom is a destination that may be impossible to reach, but that the path must be walked nonetheless.

3

Bread, Cement, Cactus

Annie Zaidi*

There are words of which it is impossible to gain the meaning until all the other words that enable it begin to crumble through disuse or abuse. One such word is love. Enmeshed as it is with kindness, respect, eagerness, loyalty, we learn to know what 'love' is through all the other words that coalesce to give us a stable life, full of hope and purpose. Another such word is freedom. We learn to know it through love, dignity, equality, acceptance, trust in institutions that uphold our right to live and thrive. Knock down the assumptions implied by any one of these words and our personal and political sense of freedom is compromised. What does it mean to be a 'free' individual,

---

* The essay reproduced here won the Nine Dots prize in 2019 and was developed into the book *Bread, Cement, Cactus: A Memoir of Belonging and Dislocation* (Cambridge University Press, UK, 2020).

after all, if you are not certain that you – with your name, your language, your belief system, your customs and your ancestry – will be treated with respect in a particular place? What does it mean to be free once you know that people very much like you are discriminated against? Enslavement, after all, is precisely this, that one set of people gets to dominate and control the life choices of another.

The quest for freedom is tied up with the quest for equality and with an emotional connection with a particular geography, be it the mohalla where several generations of your family have lived or an entire nation. It is tied up with its own lack and its inverse – to be restrained, suppressed, captured, dominated, confined, limited. For me, the question of what it means to be a free individual cannot be separated from the question of where other people think my 'place' is, in terms of both my status and the choices I am allowed by the systems that govern my life. This brief essay is a meditation on trying to discover my place in the world.

∼

I needed to see it written in black and white, up on a wall.

جہاں کوئی اپنا دفن نہ ہوا ہو وہ جگہ اپنی نہیں ہوا کرتی

'Jahan koyi apna dafn na hua ho woh jagah apni nahin hua karti'

Annie Zaidi

Travelling from Spanish to English to Urdu with its curlicue graces, that line waited to trip me up in my own language at a stall selling posters at a literary festival. It's from Gabriel García Márquez's *One Hundred Years of Solitude*. A person does not belong to a place until there is someone dead under the ground.

I bought the poster and took it to the framer's. For a moment, I stood hesitating. Framing would prolong the paper's life. On the other hand, a glass-and-wood frame might be damaged in transit. Transit, at any rate, was inevitable.

~

In North India, where my family is from, a corpse is sometimes referred to as *mitti*. Soil. Earth, if you prefer. And when someone wants to emphasize his relationship with the land, he might declare: *Yahaan meri purkhon ki naal garhi hai*. This is where my ancestors' umbilical cord is buried.

When I first encountered that sentence by Márquez, it didn't leap off the page. I hadn't buried anyone yet. I hadn't yet been told that I didn't belong in my own country, or that I had a smaller right to it. Belonging, however, had always been a fraught question. Friends from journalism school continue to tease me about the first day of class when a professor asked us to introduce ourselves, just names and where we're from. I said I wasn't sure where I'm from, and proceeded to list everywhere I'd lived thus far.

What I meant to say was that I felt dislocated, and anxious about my fractured identity. I was born in hospital and I don't know if my cord was buried. I never lived in the city of my birth. After leaving us with her parents while she went back to university, my mother quit a bad marriage and moved with her two children to a remote industrial township. The need for bread, and milk, overrode the unease of being so far from everything familiar to us.

I was just out of kindergarten and one of my first memories of the place is cactus. Another is piles of sieved sand, waiting to be mixed into cement. The colony – a word often used to describe industrial townships in India – was dry and dusty, with summer temperatures touching fifty degrees Celsius. It was flanked on one side by the Aravallis, one of the oldest hill ranges in the world. On another side was a cement factory.

Everyone here knew their place. Houses are allotted based on one's factory job. 'A' type quarters were for top management. These were three- or four-bedroom bungalows with a lawn and the services of a gardener. Upper management lived in 'B' type, middle management in 'C' type, blue-collar workers in 'E' and 'F' type quarters. We were in 'D' type, meant for those who were not quite managers but couldn't be classified as workers either. People like my mother. She was vice principal at a school for the employees' children. At the senior level, this translated into kids whose parents couldn't afford to, or couldn't bear to, send them away to boarding schools.

Outsiders were not admitted, so we never got to mix with the children of local farmers or shepherds.

The children of managers and furnace stokers attended the same school. But even a six-year-old knows how A-B-C-D goes. D type meant a two-bedroom house with vertical bars on windows, doors of hewn planks and concrete flooring everywhere including the bathroom. No marble, no glass, no tiles, no garden.

After my mother was promoted, one of my E type friends asked me, 'I suppose you'll be hanging out with the C type girls now?'

~

Cactus remains entwined with my feeling for that place. The roads were pure concrete – cement was one thing the township didn't lack – but traffic was non-existent. Only top management had cars. Most people walked. Besides, there wasn't anywhere to go. No movie theatre, no restaurant, no shopping except for basic groceries, no cafe, no park, no pool, no bookstore, no buses or taxis.

If you needed to go out of the colony, you had to fill up a requisition form and ask for a car. The district headquarters, Sirohi, was an hour's drive. There was little evidence of urbanity, but at least the town had a hospital, where I was once admitted after a serious fracture and where I almost lost the use of a leg. It had tailors and bakers. The cakes that mysteriously showed up on my birthday were made here. Sirohi was also where, twice a year, we boarded a train to visit my grandparents.

If you were desperate to go out without actually leaving the colony, your only recourse was the Aravallis. Ancient, stoic and never fully colonized, the hills were the reason the cement factory existed. Limestone deposits were torn out with the help of explosives and we were warned not to go climbing when a blast was scheduled. We never got to see the laying of dynamite, but we did hear the periodic *boom!* in the distance.

We would climb the hill nearest the colony, sometimes with a picnic sandwich. Once up there, we scratched our names on flat rocks with sharp-edged flint. Seeing my name, white on bluish grey rock, brought cheap satisfaction: I was here, alive, but at risk of death by boredom.

We were also warned not to go up hills that couldn't be seen from the colony. There were stories about Bheel men who lived in the hills beyond who had encountered children from the colony and relieved them of their valuables. I wasn't sure I believed the stories. Still, I didn't want to venture too far. Scarier than being accosted and having my earrings taken away was the landscape: hill behind hill and beyond that, more hill. Not a soul in sight.

Nobody talked about what, or who, lived here before the colony was established. We grew up with a sense that there was nothing before and it wasn't hard to believe. There was enough cactus and acacia around to suggest a desert. Once the factory was set up, nobody was allowed in, unless they were employees or their guests. The colony was gated and guarded.

The Bheel, however, must have been here before. The tribe, with its part-agrarian, part-martial history, has lived around the Aravallis for centuries. I never encountered any Bheel men, but I did see Rabaari and Garaasiya tribespeople, men and women both. Rabaari are traditional cattle herders and they supplied the colony with milk. Garaasiya came to work in the colony as casual labourers, building houses and laying roads. Over the years, I learnt to tell the tribes apart from the patterns of their shirts and skirts, their odhnis and turbans, tattoos, jewellery, the way they wore their hair. The tribes did not live in the colony though, and were never invited to join community events. Their children were not admitted in the local school.

I wonder what the tribes felt when they saw the giant white letters spanning the bosom of the hill that we used to climb: JK Puram. It was the name of the township, painted so large, it could be seen not only by us but anyone who lived in surrounding villages. It could even be seen from the windows of trains chugging through the district and it wasn't until I returned to visit nearly two decades later that I began to think of it as vulgar. It was as if the industrialists who owned the factory were announcing their control of the landscape and its mineral wealth. That giant name was planted on the hill like a flag.

Seeing it with adult eyes, I also saw why it was necessary.

The land had to be seen as belonging to the industrialists because they did not belong to the land. They didn't live here. They would not have buried their children's umbilical cords on that hill.

~

By the time I moved to Bombay, it had been renamed Mumbai and I no longer knew how to answer questions about where I'm from. For the sake of convenience, I said Lucknow because it was where I spent my vacations. I couldn't very well say, I'm from a dusty industrial township that I never want to see again. As for the place where my ancestors and their umbilical cords were buried, I hadn't yet seen it.

In Muhammadabad, a mofussil village struggling to morph into a town, we trace fourteen generations. The uncle who told me this is now gone. Fifteen generations, then.

In India, this would be called our 'native place'. Not where you or your parents live, but where you trace your roots. Mom says, our roots are here. But she is an obvious misfit and has only begun to visit after her parents died. The women of the family rarely step outside the ancestral house. Grocery, errands, jobs: men handle it. If women go out, it is usually to a religious event or weddings, or to pay condolences. A new generation of girls goes to college, but they wear hijabs and burqas.

I fight with my mother: *We* don't come from *this*! You

came from cities like Lucknow and Delhi, from secularism and cosmopolitanism, from an English-medium education. *You* wore breeches and rode horses!

Mom counters: Daddy said never to forget our *roots*. Over all protest, she builds a morsel-sized house there. Within the walls of our large ancestral house, several branches of the family have built individual units. It wears a deserted look around the year but comes alive during the month of Moharram. Shia families across the state return to ancestral homes, especially in the first ten days, to mark the tragedy within which all tragedies are meant to be subsumed – the martyrdom of Imam Hussain and the slaughter and devastation that visited his clan in Karbala. Individual grief is folded into an unending sorrow that connects you to the community.

I've visited a few times now, partly to appease Mom, partly out of curiosity. There is a railway station, too short for the long trains that come through. Once my mother failed to disembark because the compartment she was in was so far out on the tracks, the platform wasn't visible. Peering outside, she assumed the train had halted in the middle of nowhere. When I heard, I bit my tongue and didn't say what I was thinking: it *is* the middle of nowhere.

It certainly isn't the sort of place you can call an Uber. I've begun to go out nevertheless, unaccompanied by menfolk and uncaring of tradition. I neither wear a burqa nor the 'Syed' prefix that sets apart certain clans and creates a hierarchy among Muslims.

One day, I decided to brave a bone-rattling ride to visit a library in another village. Sixteen adults, each of them more patient and in better humour than me, were packed into an auto-rickshaw that was originally built to carry four. An elderly woman sitting next to me kept up a cheerful banter in Bhojpuri, which is supposed to be a dialect of Hindi but was so far removed from the language I spoke, she may as well have been talking French. Finally, she asked where I came from. I caught the word 'ghar'. Home. I said, I'm from Muhammadabad actually.

The elderly woman gave me a sideways stare. 'From Syed-wada?'

It wasn't a question. One glance and she had me pinned to my street. Fifteen generations were stamped on my face, my voice, my clothes, my gestures. Even without the burqa, she could tell that I was from Syed-wada, thus known because the street is full of Muslim families who use the Syed prefix and claim descent from Prophet Muhammad.

I didn't bother to deny it and I didn't ask how she could tell. I know my country enough by now to know that class and caste privilege is carefully preserved.

~

As a boy of ten, Grandpa moved to the throbbing heart of the province, Lucknow, and never returned to his village. He joined the movement for India's freedom. Once it was attained, he entered government service and was transferred often. He seemed to care more for the company he kept, and what he could accomplish with his time, than ancestry. He was a poet and scholar who researched the literature associated with our mourning traditions, but he didn't take his children home for Moharram.

I argue with my mother: *I* do not recall him saying that *we* belong to Muhammadabad. What he did say was that there were two things his part of the state was known for. The first was *imarti*, a deep-fried, tightly coiled whorl of flour, soaked in sugar syrup. The second was *goondagardi*. Goonda-ism. Endemic violence and bullying. But I was too young at the time to ask what it means to belong to a place that's rich in sugarcane, poetry and goons. The explanation given to me for why Grandpa rarely visited his native place was that it lacked the good hospitals his fragile heart needed.

Last year, we went to a neighbouring village where his mother, my great-grandmother, was born and where my great-grandfather is buried. Mom's cousin pointed out the exact spot and said, 'You all should put up a stone with his name on it. Our generation is the last one that remembers who is buried where.'

I felt myself bristle, then heard myself declare that I would pay for the stone and the engraving, if nobody else would. It was a curious reaction. Why should it matter to me? Is this what they call 'the call of blood'?

Mom says, wherever you can trace your bloodline, that place is yours. Yours as much as anybody else's. By that measure, the province of Uttar Pradesh is flecked with my blood. Not just Uttar Pradesh, not just India. Pakistan too. My father's side of the family came from that side of the border. Their traditions, their connection to the soil were lost when the country was carved up in 1947.

The border is something of an actual bloodline. Partition along religious lines shattered the Indian subcontinent and nobody is allowed to forget. The wound of millions being killed and displaced is scratched raw every few years. Three wars, constant accusations of cross-border infiltration and terrorist activity. India and Pakistan do not give each other tourist visas. I've had brows raised at the post office when I tried to send books to friends across the border. When citizens critique governments, they are accused of being 'ISI' or 'RAW' agents, the respective spy agencies of Pakistan and India. In India, there is a new trend of rebuking all critics of the government and its policies thus: Go to Pakistan!

I sometimes want to respond by crying out: How dare you! *My* father's family had to leave Pakistan in 1947. They were Punjabi Hindus and would never have left Pakistan if not for the violence of Partition.

I don't say it though. I don't want to make a stronger claim to India through appeals to Hindu ancestry. The stronger claim is that of Muslims who chose not to leave the land of their birth. Besides, who knows if my father's family had a tradition of burying umbilical cords?

~

The first burial I saw was in my grandmother's garden. I was a small child, upset at the destruction of a plastic parrot. Because it was shaped like a living creature, I felt it had 'died'. Death requires solemn ritual, so my brother and cousins buried the broken 'bird'.

My maternal grandmother had an affinity for soil. Despite the limitations of an urban garden, she had papayas, ladies' fingers, lemons and herbs in a small garden, and many varieties of flowers. She also had a keen sense of her own end. In preparation, she bought herself a *kafan*. Shroud. She also set aside money for her own funeral expenses. It was, she said, so that she didn't owe her children anything after she was gone.

I don't worry about expenses and shrouds. Perhaps this is because I have been independent long enough not to care about proving it beyond the grave. Still, I inherited from Grandma a certain preoccupation with burials. I wrote one novella set in a graveyard. I visit tombs, cenotaphs, cemeteries and necropolises whenever I'm in a new city. I pause to read names and epitaphs. I gravitate towards Urdu poetry, especially couplets that use burial, funereal baths and processions as metaphors.

My mother laughs when she recounts how I urged her to buy a home – anything, anywhere! – because we had nowhere to call our own. Full of adolescent drama, I'd said: *I need at least six feet of earth!*

I now have more than six feet to call my own. Not my mother's, not my father's. Mine. When it came to deciding where to buy a piece of land, I chose Lucknow.

Grandpa spent his last years in Lucknow and is buried there. Grandma followed a few years later. She was in another city when she died but had expressed a desire to be buried near her husband, so we flew her body back. Earth restored to beloved earth.

I visit the graveyard as often as I can. Whenever I find myself gripped with a fierce longing for a place of safety and comfort, I shut my eyes and conjure that cluster of graves: Grandpa, Grandma, the great-grandmother I never saw, great-uncles and great-aunts.

It is as if the question of belonging has been settled. When asked where I'm from, I have a ready answer.

4

Crossing Over

Perumal Murugan

In Indian society, freedom is hostage to the caste system. The space that each caste can inhabit and traverse is clearly demarcated. It is impossible to step out of that space and enter another. The ones that do have to pay a great price. Nandanar was one of them. Born in the Dalit paraiyar caste, Nandanar was a devotee of Shiva. He wanted to travel beyond the confines of his village, the space he was allowed, and enter the Nataraja temple in Chidambaram to worship its deity. Many obstacles stood in his way. In the end, he was set on fire. This is a tale from the Puranas. In every village, there are stories about the cruelties suffered, then and now, by those who tried to cross the limits set for them.

Did we ever have public spaces, those that are open to everyone, in our society? The answer: There have been none or only a very few. The agitation held in 1926 in Vaikom in Kerala, under Mahatma Gandhi's guidance and Periyar's leadership, was to demand for Dalits the right to walk on the roads leading to the local temple. Many struggles have been waged demanding the right of temple entry. The fight to enter the sanctum sanctorum, the abode of the deities, continues to this day. These fights have led to some reforms. Yet, many of our temples are not accessible to all even today.

Barring temples of major deities, now under state control, no significant changes have occurred in smaller temples or temples for clan deities. We have adopted a framework where each community can set up places of worship as needed, strictly within the space allotted to their caste. That is the limit of our freedom.

The Mariyamman temple in our village is called Palapattarai Mariyamman temple. Palapattarai means 'multi-caste', that is, people of all castes can go there and offer worship. This Mariyamman temple was built when my village grew into a small town. But in most villages you'll see that there is more than one Mariyamman temple, because every caste has its own temple. That my village temple is called 'multi-caste' indicates a departure from the norm.

A common cremation ground doesn't exist even today in rural India although you find them, as you do electric crematoriums, in the cities. There is a separate cremation ground for each caste rung. In some cases, there are no proper roads to reach the cremation grounds for some low castes.

Corpses of people belonging to one caste cannot be carried through the colony of another caste. Where humans are allowed to enter, a corpse won't be allowed to pass.

To this day, there are no public spaces in our villages: only separate temples, separate taps for drinking water and separate cremation grounds. In the cities, there are public spaces like parks, temples for big deities, and beaches. But even they are not available in proportion to the size of the population. Increasingly, even in cities, spaces are becoming private. Many parks are under the control of private bodies. City people increasingly stay within gated communities, where everything – parks, playgrounds – is private.

In Indian villages, there are separate settlements for each caste – barely any land is allotted to the landless castes. Village administrations are adroit at allocating government schemes by caste. The successful central government scheme for providing 100 days of employment to rural households is a good illustration of this phenomenon. Under this scheme, people are divided into caste-based groups and jobs are allocated accordingly.

A caste group will clean only the area where they live, along with the temples and streets in it. They don't enter areas inhabited by another caste group. If someone from one caste enters the living quarters of another caste group, the whole village will hear of it. Permission is given for entry into the fields only during working hours. In the cities, such restrictions work more subtly. Apartments in many high-rise complexes in Chennai are sold only to people of certain castes. Even houses are given on rent only after inquiring about the prospective tenant's caste.

Segregation was practised in the dining halls of some restaurants, with a section reserved for 'Brahmins only'. Even in Shaivite mutts headed and run by non-Brahmins such segregation was observed in dining halls. In many villages, tea stalls followed the two-tumbler system; in some, the practice continues to this day. After it was deemed illegal, the practice has taken a different form. The stall owners now serve tea in single-use disposable plastic cups.

Today, such caste-based discrimination in shops, eateries and commercial complexes has receded to a great extent; however, the implicit understanding that certain caste groups cannot own and run shops or eateries persists. When they do, people of other castes don't patronize those establishments.

The dynamics of caste plays out everywhere. Even public transport. In rural buses, if a person from a dominant caste gets on board, there is an expectation that a lower-caste person should give up his seat for him.

This is considered a sign of respect. When a student gives up his seat for a teacher, or a person gives up their seat for someone in a slightly higher position, is it really a mark of respect? The person who boarded first is sitting comfortably. Why should he give up his seat to make way for someone else?

I know a teacher who was bent on taking revenge on a student who didn't get up for him. What kind of attitude is this? Though this practice is generally considered as 'showing respect', what's behind it is a casteist disposition. The inclination to see everything on a high–low scale and to deal with others solely on that basis couldn't have come from anywhere else.

As always, we deal with these inequalities by building walls around ourselves. Those who can afford it prefer to use private transport. Many cover even a distance of 200 kilometres daily on their two-wheelers, while anyone who is somewhat well off prioritizes travelling by car. The desire for 'private' is far greater than that for 'public'. Movie theatres used to be a public space open to everyone. No longer. Rural 'tent' cinemas were closed a long time ago. Even in small towns and big cities, most single-screen cinema halls have shut down. Now only expensive multiplexes, where ordinary people cannot enter, are left.

It is true that both education and employment opportunities have expanded the scope of public spaces. Government colleges have reservation though in private universities this is not the case. Educational scholarships, too, are provided on the basis of caste, and it's the same in the case of job opportunities. Nonetheless they remain public spaces, open for all. Similarly, in the unorganized sector, people from different castes end up working together.

As a result, at universities and workplaces there are more opportunities now for men and women to meet and interact. Naturally, there are more instances of couples falling in love.

But the acceptance of love and love marriages hasn't evolved. Here too caste stands in the way. In fact caste-related honour killings have increased today. It is now possible to commit such killings easily, even in busy places like public thoroughfares and residential colonies. Our society has provided no safe spaces for lovers. Love allows people to transcend barriers. But our caste system won't allow crossing over.

Caste mentality affects the way we work. Take an ordinary office set-up. This is usually very hierarchical. In a sense, it is comparable to the different rungs of caste hierarchy. Even chairs are allotted by hierarchy. Starting from high-back chairs to shorter ones and plastic chairs, the shape and quality of your chair change with your position in the company. In all offices, the attendant is given nothing to sit on. They are expected to stand or move around the whole day.

Even freedom of expression at work is permitted strictly by hierarchy. In most offices, the practice is to receive instructions from above and implement them. Consultation meetings are held only in name. In those meetings, what the superiors say must be politely accepted by the subordinates. One may express agreement with one's superiors, but contradicting them will be interpreted as crossing one's limit. Subordinates don't have any right to contradict an idea or to propose an alternative.

Those who do so will be considered suspect and the authorities will henceforth keep an eye on them. Therefore, those who have different ideas do not speak about them;

they become silent and listen passively to what they are told. The tendency within caste hierarchy to think of dissenters as adversaries and mavericks is manifested in the same way within this power hierarchy too.

What about an individual's freedom of expression in art or literature or cinema? By the old measure, an individual was allowed to speak or not in accordance with the position allotted to him in the caste hierarchy. The same measure is in effect in a different form today.

We can express our agreement with ideas that have been accepted by the public. We can propound them as well. We have the freedom to do so. But we cannot contradict those ideas, nor put forth alternative ideas. We cannot criticize religion or express an opinion about a particular caste. We can't even start a minor debate around religion. We cannot write about language. We cannot write about a character who pursues a particular occupation. We cannot write anything about the customs and rituals followed in our society. This is who we are today.

One of the characters of a film was a lawyer. Immediately, there was opposition from lawyers claiming that the film demeaned lawyers and their profession. If the character is a doctor, doctors would rise in protest. There will be a demand to ban the film, threats to shut down its screening, then a compromise will be reached – that's how it works.

People in the film industry have a strategy to get around this problem. If the film has a lead character who is a police officer who cheats, it also has a junior police officer who is honest. The minor character exists to show that there are good people too in the police department.

In our country, caste informs the identity of each and every individual. Yet, caste mostly doesn't find a place in our films. Caste identity is present only when a character is to be exalted. In other circumstances, it might be hinted at, but the tendency is to avoid mentioning caste and generalize it instead. Film-makers do this because the use of caste names could invite problems.

Take the recent controversy in Tamil Nadu over a prayer song called 'Kanda Sashti Kavacam', composed in celebration of the Tamil god Murugan. The song seeks Murugan's protection for every part of the body:

> May the iron spear guard the penis and vagina
> May the grand spear guard both buttocks
> May the shapely spear guard the round rectum
> May the heavenly spear guard both sturdy thighs

Finding the reference to body parts like penis, vagina, buttocks and rectum obscene, a group called Karuppar Koottam (Throng of Blacks) released a video mocking the song and posted it online. For this, members from the group were arrested and cases were registered against them. People also wrote against the group's stance – by maintaining that it was not obscene to mention penis and vagina since they were no different from other body parts like hands and feet.

Some resorted to more violent methods like hate speech and agitation. Karuppar Koottam, who released the video, were non-believers. 'How could non-believers dare to speak about god? They have demeaned god and thereby hurt the sentiments of believers,' the protesters claimed.

The case of 'Kanda Sashti Kavacam' could have led to a healthy debate about the definition of obscenity. Instead, people were busy pointing at the caste, religion and ideology of their interlocutors.

What can we say or write in such an environment? If we speak of only those ideas that have popular acceptance in our society, no problem is likely to arise. If we speak or write against the grain, cases will leap at us, threats of violence will hail down and there may be actual violence. The limits of freedom now are exactly as they were in the past. We can say that only their form has changed, or they have shrunk even further.

In everything that has to do with freedom, a casteist attitude is clearly present. Most people from the dominant castes articulate ideas that reflect popular wisdom and remain its ardent supporters. Because it's the ideas related to popular wisdom that help them to consolidate their caste-based dominance. Even the few individuals from the dominant castes who speak against popular wisdom are protected by their caste; they are allowed to get away with their dissent and handled gently.

At the same time, those who speak against popular wisdom are mostly from the depressed castes. They are compelled to speak that way in order to rid themselves of the stigma of caste. Such people mostly do not have any protection. Even people of their own caste do not offer them protection, because people from the depressed castes too have minds that are imprinted with ideas derived from popular wisdom. They are imprinted over and over again. Periyar had spoken relentlessly about god and the superstitions followed in his name. His speeches were savage, sardonic. But the world in which he could speak so openly does not exist today.

Translated from the Tamil by N. Kalyan Raman

5

The Freedom Exchange

Yashica Dutt

'So what if she is a girl, I'll (toh) give my children freedom,' I'd hear my mother say to the neighbour, as I pretended to be invisible behind a pillar. Hiding under the bedcovers that night, I'd hear her pay the price in slaps and blows from her husband.

Even before I knew what freedom meant I knew it was something that wasn't mine to take. It was a commodity that someone else, my mother, my culture, my society could choose to bestow on or withhold from me. I was the firstborn in a family of 'collector saabs' and their children. In the not-so-recent past, my family members had scrubbed the bathrooms of people who recoiled at the sight of their own excrement and at the stranger who was cleaning it. My freedom was fleeting and finite.

The Freedom Exchange

'You're giving her too much freedom,' my mother's in-laws would say when she applied nail polish on my tiny five-year-old hands. Or when she bought me the same frock that she'd seen the Rasna girl wear on TV, before any other kid in the colony wore it. They said it repeatedly when my mother refused to let them send me to a mediocre Hindi-medium school because she wanted me to go to the best convent school in Ajmer, even though no one in the family had attended an English-medium school. She got her way, threatening to leave her husband, who didn't like to work and drank to the point of mania every night, and I was sent to Sophia School.

And so my mother surrendered her freedom for mine. She knew that the road to freedom for her daughter started from the gates of a hundred-year-old Catholic convent. It was one of many trades – her freedom to be happy exchanged for her dreams for a daughter's life. Her own dreams ended when she married into a family of afsars (officers) from 'our caste'. As a young wife, she spent her evenings shivering, swathed in a thick sheet, because her parents had sent her to her husband's home with no warm clothes suitable for Rajasthan's freezing winter and her new family didn't bother to buy her any.

A respectable job offered her the possibility of escape. My mother would slip into the kitchen at the far end of the house after a long day of chores to study for the IAS exam, but was often dragged by her hair to the bedroom and beaten for 'showing off'. The only way she could ensure a good education

– the portal to a better future – for me was to lock herself up in this hell and throw away the keys. And so she did it.

This was the first of the many freedom exchanges my mother made for me. It was also the template memory that I returned to when I thought about what freedom meant to me – a thin thread, suspended between the limited choices my mother was given and the options I might discover. My mother bargained, using the small store of freedom she stole from the overlooked cracks of her life, to turn liberty into one of the defining ideas of mine. It became how I understood the world around me, the founding principle around which I would build and arrange my life.

Freedom for her and then to me also meant no discrimination between a boy and a girl child. At a time when many of my classmates were being groomed to cook, clean, set the table, serve, wait for the men and boys to eat, finish their food, clean again and then finish homework, while their brothers alternated between playing cricket and the video game Contra, my mother's insistence that I didn't have to bend over the stove or squat down to mop was a small revolution.

I didn't have the same breadth of relaxed regulations as boys my age, or even that my own brother enjoyed a few years later. And still, I grew up convinced that I was on an equal footing with them – perhaps better than them, even – and any other men I would encounter in the future, able to hold my own with acumen, wit and intellect.

The Freedom Exchange

By the time I got to college, I was unwilling to negotiate any of my freedoms. I had seen my mother squeeze it out for me, drop after drop, for almost every day of my life. I intended to guard it as my precious inheritance. I was going to shape my destiny, take any path and chase freedom in all the choices I would make. But these choices extracted a toll. I would also live with the shame, guilt and agony of the exchange my mother had to make for that freedom.

To shape your destiny, you need a clean sheet. And so I negotiated my own freedom exchange: I pretended to be someone I was not, someone who was 'upper' caste. At school I had concealed my caste, telling nosy aunties that I was a brahmin. And I continued the act at university.

Freedom to me meant to be free of the burdens of caste and gender. My choices would reflect only my experiences – my decisions were a product of free will. That push and pull, though tedious and constant, granted me a modest clearing in the forest, a fleeting respite when I was not tethered by my identity as a Dalit woman.

When I couldn't make it into the 'Residence' at St Stephen's College, I was secretly thrilled about ending up in a girl's-only paying guest accommodation that had far fewer restrictions. I soon traded that for several rented accommodations in quick succession, ultimately settling into a studio apartment where I could safely nurture the illusion that I had somehow tricked the hawk-eyed glare of patriarchy, just like I was hoodwinking caste.

When my first book, *Coming Out as Dalit*, was published, I realized how grossly I had underestimated the vice-like grip of both. I was sharply surprised to learn that I was criticized the most for 'exploiting' the Dalit narrative, for my seemingly 'cloying' centring of emotions and my 'brazenly naked ambition' to seek credit for my work without feeling the need to hide the toll it took on me. My critics insisted, on Twitter and elsewhere, that because my outfits outsized their expectations, my words didn't carry traces of the small town I grew up in. That I was 'not the right kind of Dalit' because I lived in New York.

These critiques often came from people who didn't find it necessary to read my book to attack my ideas. After months of trying to make sense of this hurtful criticism, directed more at who I was rather than at what I had written, I saw how fragile my fantasy of freedom had been. It felt like hairline cracks were running through that long-held fantasy that I was free, until it shattered completely.

I was not free. No Dalit woman is. Most have far fewer 'freedoms' than I do, and I still could not claim to be free. I woke up day after day until that realization curdled slowly but firmly into my truth. My work would never be judged like an 'upper' caste man's. A man's ambition was natural, desirable, expected.

But as a Dalit woman, I needed to prove that I knew everything there was to know about the experience of a quarter million Dalit people to earn the right to talk about my own story. My legitimacy would be decided by other people's assumptions: was I too 'rich-sounding', too 'urban-looking' or too 'polished' to recognize the stench of the fecal matter my ancestors had died trying to scrub from their elbows?

In the complex matrix of caste and patriarchy that permeates Indian society, Dalit women lie at the absolute bottom. They are often punished simply for existing. In 2019 ten Dalit women were raped daily, according to the latest National Crime Records Bureau data. Their rapes, assault, violence and deaths, as the Hathras case exposed, are more dispensable and far less valuable than the pride of 'upper' caste men. After the rape and murder of the nineteen-year-old Dalit made international headlines, Thakur groups marched for the rights of the upper-caste men, alleging that the rapists whose caste matched theirs had been falsely accused of the crime, though there was nothing in the evidence to support this contention.

The victim had been raped, had her spine crushed, her tongue slashed. She was ferried between hospitals because the authorities refused to transfer her to Delhi while also refusing to file a first information report, and after her death from her injuries, she was hastily cremated, her family members prevented from carrying out her last rites even as her mother begged to see her dead daughter one last time. That young Dalit woman received less dignity than the 'upper' caste men who killed her.

And she was hardly the first Dalit woman to suffer that fate.

In 2016 Delta Meghwal from Bikaner was allegedly raped and murdered under mysterious circumstances, her body found in a water tank and cremated before an investigation could be conducted. Both these Dalit women also suffered because they were poor and lived in rural India – statistics show that at least ten Dalit women are raped every day, most of these cases not reported to the police, justice rarely delivered to the victims or their families. But the unique sense of indignity and heartlessness that fuels caste hatred is hardly limited to those with lack of resources or access to urban centres.

If that wasn't true, then several thousands of Dalit women, including myself, wouldn't be forced to hide our caste or live with the terror of being 'outed'. Many of us wouldn't endure the emotional, mental and even physical abuse that we are subjected to in our interpersonal relationships precisely because of our status as 'lower bodies meant to be put in their place', both with Dalit men and otherwise.

More Dalit women would have positions of leadership in the corporate workforce, 94 per cent of which are currently occupied by brahmins and bania castes, as Christina Thomas Dhanaraj wrote in a recent report. In cases of sexual assault and domestic violence, we would be believed and supported unconditionally, instead of being asked to stay silent to protect 'our men' – erased by even 'upper' caste feminists who cannot see how it is our caste that hurts us.

Centuries of deliberate sandpapering of caste into India's culture left no space for Dalits to survive. But cracking through the cement, 'like weeds we grew' anyway. When India became independent, carrying close to 360 million citizens over the threshold into equality, freedom and liberty, most Dalits were chained to their caste-imposed professions. They have since had to jostle for every inch of the social, cultural and often even legal freedom from their caste, which still continues to elude us in its entirety.

Whether it's the spectrum of violence that just as easily swings from degradation to murder or the prickly and arduous struggle to cut loose from the confines of this shamelessly unfair system, our freedom is a bargain we often end up making with our dignity or our lives. As we face blatant discrimination, brutal assault, mental trauma, systemic inequality and the countless morbid mechanisms in place to ensure that we don't threaten 'upper' caste entitlement with our equality, the struggle for Dalit Independence is far from over.

We struggle to rise from the margins, scrounging for access to the sole source of water in the village, prepping for exams under dim bulb lights, enveloped by the putrid stench of garbage in neglected bastis and colonies, cautiously herding our hushed wedding processions to pass through undisturbed, failing to justify to our 'upper' caste classmates why we belong here as much as them, scrambling for compliance if not deference in our administrative positions, grappling to find our voices in crowded newsrooms. Freedom for us is fought for every day.

With barely the freedoms to live, love, breathe, read, express, exist, we also don't have the freedom to just be. We don't have the freedom to define, create, present ourselves away from the labels that have been laid out for us. Poor Dalit, manual scavenger Dalit, basti Dalit, corrupt Dalit, Reservation-grabbing Dalit, Mercedes-driving Dalit, unthinking Dalit, New York Dalit – the dominant savarna culture needs to confine us to one box or another to make sense of us. We must always belong to a category they understand.

Like microbes in a Petri dish, Dalits need to be studied, examined, observed but never on our own terms. The unidimensional perspective of the 'savarna gaze', much like White Gaze, filters Dalits into reductive, unimaginative categories, flattening our differences and robbing us of our humanity at the most basic level. This desire to define so we can be scrutinized, investigated and controlled has stripped us of our freedom to be individuals.

The 'savarna gaze' that affects non-Dalits and even some Dalits demands that we look, speak, present and behave only in ways defined for us to claim our existence. It insists that if we fail to fall into these lines, we lose the right to speak for ourselves or anyone else that might be like us. 'Savarna gaze' traps us into the uroboros of 'authentic Dalitness', interrogating our suffering, mapping our trauma and measuring our pain to validate if we even belong to ourselves.

Looking down at us as the stakeholder of 'whose story gets to be told', that gaze creates contests for our grief, content in its deceit that those of us who win that 'trauma trophy' might be too hurt, or worse, too dead to talk about their suffering.

And those who can speak will never fare well on their (fake) scale of 'who's most miserable', and therefore never valid enough to be considered seriously anyway. Despite the categories, the labelling and identifying and pitting us against each other, none of us will be good enough for a system that profits from keeping us at the margins.

The ruinous system of marking people as untouchables robs us of many freedoms. But among them, the freedom that perhaps most evidences our humanness is the freedom to fail. Even though 'savarna gaze' itself sits on a peak of opportunities that were either handed down to 'upper' caste people or especially created for them, it demands from us perfection. Every Dalit person who succeeds is forced into exceptionalism to shatter the cages of caste that are fabricated to crush us. Unlike the 'upper' caste with their support networks, endless opportunities and pliant safety nets invisibly stretched out to fall upon, Dalits only get one chance.

We don't have the recourse of unpaid college fees when the bursar, almost always 'upper' caste, is convinced that Dalits don't deserve higher education and is restless for us to drop out. Many of us succumb to mental illnesses that often shroud Dalits in their darkness, because they are so worn out from fighting a hostile system that refuses to acknowledge us as humans. Any deviation from perfection is used as more evidence that Dalits deserve nothing better than the work we were ordained to do according to the tyranny of our caste-based professions. As Dalits, we are constantly reminded that we are worthy only if we are exceptional. The freedom to be fallible, to be ordinary, to make human mistakes is one that non-Dalits routinely take for granted – but it is not even a possibility for Dalits.

As Dalits, we are constantly reminded that we are worthy only if we are exceptional. Caught in the wheels of this savagely ruthless machinery, the myth of a perfect Dalit is constructed so our humanity can be ignored. When we inevitably fall short, we too can be spit out, ignored and crushed, like every other Dalit in history. It's what we have seen with Rohith Vemula, Payal Tadvi, Balmukund Bharti and countless others who were institutionally murdered: the only kind of Dalit who can tell their story authentically is the one who is already dead.

Less than a year into her marriage, almost seven months pregnant with me, my mother decided to throw herself off the roof of my grandparents' house. Perhaps she believed that this act was the only kind of freedom that was available to us. She wasn't wrong. The freedom to raise not one but two daughters on her own terms was one she had to pry from the cold, undead hands of casteist norms, at the cost of almost giving up her life.

Most Dalit women, rural or urban, educated or not, with resources or without, carry these traumas in their bodies. The body retains the memories of these battles and transactions, losses and small, hard-wrested gains, carried

The Freedom Exchange

out for generations when their mothers, grandmothers, sisters, female relatives or themselves had to physically wrestle with this society that only allows them to exist as examples of exploitation to seize their dignity as fully realized humans. It's not romantic, heroic or valorous, these freedom exchanges. It's the price we pay to live. But should we have to?

6

Krantijeevi Tarangini

Vivek Shanbhag

'Hometown on fire. Burning meat in the air. He sips on sherbet in the city.'

What comes to your mind when you read these lines? What place is this, why is it burning, who has gone to the city, why is he drinking sherbet? Wouldn't you be beset with questions? Would it not be worse if the post were your friend's, who refused to explain it? Wouldn't you be exasperated?

These are Tarangini's status updates – peeves me and those like me. It is so tedious to decode her lines. Even when you feel you've understood, what you have arrived at isn't more than the meaning you've ascribed. Only she can say what any of it really means. From the responses that are posted, it is evident that many who follow her spend sleepless nights on these intriguing lines. You can see the questions, threats, barbs, likes, abuses . . . well, she responds to none.

Krantijeevi Tarangini

After I connected with Tarangini, I began to read her posts and comments every day. Initially, I was curious, amused as well, but before long it had turned into an addiction. It isn't easy to resist these bizarre lines, the temptation like the pleasure derived from pouring hot water on an itchy patch. You feel like making the water hotter, you also begin to enjoy the itch. The first thing I do these days when I wake up is check her status.

'Done scratching your back? Now leave for the whorehouse.'

'Carry coconut oil. Died yesterday, today he wants to hold hands while crossing the road. *Thoo!*'

'Run with the millstone. Run, run.'

Is it possible to forget such lines? I try to disentangle them, and they grow roots in my mind. They tunnel deeper, I try to use logic as a shield. All in all, it is an unnecessary perturbation. Perhaps it's the language that touches the innermost desires, deceit, lust and sin nestled in the human mind. The thought itself is unnerving.

'Why is your stuff so absurd?' I asked Tarangini.

'Nothing is absurd. When you try to express what's boiling up in you, grammar collapses. That's it. If grammar is your concern, then I will not argue. Let's leave it to our teacher, Joshi. Those who feel as intensely as I do will get what I'm saying. I don't care if others don't. My words meet their mark, I am certain.'

Tarangini is my childhood friend, two years older. Sanjeev, her younger brother, was my classmate. There were two doctors in our town, and Tarangini was Dr Dattaram's daughter. Dr Dattaram was famous for his modern outlook and lavish lifestyle. Their home was never short of guests. Cooks and servants outnumbered the family.

A compounder, Chandappa, also lived in their house. He had his corner under the staircase, his bedding rolled and stacked, but not once did I see him sleep there. He hovered around Dattaram, always available at calling distance. 'Chanda,' Dattaram would call; 'O . . .' Chandappa would appear before him. Young boys refused to visit the clinic when Chandappa was alone, for he asked them to pull off their shorts and cough, holding their testicles. If they demurred, 'Why are you shy? Should I take off mine and show you?' he would say, freaking them out completely.

Dattaram's clinic was always milling with patients, he didn't have the time to so much as scratch his ass. They waited in the clinic when he went home for lunch in the afternoons. It was never before 9 p.m. that he got home. His ritual was to take a bath, get into a fresh set of clothes, sit out on the terrace with a glass of whisky and a cigar, all by himself. The clinic was closed on Sundays, but patients turned up at his house in emergencies. Dattaram never turned a sick person away; if need be he drove them home afterwards.

Along with medicines, his patients got a lesson or two on the importance of a progressive outlook. These might feature the importance of sending children to school, a scathing attack on superstition, putting an end to caste practices. Not that people agreed with his views but, since they felt deeply indebted to his healing powers, they abstained from voicing theirs. If a doctor as qualified as him – an MD – had set up practice in such a nondescript place, what could it signify but his patriotism? The way he dressed – white shirt and tie, sparkling shoes – his dignified speech, all of this made people wonder why he hadn't gone to Pune or Bombay. They regarded him with both wonder and gratitude.

The modernity in his personality was reflected in his everyday conduct. His wife addressed him by name and in the singular pronoun in public. He would reply to her in the same lovey-dovey tone. He talked openly, in the most alluring fashion, of his daily habit of having a glass of whisky. In tender moments, he would not hesitate to put his arms around his wife's shoulder or hold hands in public. He didn't seem to care how such a display of affection went down in a small town.

People felt it was unnatural when Dattaram spoke to his children as if they were his friends. Particularly with his daughter, Tarangini, who had been given enormous latitude. My grandmother, who knew of this from hearsay, had remarked: 'If you carry someone on your head for too long, they will do all their jobs right there.'

Tarangini wore the most fashionable clothes, and Dattaram, far from being opposed, was in fact very enthusiastic about getting them for her from Bombay. She was the first girl to wear trousers in our town. The doctor's attitude towards his daughter attracted derision. 'Now these things look good, but later when it turns into a habit . . .' they would say, or 'a good seed makes a good crop', so on and so forth.

He made things difficult for the organizers who invited him as a guest of honour to public programmes – he would lecture the audience on his pet subjects such as superstition, democracy, nation-building, equality, casteless society, etc. He criticized the wrongs of all political parties, hence one could not get a fix on his affiliation. It led to all kinds of guessing games in town. He spoke of atheism, and people assumed he was a communist. But then what of the generous donations he made for Ganesh Chaturthi?

Tarangini earned herself the moniker Krantijeevi. This is an interesting story. In the last year of high school she took part in a public speaking competition. The subject was 'The status of women in society'. In the animated flow of her impassioned speech, she inadvertently said 'Krantí*jeeví*' instead of 'Krantikari', meaning a 'revolutionary'. Not once, but twice! Everybody pounced on it. That's it – the name Krantijeevi stuck to her for as long as she was in school.

Dattaram would tease her about it too. The speech had several of the doctor's pet themes but there was one thought that was novel and truly revolutionary – it stayed with me. 'It's a woman's right to decide to have a baby. A man cannot force it on a woman. To have a baby out of wedlock is a woman's right too.' I didn't get the full import of it then. Years later, when I thought about it, I wondered if she had put any of it into practice, and if she had, how.

During the competition, a few boys from her class were sitting behind me.

'Wow, what an item doctor has produced,' they leched. I wanted to turn around and protest, but what if they said, 'Hey, what's she to you?' I was at a loss to say what my claim on Tarangini might be and thought the better of it. Even now, when people make crass comments about her on social media, I feel like reacting strongly, but I am overcome by the same hesitation.

During the summer vacation, Sanjeev's house used to be full of their cousins. There was a quiet contest between us in the classroom in which Sanjeev invariably prevailed. Their house was always open to me – he probably experienced the heady delight of the winner when I hung around with him. In those days, Tarangini joined us. I loved her proximity. When I was in class one, I was attracted to my teacher – it was an age when I hardly knew what that meant. Growing up, no longer so innocent, the girls I took to were younger and younger. In my callow youth, I didn't think it was a big deal to like women a couple of years older than me. But now, in my fifties, I feel age does matter. Don't get me wrong. Political correctness doesn't go with Tarangini; one should be prepared to examine the true nature of things.

One day, probably a Sunday, Dattaram was relaxing in his drawing room after lunch, reading a book. The children, in vacation frenzy, were bringing the house down. Dattaram could not concentrate. He chided them and the noise came to a halt. Now they were to sit before him and receive his long lecture on everything from the freedom struggle to the human anatomy, to galaxies, the electoral system, and more.

At one point he added: 'You must fall in love. Or the world will never appear differently to you. Without it you will never desire revolution.' I cannot remember the context in which he made this statement, but I can hear it, even now. The word 'love' is thrilling to youngsters, and the source of parental consternation. So, to speak about it so unabashedly was also a form of protest.

My eyes had turned towards Tarangini. She was holding her painted fingers up to the sunlight, engrossed in their gleam, fully oblivious to this world. Her lips had formed a pout, an expression natural to her whenever she was absorbed in something. She suddenly looked up and looked in my direction. I felt distraught and looked away.

Tarangini went to college in a different town. She went on to Dharwad to pursue her master's. My father was transferred and I went to Bagalkot to do my engineering.

In the early days, lonely and homesick, I wrote her a letter and posted it to her hostel address. She sent back a short reply. I read it again and again, soaking up every word, squeezing it for as many meanings I could find.

'Study well' was her last line. I strummed on those two words endlessly to see if the resonance brought up more. With those two words I wove a dream – of studying well, becoming something, and offering all my success to her. Over

Krantijeevi Tarangini

the next two weeks, I found other attractions on the campus and the excitement of her letter faded into the background. About one year after this episode, I had the opportunity to attend a wedding in Dharwad, and I went to the university ladies' hostel to see her. It was five-thirty in the evening. The watchman at the entrance took down my name on a piece of paper and sent it in through an attendant.

As soon as Tarangini appeared at the end of the corridor, I recognized her. But, until she walked closer, she did not recognize me.

'It's you, is it? It didn't occur to me that it could be you even when they gave me the slip with your name!'

She was wearing a loose white cotton shirt over a light green salwar. She had pulled her thick, curly hair into a tight bun.

'Come, let's sit here.'

I followed her.

We both sat down on the stone bench in the garden outside. Only now I noticed that she had a bunch of tamarind in her hand. Putting her legs up on the bench, she dropped the pods into her lap.

'Want?' she asked, holding out long green pods.

'No . . .' I noticed a string of red beads around her neck.

'I just love these. The fairs here sell heaps and heaps,' she said, as she peeled the pods and ate one by one the white pulp within. I can't remember the details of our conversation. Though she was engrossed in eating, it was she who asked the questions.

Once in a while she looked up at me but her attention was focused on ripping the hard-skinned ones with her nails. She asked, 'How come you are here in Dharwad? Whose wedding is it?' I should have taken some tamarind from her, I later felt, instead of sitting idly watching her eat. Amidst all this, I raised an objection: 'You never wrote to me.' 'Had you written another letter, I would have replied,' she said. Some pulp was wedged under her lower lip. She didn't bother to wipe it away and it stuck out like a strange, spare tooth.

My visit was ruined by that image. It's hard to explain, but she was so uninterested in wiping her mouth clean that the conversation – questions, replies – became too irksome and I lost interest. I had gone to meet her in my best clothes, in what I had worn to the wedding that morning. My sandals were new too. I had taken care to place a clean handkerchief in my pocket, just in case I might need to use it.

I had gone in without thinking of what I wanted from this meeting. Suddenly I felt that my time and energy was being wasted. I know I sound rude, but if I want to be truthful, this is the only way to say it. A hunter who would rather not waste his arrows looks for his spoils within the limits of his bow, doesn't he? You can look the truth in the eye, but how might it seem to the eyes of one who sees everything as black and white?

I lost touch with Tarangini. I had no reason to write to Sanjeev. Now and then, I heard some news about them. Sanjeev moved to Mumbai; his parents were no more. Tarangini lived

Krantijeevi Tarangini

in Bangalore, was unmarried, etc. Years later the newspapers told me that she had married the actor-producer Haidar; old friends informed me of this as well. It was confirmed when I saw the couple's photo in the newspapers. According to friends she was not his first wife. Anyway, that information was not in the newspapers.

When I was in class ten, Haidar was shooting in our home town. It was a film that he was producing and acting in. Film shooting then was not as commonplace as it is now. Half the town gathered to watch the shoot, hanging around the sets at all times of the day. The crew had taken help from Dattaram, and so a small role was offered to Tarangini.

She was one of the friends of the tragic heroine who kills herself. The scene ran barely half a minute. The heroine is perched atop a gate, with her legs stretched to one side. Coyly, she explains to her three friends the love games her boyfriend plays with her. Tarangini, playing one of the friends, bites into a raw mango and says: 'That's how he is. No shame. He does it to me too.'

A cruel scene. The director did multiple retakes, unhappy that the heroine didn't look devastated to the right degree. To us, the acting had no flaws. Finally, he spoke angrily: 'Think. He is your man, and he does the same thing to her as well. How shocked you would be. Think.' The director had barely turned his back than the heroine mumbled, 'Let him have his way, sir. I will also have mine.' Those standing close by began to laugh; the director was livid. Finally, the take was approved – I'm not sure whether the director gave up, or whether it actually met his expectations. Now when I heard about Tarangini's marriage to Haidar I remembered this episode. They would be at least fifteen years apart. I wondered if there was some connection between the shooting and their marriage.

After their marriage, I carefully read any news of him that cropped up. He no longer appeared in the entertainment sections, but continued to be in the news because of his entry into politics. He was the chairperson of one of the corporations, and once, during a press meet, a reporter provoked him.

'Yes, yes, a Muslim certainly has connections with Janmashtami! If you come home, I'll show you,' he retorted.

It appeared as a box item, as it would.

It was through the newspapers that I learnt of his tragic death. On the way to Mangalore, his car had met with an accident. No sooner had I read this than I wanted to meet Tarangini, but hundreds of reasons came in the way. As the days passed so did the desire, till I found I had forgotten about it.

It has been four years since he passed away.

About six months ago, I received a message: 'Add Tarangini to your friends list'. Almost every day networking sites throw up suggestions which I mostly ignore. This time, I paused. Her picture was not public. Yet, I knew it was the same Tarangini. Memories raged within me; I melted, and immediately sent a friend request.

Two weeks later, I received the message that she had accepted. Just to make sure it was her I left a message: 'Are you the same Krantijeevi?' The next instant she asked for my phone number. She called right away.

Almost immediately, a barrage of questions. She soon had all my news. She was happy to know that I lived in Hubli.

'Everyone says Bangalore. Thank god you are in Hubli. Unfortunately for me, I am in Bangalore. Let me not start my story here. I'll fill you in when we meet.' It seemed like she was happy to have connected with me.

'Next time I'm in Bangalore, I'll certainly meet you,' I promised with joy.

It was after this that I started noticing her bizarre posts. The first time I read one, I was befuddled and looked through her entire account. I didn't get much information. Her old posts disturbed me. The responses were even more troubling. There was a world around Tarangini, and it was neither innocent nor easy to understand.

'Sleeveless beauty. All these days you swallowed the earth, now you throw it up', said one status line, to which came the response 'It is only from a waif that such words come forth'. 'Not snake, the mongoose will win', 'Sluts get sluts, and widows widows.' Yet another said: 'K.R. Market, Murderess.'

Once she put up a line she would never reply, as if the last word was hers. Even to the slurs of filth, cunt, slut, cocksucker, she refused to respond. What is the meaning of all this, who are these people, is this a coded language that only they know how to read? Sometimes there is pleasure to be had in the putrid, and I developed a strange intoxication from all of this.

I visited Bangalore twice after our conversation, but hadn't the time to meet her. On the third visit, a meeting was cancelled and I remembered Tarangini and sent her a message. When you are alone, and you have the time, you foster lewd thoughts. We decided to meet that evening.

She gave me the address of a restaurant. 'It's a quiet place. We can relax and have a comfortable chat.'

I shaved again before I left. I coloured my hair each time I travelled to Bangalore, and was pleased that it had come to good use.

I reached ten minutes ahead of time, chose a table by the window. Waited for her. It was an air-conditioned upmarket restaurant. Apart from soft music playing in the background and some whispers, it was quiet. I turned the pages of the menu, and felt numb at the prices. The bar menu especially. There was no logic to the cost.

Tarangini turned up in a dark blue sari paired with a sleeveless blouse. Since I was expecting her, I recognized her as soon as she walked in. If we had crossed each other on the streets, I wouldn't have recognized her. I stood up and waved out. 'You've changed. In my memory you were different,' she said, as we shook hands. She had watched her figure, looked slim and strong. She pulled the heavy chair effortlessly and sat down. It was impossible to guess her age from her body language. She wore a dark brownish lipstick.

'You have changed too, not much though. One has to look at you for a bit, and then one can tell.'

'Clever!' she replied. I didn't much care for the tone of her voice.

'You look nicer now,' the line came to my mind, but I couldn't bring myself to say it.

I decided to order depending on what she chose to drink. Without even looking at the menu, she ordered vodka and orange juice. I did the same.

'Where's Sanjeev these days?' I hadn't thought about how to begin the conversation and her brother came to my rescue.

'He's in Mumbai. His wife works in a bank. Their daughter is ready for marriage. All of them are floating in worldly happiness.' The sarcasm in her words disturbed me.

'It's ages since I saw him,' I said blankly. 'After we all moved to different cities . . . at least I got to meet you that one time in Dharwad,' I blabbered.

She didn't answer. I decided not to speak of things that she disliked, and brought up Bangalore traffic, garbage, booming real estate and other sundry issues. We just skimmed the surface without trying to get to the core of things. Slowly we started warming up, and the drinks arrived. 'Cheers to our reunion,' I said, raising a toast. Our glasses clinked.

'Tell me exactly how many years is it since we met?' she asked, before taking the first sip.

'That is what I was calculating, thirty years perhaps.' She nodded her agreement.

Immediately after the first sip, I leapt to childhood. 'I have never seen another household which was as modern. You all were far ahead . . . of even what's OK today!'

'What you say is true. Appa's thinking was distinctive. But in practice it was less rosy.' She was looking perhaps for the right words. She had rested her elbow on the edge of the table. The skin on her arms was firm.

'When I look back I get goosebumps. Appa was staunchly anti-tradition. He was stubborn as well. Something at home would enrage him every day. Nobody ever asked my mother what her views were. Do you remember Ajji? Appa's mother? She rarely came out of her room in the far corner of the house.

'That was the best room in the house. During exams I studied there; in fact, sometimes I slept there. I remember the fight Appa and Ajji had. My father performed the death rites for his father, but the anniversary rituals were beyond him. That used to upset Ajji. She secretly ensured that someone in her parental home performed them.

'My father got wind of it – I was in college at the time – and it led to a huge fight. In the heat of the argument, he declared, "I performed the last rites for Appa, I won't do anything for you, and neither will my children do anything for me." Ajji got scared that she would turn into a ghost. Appa had spoken of death and *that* was a bad omen.

'What he said was extremely cruel. After that day, she became delirious. Unable to see her suffer, I promised that I would get Appa to perform her funeral rites. When she passed away, I was in Dharwad. My intervention was not necessary. Appa performed her last rites. Ironically, Sanjeev not only performed Appa's death rites, he does the annual ceremony as well. Ask him and he will say, "Appa had no faith but I do. I do it for myself." It took a bit of probing but I found out that both he and his wife were scared their family would be haunted by ghosts.'

The first drink was over before we realized it. She ordered a second round with fried cashews. 'This is something Haidar got me hooked on,' she laughed, screwing up her eyes.

As if she had heard the question that had arisen in my mind, she said: 'Yes I would drink when Haidar was alive.'

'How did he latch on to you?'

She was amused by the way I had asked the question. 'What do you mean latch on?' she laughed.

My questions, her answers, incidents, episodes, summaries, diversions . . . till we had finished dinner the conversation was all about her.

Her perspective: I realized how different I was compared to other girls when I went to Dharwad. So secretive! What they practised clandestinely, I did openly. That was how Dad brought me up. It had its good and bad effects. I experience both, even now. My mother hounded me to get married after my studies. My father wanted me to get a job. Succumbing to Amma's wishes, Appa began to look for an alliance.

Till then he had had no clue how difficult any of this was. I had earned a bad reputation in our circles. People had heard all kinds of stories about me. From the clothes I wore as a little girl to the boy who travelled back with me from Dharwad after my exams. It was awful, I can't even begin to say what. Nobody dared take home this girl who was a threat to the establishment. It was not easy to find a boy outside one's caste. One day Appa sadly said, why don't you find someone for yourself? He had probably put down an inter-caste wedding for me in the script of his revolution.

Marriage is not a woman's ultimate destination, Appa would hold forth, and now I could see him crumbling under the weight of his statement. Now he stumbled on all that he had once laid down so I could blossom naturally. Early on he would say, 'One must be fortunate to marry my daughter'; he stopped when he realized how foolish he sounded. He even stopped objecting to my mother's oblations at various temples, so you can imagine how much he had mellowed.

Eventually I got a proposal from an engineer. He had a big job. My father was very happy that he was an atheist. He sang his praises. Their entire family came home to meet me, a good-looking guy. From the light-hearted banter of that evening, it seemed like there was consent for the alliance. My mother wore a relaxed smile. Finally, he said, 'I want to speak to the girl.' My father, you know him, 'Oh yes, why not?' And he took us upstairs to his room, closed the door behind us and left. It was just the two of us. We sat on the bed, facing each other. It almost felt like an entrance exam. Well, I'm not complaining about it.

'Does God exist or not?'

'God alone knows.'

'What if the man develops another relationship after marriage?'

'Let's take a call then. It could happen to the woman too.'

'You don't believe in chastity?'

'If the man believes, the woman will believe.'

'What do you think of sexual relationship before marriage?'

'What of it? If it is there, it is there. And that will become something of the past.'

'Can other men touch you?'

'If I consent.'

'If I touch.'

'Not without consent.'

'Even after marriage?'

'Yes, even after marriage.'

'Suppose I touch . . .'

He had a smirk when he placed his hands on my shoulders. What do you know about a man's power – that smile carried pity and contempt for my ignorance. I stood up and slapped him.

That's it. The news spread like a bad smell. My father didn't look for another alliance.

After a year's struggle, I found a job in Bangalore. My parents had died by the time I met Haidar. One evening, I went to the West End Hotel for a programme. I saw Haidar from a distance. I walked up to him and introduced myself.

I reminded him about the shoot. You may not believe this, but that night we dined together. We instantly hit it off. Back then, when his film was shot in our town, who could have imagined that one day, in my future life, I would meet him?

Once again, I became a teenager. Night and day, we messaged each other. I longed to see him. His feelings were just as intense.

Haidar was married and had a grown-up son. He did not live with his family; once in a while he went home. He never concealed anything from me. Since people recognized him, it was difficult to be in public places. We travelled out of town, travelled everywhere.

Since family for me was just Sanjeev, I sent him a mail about our upcoming marriage. Immediately he called back, 'Don't be hasty. I'll come over this weekend.' Did I need his permission? I got angry.

'I have to shop for the wedding this weekend. Don't come,' I said. He insisted. This man, who had not bothered to once ask me how I was, suddenly woke up to his fraternal feeling as soon as I announced I was going to marry a Muslim. He came running, brought his wife along for support. They both sang the same tune – think about it, think about it, they kept harping.

They started off with the age difference. They didn't have the courage to bring up Haidar's religion so they pushed their agenda with a gentle term, 'cultural difference'. Their real worry was whether it would harm their daughter's prospects.

Sanjeev's wife even put it across mildly. I had lost touch with Sanjeev when I moved to Dharwad, but there was always in my heart a measure of his nature. That was jolted.

I did all the arrangements for my wedding by myself. I went alone to buy the wedding sari.

~

Amidst all this, I told her briefly about my wife and children. I would have liked to say something spectacular about me, something that she never imagined I was capable of, but there was nothing. 'Gulab jamuns are really good here,' she said, a temptation that was hard to resist. We ordered jamuns and waited to be served.

Like a mind reader, she answered the question that had cropped up in my mind.

'I didn't convert to Islam. We had a registered wedding. Haidar had no belief in religion or god. I am not sure if I am a believer or non-believer. Strangely, Haidar's first wife had no objection to him marrying me, she had objections to me not converting. I think she was jealous of my freedom.'

'I don't know this side of Haidar. All I remember is his Janmashtami statement,' I laughed, remembering what I had read in the newspaper.

'There's more to him. I'll tell you. He was an agnostic. An intense lover. Generous. But like other men, there was a raging machismo within him. He never touched me without consent, didn't forcibly drag me to bed, but if I disagreed with him, he used to thrash me. I was a pathological dissenter, so I used to get beaten up quite frequently . . .

'Don't look surprised. That day when you asked me if I was Krantijeevi, my heart skipped a beat. I remembered it after so long and you reminded me. This nickname has dogged my life in an ironic sort of way. As if fate is playing a roguish game.'

I had wanted to remind her of the high school speech to make fun of it. But when she explained how the memory had touched a nerve, I decided to let it go. Just the way her online enigmatic messages disturb us, this nickname prickled at her.

'Do you still work?' I asked, trying to steer the conversation in a different way.

'I quit my job as soon as I got married. Haidar ran two colleges. I continue to look after them. Haidar has left behind a lot of property, a house, cash. His affairs are murky. It is a challenge to run them but an exciting challenge. Men, money, glamour, political clout . . . it is a different world out there. Women perceive men so differently. But what matters to me most is consent, it is sacred. Haidar understood this. That is the only reason why even when he thrashed me I didn't feel angry.'

The jamuns arrived in small silver cups. As she had said, they were delicious.

'I am unable to fathom your social media persona,' I said, in a tone that displayed no emotions.

'All the dirt of the human mind is dished out there. The

anger, intolerance, hatred, malice – it is all true. But the love that is displayed there is something you should be wary of. It is false, a lie. First of all, people's hearts have gone dry. They can see only their own selves.'

I tried to collate all that she had said – consent, freedom, etc. – but simply failed to link them together in the context of her experiences. In fact, I am very scared of women who expect sincerity, transparency and pure love in relationships.

I picked up the bill; even as a matter of courtesy she didn't offer to pay.

There was a tree by the restaurant. The road was beyond. She stood under the tree and called the driver, puckered her eyes and pursed her lips. I was seeing this expression after years, it softened my heart. Before I could say this to her – 'Your hotel is in the opposite direction or I could have dropped you,' she said in a rush, fixing her eyes on the road.

'No problem, I'm sure I will find an auto.'

I remembered the Dharwad meeting and felt awkward. Like that day, I had no clue about what I had expected from this meeting. Like then I became withdrawn.

Her car stopped a few yards from us. Bye, she said. I gave her a hug and saw her off.

I took an auto and reached the hotel. I was very sleepy, but before going to bed, I checked her status. There was nothing. I slept in peace.

The next morning I opened my phone as soon as I woke up, to see what Tarangini had said.

'Even a moment is more. Testing me? Motherfucker!'

I didn't expect this. I flew into a rage. What a thing to say! As I framed a response, the worst possible abuses went through my mind. Really, who was she saying this to? I recalled the previous night's happenings, moment by moment.

Her car came, she turned towards me and said, 'Bye.' We were standing close to each other. I moved closer to give her a hug. I had never hugged her before. Her strong perfume overwhelmed me. It took me a second to move away. Probably a millisecond late. As soon as I realized that, she had taken her hand off my back. I too moved away. Then she said nothing. I dryly said, 'Stay in touch.' She nodded, put her hand out of the car and waved.

Who then is the target of this statement? Am I overreacting, imagining things that never happened. Fine, it perhaps was a second more. There was room for more than one meaning. Isn't it this little space that holds the things that we choose to hide even from our own selves from which we pick a meaning that suits us? Comments had started flowing in.

'Let all the motherfuckers fail in the exam!'

'Does that mean no entry to latecomers?'

'Yad bhavam tad bhavati.'

So many like this, entirely prompted by the turbulence in the commenters' minds, their guilt triggering their anger ... that's all that mattered. Or maybe they knew something I didn't. But the truth is that whatever the words sowed was growing within us.

She has never responded. When I sat down to type a response, I remembered that some strands of her hair had escaped her bun, caressed my face. For a few seconds my senses were a blur. That's what caused my delay. Of course, what else?

'First learn to tie your hair properly.'

I wondered if I could add expletives to the line to match her assault.

Translated from the Kannada by Deepa Ganesh

7

Akhil Katyal

An Evening Walk
while a friend is in prison

The small countries
of a dog's paw-prints.

The liquid yellow
of the laburnum.

The last round
of the river-bound bus.

All this ordinariness
belongs to you.

The criss-crossed purple
of the sabz burj.

Akhil Katyal

The Shah-Jahani arches
of the Bangla Sahib.

The song of the clay-pot
that crosses the Chenab.

All this ordinariness
belongs to you.

The sandstone heat
near every home.

The way the sun eats
the South Block dome.

The inevitability
of your freedom.

All this ordinariness
belongs to you.

(for Natasha Narwal)

Akhil Katyal

Question and Answer

Answer:
Those who don't sing his song.
Those who see through his skin.
Those who don't make easy gods.
Those who lick the skies clean.
Those who throw fists at iron.
Those who shiver over nights.
Those who hold proofs of light.
Those who have him by his tail.

Question:
Who does the dictator send to jail?

Akhil Katyal

These Days

the sun
climbs so slowly
even the fallen seeds
throw long shadows.

Above them
the hours spread
like locusts

like hunger

like an illness
refusing to relent.

A government uses
this convenience to
make some arrests.

Akhil Katyal

Falcon

wings sharp as sickles

needle-sighted birds
older than Gilgamesh

older than all kings

seeing
further than any of us,
through dust and
darkness, and lies

hawk-eyed
fathoming all skies

catching in their arms
what our hands cannot reach,
what we hunger for

clawing at every night
prophetic, brave
giving flight

Akhil Katyal

moving flames
of the sky

known by many names,
one: 'the royal white falcon' is

Shaheen

the bird
that leads to victory

8

The Women on the Wall

Raghu Karnad

I saw the figure of a woman clad all in black, her face as well, lunging at a wall to pull herself up. Also balancing on the wall were two policemen, clad in riot gear. They stood against each other, khaki and black, after nightfall at the end of 26 January 2020. In the moment before that I was scared, suddenly realizing what a lathi-charge was, and how it would feel if an inch-thick rod was swung through a long, hard arc into my cheek, my spine, my girlfriend's wrist. I was trying to reach for her through the crowd, and also to keep live broadcasting, and also to run – but then we saw the woman on the wall, and I think we all stopped.

That afternoon a new protest sit-in had begun at Nizamuddin West. It was the latest of nearly twenty that were underway across Delhi – and more, across the country – of Muslim Indian women occupying public areas, all on the model of Shaheen Bagh, resisting the government's secretive citizenship agenda. This sit-in was especially visible and daring right beside a major turn-off from Lodi Road: the first of the permanent protest sites in central Delhi.

By evening, it had grown to a few hundred people, singing and lecturing under the halogen street lights, and the police had also arrived in force. Around midnight, soon after we got there, locals began to extend a tarpaulin over the protest site, a bare measure against the chilly rains of late January. The police lost their patience. An order was given, and they came in around their barricades, lathis raised and tear gas ready. The protest leaders, mostly older women, did not flinch. They moved forward to meet them.

Two policemen, decked out in helmets, visors, vests, scaled the wall that enclosed the mohalla, and edged up to pull the tarp off its pole. Then a young niqabi was up there too, calling out without pause, as if her balance depended on it, *'Azadi.'* Behind her, all the voices swung up into the air – *'Awaaz do'* – like poles raised to hold her – *'Hum ek hain.'* The armoured men halted, their shoulders drooped. A blurred minute later, they climbed back down. In another ten minutes, the uniformed company were back behind their barricade, and the protest was allowed to continue. It was small and very exposed. I wondered if it would last the night. But it lasted two months, another satellite lit by the radiance of Shaheen Bagh.

If you went, you will be able to say that you were witness to a miracle. For a hundred days, through the coldest winter in a century, a group of women in an urban ghetto of Muslim Indians slept on the road, with only cloth to separate them from the street and the freezing sky. They held the banner for their country's Constitution, its unity and its founding charter – and all the poisonous acts of the most powerful men did not hurt them.

From where the women sat and slept, art grew over the broken road and up like vines to cover the soot-stained pedestrian bridge. Revolutionary slogans and national flags flew together, forgetting their differences. Pilgrims like us came from further and further away.

From about halfway through the hundred days, soon after its celebration of Republic Day, it fell to Shaheen Bagh to lead and sustain a national movement – the largest peaceful protest movement by Indians in decades.

The ruling establishment, furious now and desperate to win an election, rounded on the women and their supporters. They were slandered on TV every night; bullied in election speeches by each of the country's most powerful men, from the prime minister to the home minister to the chief minister of Uttar Pradesh. Fringe gangs made public promises to attack them, and radicalized men visited with handguns drawn. The women stood their ground.

They endured the terror of a riot across the river, which began as a pre-planned programme to destroy their smaller sisters, the mini Shaheen Baghs of north-east Delhi. Through every form and level of provocation, they were peaceful.

After one hundred nights and days planted and flowering on the street, Shaheen Bagh was uprooted on the morning of 24 March 2020. So were other protest sit-ins in the National Capital Region and elsewhere. It took a global pandemic – one that shut down the country entirely, along with much of the world – to justify and practically enable removing them.

~

What Shaheen Bagh created was so rare it was almost old-fashioned: it created moral example. It was faultless in its demands, its conduct and its inclusion. The *naara*s there were sung in Urdu but also in Malayalam and Assamese. On the thirtieth anniversary of the flight of the Pandits from Kashmir, there were Kashmiri Pandits on stage at Shaheen Bagh, defeating enmity with empathy.

Fixed at its centre, however, were the women. On an evening in late January, in the descending darkness, I was drawn to a beaming white headscarf and shawl behind the stage, and so I met Tarannum Begum. Where the embroidered border of her veil lay on her chest, she wore a round pin with the Indian flag and the words 'Save Our Constitution' in English and Urdu.

Tarannum had been there since the beginning: when the police stormed Jamia, where her own children were students.

Outside the university gates, where the community stood in anxious support, they were lathi-charged. They ended up gathered on this stretch of road, where four women and six men stayed out the whole night.

'People think women are weak because they keep quiet,' she said. 'But they know everything, and now they had to come out – to save our citizenship, our Constitution, our Hindustan.' Each day more people joined them, she said, bringing tea or dinner, putting up a makeshift stage, until they were surrounded by hundreds. The night I met her, it was thousands.

It was an antibody bursting to life inside a nation infected with hate and sick with despair. The place was so healing that even the Delhi police were reliable in protecting it from overt threats. (Even if, as Mark Tully noted, the police were also 'unnecessarily barricading roads to spread chaos for commuters, thus creating hostility to the sit-in'.)

Everyone else became reliable too. When extremists promised to attack and disperse the women on 2 February, Sikh farmers gathered and travelled to their barricades, to offer their physical protection. Behind them were artists of every background, from underprivileged poets to celebrity supporters from Mumbai and Delhi, offering their presence as a hedge against violence (and against the factual distortion that was guaranteed to follow). For a week, the tiny stage at Shaheen Bagh received a stream of pop stars and classical singers, actors and entertainers that would have passed for a music festival.

Yet there was also a risk to our dependence on Shaheen Bagh, a danger that would play out and culminate in a riot.

~

Outside of the North-Eastern states, few of us were paying attention to the BJP's citizenship agenda – centred on a pair of programmes, the CAA and the NRC – until 15 December. That evening, the Delhi police decided to repay an unruly street protest by storming the campus of Jamia University and battering the students inside. A well-loved library was stained with blood and tear gas.

That action opened many eyes which had glazed over from too much bad news. A sudden monsoon of protest formed, which would swirl over the country for weeks. It was called, inadequately, the Anti-CAA Movement, but the CAA was only the spark, and the Anti- did not capture its surging affirmation of a society that was inclusive, kind, diverse and unified. As proof, it claimed a long-neglected legacy, the national flag and anthem (leaving pro-government protesters to adopt the slogan '*Desh ke gaddaron ko / Goli maaro saalon ko*').

By 19 December, marches, rallies and crackdowns were unfolding every day, in every major city and an unknown number of towns. Here were Indians of every class, religion, region and age. There were moments of honour for college students, Dalit organizations, scientists and military veterans, middle-class families, movie stars and stand-up comics, trans and queer folk, labour unions, bar associations, retired bureaucrats and Indians overseas. They formed the broadest imaginable social alliance, centred on Muslim Indians but going beyond them – and offering its collective social capital for their protection.

The scale of the protests was impossible to ignore, but the scale of what they accomplished has been underrated – except by the BJP. Even as bodies were dragged and battered in the streets, the movement took hill after hill in representing its argument and its cause. It dismantled the smoke and mirrors surrounding the citizenship agenda faster than the government could erect them. Unexpected allies merged with the clamour of Indians laying into the government, defending and affirming the energy in the streets.

Public figures who spoke to the right-wing base began to cross over to its arguments. A populist celebrity author, Chetan Bhagat, demolished the case for the citizenship test in a newspaper op-ed. A right-wing news anchor, Anjana Om Kashyap, broke from the party line to explain how a mass programme to disqualify citizens required a law to selectively readmit them. A conservative intellectual, Pavan Varma – also a senior office holder in a party allied to the BJP – called on his chief minister to 'categorically reject the CAA-NPR-NRC divisive scheme'. An aged saffron lion, Murali Manohar Joshi, rose from his winter to condemn the vice chancellor of Jawaharlal Nehru University after a night-time mob assault on students.

Legislative responses kept pace: a dozen state cabinets and assemblies eventually passed resolutions against the new law, or joined suit against it in the Supreme Court, or refused to carry out the groundwork for the NRC. Even on 25 February, while the protest sites were coming down in cinders in north-east Delhi, the assembly in Bihar – a state where the BJP was in the government – voted unanimously not to implement the present NRC.

~

Like the decision to claim the national flag, the diversity and elite participation was armour for the protests, or at least protective cladding. In states where the BJP controlled the police (especially Uttar Pradesh, but also Delhi and Karnataka) it did not save working-class Muslims from the lathi and the bullet, from being killed and maimed by police actions, or from more creative punishments afterwards. But it did save the victims from being framed as villains, and their message from being twisted into its opposite by the captive media.

Part of the marvel of the first month was how the protests had sparked and then spread with no organized centre. By the middle of January, however, the stamina of elite participants was waning. They were still there, but retreating from the streets and squares back on to social media. Students had to be in class now, others back in office. The movement needed a strategy to consolidate, sustain and protect itself, as well as genuinely coordinated tactics for each day. In 2013 a kind of conscious, semi-cynical institutionalization had allowed India Against Corruption to last and to grow, to great political effect. That was against easier odds, and a much milder political incumbent. In January of 2020, nobody was cynical enough.

The burden, and the danger, of carrying forward the anti-NRC effort shifted on to Shaheen Bagh and its little sisters. 'Necessity stayed on the street,' my colleague Naomi Barton observed. 'Privilege went home.' The women of the smaller Baghs were unwavering, and they were vulnerable. Supportive outsiders pivoted towards them – attending to SOS calls from the sites, negotiating with police, corporators and politicians, dragging the media back to open their eyes to the struggle. They poured time and resources into helping sustain the sit-ins, and away from larger actions designed to maintain the broad base of the protests.

It was an optical hazard, as well as a strategic one. Even for sympathetic newspapers, the mini Shaheen Baghs didn't produce the right imagery. Each day looked more or less like the next, and to outsiders, each Bagh looked like every other, apart from Shaheen Bagh itself. Even in their dozens, the sit-ins could not command attention, at least not proportionate to the courage of facing all those freezing nights.

The imagery was also now dominated by women in niqab, giving interviews through heavy cloth, faces and even eyes unseen. To a discerning liberal audience, this was evidence that the movement was empowering those who most deserved it, working-class minority women. It bore out the millennial credo that the elite will not save democracy for the marginalized, but the other way around. And if you were there, as on that evening in Nizamuddin, you would learn to see past the veil and your own nervous prejudice – to see revolution in the figure of a woman clad all in black, her face as well.

But to other Indian audiences, the visuals were troubling and suspicious. The simple garment of conservatism was easily painted, by hostile media, as proof of radical Islamism – and thus, their patriotic protest as an anti-national threat.

By early February, the image of the anti-NRC movement was starting to lose its spectacular diversity and to look exclusively Muslim – just what the ruling establishment was waiting for. A strange alignment occurred between the BJP's spin ('All the chaos is only Muslims, nobody else') and the woke self-abnegation of its critics ('All credit must go to Muslims, nobody else'). At the very start, the prime minister had said, 'You can identify them by their clothes' – and the Internet blew up with photos to challenge his communal stereotype of the protesters. In February the photos did not do that any more. New malice was unleashed.

On 11 February Delhi would elect its state assembly. The popular incumbent, the Aam Aadmi Party led by Arvind Kejriwal, hoped to reprise its feat from five years earlier: in 2015, right on the heels of Modi's national victory, it had stolen the saffron party's base – the Hindu middle class – away from militant nationalism, and won by a historic landslide, proving a new model to take the wind out of the BJP's sails. Since then, it had laboured at improving schools, clinics and access to water, and broadly at making government seem sensible and accountable.

Modi's new victory in 2019 was presented as proof of a national consensus against the secular ideal, and a mandate to begin building a Hindu rashtra. The citizenship protests had blown that narrative apart, and left the ruling establishment dizzy and embarrassed.

Come February, more desperate than ever to discredit the protests and to win in Delhi, the BJP conjured a dark mirror image of Shaheen Bagh as a nest of communal treachery and terror. 'They'll enter your house, rape your sisters and daughters, kill them,' one member of Parliament warned voters, speaking to a leading news agency. 'There's time today. Modi ji and Amit Shah won't come and save you tomorrow.' The lumpen slogan 'Shoot the traitors dead' was taken off the streets, and roared at a party rally.

Still they failed. Arvind Kejriwal swept Delhi a second time, and now humiliation demanded punishment.

Two weeks later, when the mini Shaheen Baghs in north-east Delhi tried to raise a new challenge, occupying portions of major roads, there was no armour left to save them from carnage. A defeated BJP candidate promised he would root them out himself. Within hours, the sit-ins were stormed and burned to the ground. Riots followed, and later the security forces were allowed in – to hold some communities indoors, while others laid the offending neighbourhoods to waste.

After nightfall, at the end of 26 February, I stood with a detachment of well-armed policemen by a nala near the Loni border. The riot was over, officially, but we were looking on as masked men set fire to slum dwellings and small transport vehicles whose owners had fled.

The masked men turned their eyes on us and began calling, '*Media ho ya mullah ho?*' Then they were covering the ground between us, and I was frightened. I searched the eyes of the police officer for some assurance. He said, 'You'd better run.'

We ran, and the next morning the captive media arrived, to make sure the country understood each way that Muslims were to blame.

~

Still Shaheen Bagh stood – through threats and atrocities, through the winter turning warm at last, through Holi. What it took to truly justify its end (or its physical dispersal) was nothing less than the worldwide suspension of social, commercial and economic behaviour that we called lockdown.

The new logic of everything, brought about by the novel coronavirus, had already swayed the most loyal advocates of Shaheen Bagh. At the mini Baghs around the country, there were arguments and urgings about winding up, with dignity and political advantage intact. The women – the only ones to truly understand the scale of their effort so far – made the proper adjustments, reducing their numbers and rearranging their sites to meet practical sanitary requirements. Still hostile media-men stalked through, raving at the women's resolve, and ignoring the real bomb of human density that was every other square mile of urban India.

On the morning after their hundredth night, when all the city was in curfew, the police finally came and pulled up the garden. And again the captive media followed, now at its leisure, to begin the work of rewriting this chapter, and recording it as a radical Muslim conspiracy to create a riot.

The argument of Shaheen Bagh was never defeated though, and the love – that is one word for it – which bound its participants was not found wanting. And the 2020 movement for India's Constitution, even in abeyance, resembles the original struggle that brought about that Constitution. Those freedom fighters also rose, were suppressed, and regrouped in new forms years later, guided by the certain thread of justice. Most historic movements have lost ground, then returned even stronger, in cycles – as we witnessed on the other side of the global lockdown, when the United States poured into the streets in defence of Black Lives – a banner once broken, now flying higher than ever.

At the end of a hundred days, Indians went from radical gathering to radical distancing – from physically converging as a public to lay claim to their republic to waking up isolated

The Women on the Wall

in a world of private boxes barred from touch. But the two are not opposite. A spirit of collective action and care, of protecting one another, drove them both – the danger of the time in lockdown was that India would spend the time only thinking about its solitude, and forgetting its solidarity. But social distancing does not need to mean the loss of political togetherness – the gift to India from the garden of Shaheen Bagh.

9

Why I Choose Hope

Rana Ayyub

In July 2020 India was struggling with a debilitating lockdown announced by Prime Minister Modi in March to bring under control the impact of Covid-19 in the country. Thousands of migrant workers were marching towards their home towns, in bare, blistered feet, under the scathing sun, their children eating leftovers off the streets, taking breaks to quench their thirst with water from cheap dented bottles. The migrants who had been the backbone of our modern cities, oiling our infrastructure with their sweat, were abandoned both by the government and by the upper middle class that had stocked its refrigerators with avocados and mangoes of the season. In a four-month-long relief work initiated by me through the crowdfunding platform Ketto, I tried to placate my own conscience and of those like me who felt helpless watching the devastating images of human plight on the front pages of our newspapers. For a moment, I felt good about the country, the wonderful souls who were contributing generously to make sure that a pregnant woman who survived on one banana in forty-eight hours felt needed and cared for.

In a parallel reality, another pregnant woman, a gutsy, fearless twenty-seven-year-old woman with conviction, fighting against an unjust society, a fascist regime, was incarcerated in Tihar Jail. When arrested in April for being part of the students' movement against the divisive Citizenship Amendment Bill, Safoora Zargar was three months pregnant. In jail, she suffered from anxiety disorder and was made to sleep on the floor. But the first trimester of pregnancy with its share of sickness coupled with the fear of contracting the virus deprived her of sleep and she spent the nights reading verses from the Quran.

With everyday humiliation, a slander campaign on social media that would cast aspersions on her character, ask questions about the father of her unborn child, it was brutality aided by a modern-day witch hunt. When I met Safoora in July, a week after she was released on bail, she looked frail for a woman who was six months pregnant. I was meeting her for the first time though I had heard stories of her activism, her courage, her penchant for speaking up when those around her chose an uneasy silence. Her husband and her younger sister shielded her from us and the rest of the world. She was reluctant to speak and understandably so as her heart and mind were at swords. Safoora was not a woman who left her thoughts unexpressed, but she was equally uncomfortable with the thought of troubling her unborn baby with the consequences of her words.

Her mother had recently undergone a brain surgery; her husband, the only working member of the household, feared losing his job and was working late hours. She herself could still not sleep; her sister told me that she would wake up in the middle of the night with sweat trickling down her face, a crippling anxiety attack that restricted her movement.

I sat with Safoora for hours, whose face did not for a moment betray her anxiety. She was worried for her young classmates whose lives she feared would be destroyed. As I walked into her housing society near Jamia in a predominantly Muslim society, my face covered with a mask and my glasses, a resident stopped me. 'Are you Rana Ayyub?' he asked. I replied in the affirmative. He pointed at the top floor and said, 'We are proud of her.'

In September Safoora developed complications and later gave birth to a boy. She named Hasan, Arabic for benefactor. Hasan will grow up to hear stories of his revolutionary mother whose bail could be cancelled any day as I write this depending on her 'behaviour'. The court demands silence of those it has given bail to on humanitarian grounds. This is torture, I tell her, and she smiles and looks away. To silence a young, outspoken woman is perhaps worse than walking barefoot in Tihar with hardened criminals. But this is the punishment India has chosen for some of its brightest minds who unlike many of us in a population of 1.2 billion have a spine and a conscience.

It is not easy to live in this New India. It is not easy to live here without the privileges that make it easy to breathe in this democracy. The less privileged include our poor, our women, our Muslims, our lower caste, our adivasis; to be one of them and to protest against the brazen injustice that is being done to them is seditious.

Safoora Zargar and her revolutionary fervour reminds me of Bapu Patil, Anil Mamane and hundreds of other students whom I met in 2010 as an editor with *Tehelka*.

I was working on an investigation on the misuse of the draconian Unlawful Activities (Prevention) Act (UAPA) in Maharashtra. I met them everywhere, in jails, at the office of lawyers, at police stations, at universities, at their homes with copies of Karl Marx and Ambedkar placed neatly by their bedsides. I met Kanchan, a twenty-year-old woman with short, curly hair and an infectious smile. Her husband had been arrested on charges of being a Naxal and the evidence against him was a pamphlet with quotes by Lenin. The chawl they lived in was coloured blue just like the many Dalit localities in Nagpur. In her struggle to get justice for her husband who had been accused of aiding and abetting Naxal activities, Kanchan had become the hero of the story. I tell her that she and her husband are looked at with suspicion, to which she responds, *'Arre didi, 5 foot ki ladki hoon main, 40 kilo wazan hai, main kya kar loongi, sach bolti hoon, sach ke liye khadi hoon, ab sach se thoda dar toh sabko lagta hai'* – Sister, I am 5 feet tall, weigh 40 kilos, all I do is stand for the truth – and the truth, everyone fears it a little.

Both Kanchan and Safoora are fighting a truth that the Congress and the BJP when in power find unpalatable. Charged in the Bhima Koregaon case, Kanchan's colleagues including her human rights lawyer Surinder Gadling along with hundreds of intellectuals and activists of the Kabir Kala Manch are still behind bars. It is these voices that have been stifled and silenced that have given me the strength these past fifteen years to write a truth that is both unpalatable and unpopular. More often these voices are young and have much to lose and yet they fight to save our collective conscience.

We Indians are living at a time that is testing our resolve as a journalist, as a crusader, as an activist, as a teacher, as a politician, more importantly as a citizen who believes in the guiding principles of our Constitution. Our essential humanity is being mocked, our love for the nation is seen with suspicion, our commitment to justice is being viewed through the skewed lens of hypernationalism. I am often accused of being brutal with my words and radical with my truth. I am often advised to tone down and make peace. I am mocked on social media for being more an activist and less a journalist. I often wonder, how does one speak the uncomfortable truth without losing friends and allies?

On days you wake up and feel helpless and claustrophobic.

You do not recognize your well-meaning friends who share WhatsApp forwards of Muslims spreading the coronavirus. You are in a moral dilemma each time your security guard says 'namaste didi' because he proudly claims to be a Godse-wadi in his display picture. Your friends tell you to leave the country and accept the prestigious fellowships being offered to you. This country is not worth living in, announce your privileged friends sitting at the posh SoBo House overlooking the stunning Arabian Sea.

It is a privilege that has not been accorded to either Safoora Zargar or Sharjeel Imam or Kanchan or Devangana Kalita or Umar Khalid and thousands of Indians who cannot look away like friends their age. They have chosen to abandon their individual dreams and plans, the comfort their education could have possibly earned them.

In April, days into the lockdown when life had come to a standstill, my brother Arif and I stepped out to meet a farmer who was offering export-quality mangoes at a thousand rupees a dozen. Having picked up enough boxes that fit into our SUV, we passed by a railway station complex that had now become a shelter for migrants who had lost their jobs. A toddler was playing in the middle of a deserted road in the scorching sun, his ribcage visible under a thin layer of skin. He was nibbling on a banana peel. His mother, seven months pregnant, had passed on that one banana to him, her first meal in two days.

It was a sight that was not just disturbing but deeply embarrassing. With those export-quality alphonsos in my car, a deep sense of shame and elitism overwhelmed me. It was then that the restless youth of this country, many left jobless by the lockdown, came to my rescue. A call for help on Twitter got me access to young boys, many from the slums of Dharavi, Sion, eager to join in what ended up being the most therapeutic assignment of my life.

A relief operation that lasted four months helped 6000 migrants reach their homes, provided ration to 50,000 families and also helped families whose homes were destroyed by the cyclone and floods in West Bengal and Assam, which happened around the same time. It felt as if the universe had a sinister plan.

I am writing about this because these four months gave hope to the cynic in me, it gave me hope that all was not lost. The young boys, many fasting for Ramzan, living in chawls, not sure if they could provide for their family, left everything to immerse themselves in the relief work. They would start by unloading the sacks from the trucks to the warehouse, packing them, making lists of the neediest, travelling in tempos to places that were worst hit by the pandemic. I was the one getting accolades on social media, but the real heroes were these boys who believed in the essential goodness of humanity. Three of them contracted Covid-19 and two elderly volunteers lost their lives, but they left behind an immense sense of hope that all was not lost.

In a country blinded by hate, I saw glimpses of selfless love. In the evening when the volunteers would sit together for iftaar, they would bring food from their homes. I, the only woman, was given the centre of the table, and the youngest volunteer, one of my favourites, would make jaggery tea for me.

With my history of depression and anxiety, the months leading up to the lockdown were traumatizing for me. I had witnessed naked hate on the streets of Delhi in February that led to a communal pogrom. As a child of the 1992 riots, when a mob barged into our homes with swords, a Sikh family had helped me and my sister escape gang rape. At the age of nineteen I was in Ahmedabad during the Gujarat carnage, helping the relief work to allay the crippling feeling of being 'helpless'. Delhi of 2020 ripped through the layers of post-traumatic stress disorder.

I had been put on an increased dosage of escitalopram and clonazepam to help ease my nightmares. The lockdown that was announced a month later, which left me, like everyone else, with no access to the world, disconnected from friends and confidantes, was likely to worsen my condition. Humanity was my saviour – the relief work aided by the young men rescued me from the clutches of my past.

I asked a student who is now behind bars on charges of terrorism for his speech during the citizenship protest, a speech that spoke of pluralism and humanity, 'Why do you do what you do?'

He answered, 'Do we have a choice?'

Given a choice this student activist would yet again risk his comfortable life for the cause of freedom and justice.

Rana Ayyub

Each day in India is a slide into majoritarianism; each day in the country is an attack on our personal liberty. Each day in this country is an attack on the believers of love targeted through vile allegations of love jihad. Each day is an assault on our mental health as our news channels conduct a medieval witch hunt against women they hate. But fight we must. To quote Martin Luther King, 'I believe that unarmed truth and unconditional love will have the final word.'

10

Agendas

Roshan Ali

The tiny man at the immigration counter in his pale blue shirt glanced at my passport and then looked at me from under his frowning eyebrows. His stiff, black moustache twitched with suspicion.

'Ye kaisa naam hain?' he asked.

'Sorry sir my Hindi is not good. I am from South.'

'Achha what name this is?'

'Alif Algernon sir.'

He raised his eyes from the passport and examined my face.

'Muslim?' he asked.

'No sir, actually . . .'

'Alif is Muslim name I know. But yaar what is this *allergen*?'

'No sir, not allergen – Algernon. My parents had weird ideas.'

He wasn't listening.

'And also what are you say you don't know Hindi? Hindi is language of India.'

I was looking at his face trying to figure out the motivation for this rudeness when he asked again, 'Muslim or what? What is religion?'

'I was trying to tell you, I don't have a religion.'

He laughed and spluttered, then coughed for a whole minute.

'How you can not have religion?' he asked once he had recovered. 'Your name is Muslim, Alif, so you are Muslim. Don't tell lies. You just want to get into Delhi quickly.'

I paused, trying to process what he had just said.

'Sorry sir just want to clarify,' I said after a brief, tense silence in which he flipped rapidly through my passport trying to find something in it that would confirm his suspicions about me. 'Why can't I go into Delhi if I'm Muslim?' I asked.

He looked startled. 'You not seen news or what?'

'Not for two months. I am coming from a research trip to Borneo.'

'Phone?' he accused, pointing at my pocket, with a neat, small, white hand.

I pulled out an old Nokia 1200.

'No news,' I said.

He shook his head.

'There is riots in Delhi mister,' he said. 'Many people died.'

'Riots? But these things keep happening.'

Agendas

'Hindu–Muslim riots Mr Alif,' he continued. 'But everyone knows who made the violence.'

I tried to appear moved. He looked carefully at me again.

'But you are not Muslim I think. You have converted to Christian? It is death penalty for you in Muslim country,' he said and looked pleased, his reddish smile beaten into meaninglessness by his dehumanizing task of treating people as pieces of paper.

'That's very bad sir,' I said, twisting sadness into my face. 'But I am not here for anything like that. I'm only here to meet my uncle.'

'For what purpose?'

'My parents died last year and they left me some money.'

He guffawed and fingered his crotch.

'Why did your parents leave money with him?' he asked angrily, waving my passport in the air. 'You are a grown man. Why didn't they give you money? Don't tell me all this nonsense.'

'Sir please believe me. I was estranged from my parents. We hadn't spoken in many years.'

He suddenly looked straight into my eyes and then I think he pitied me because his moustache drooped (whereas earlier it was standing in an arm-straight-out-in-front-palm-facing-downwards kind of attention) and his face softened.

'I hope so you are not lying to me,' he said, sounding almost sad. 'It is a sin to lie about your parents' death.'

Then he stamped my passport with an efficient flourish,

like he had done a thousand times before and shouted 'next' past me, into the line of nervous, waiting people.

And just before I walked away from the counter, he looked at me sideways and added, 'Bhai I know you don't care about all this but if you have any Muslim family members please tell them not to anger the Hindus. We are more in numbers and we love the country.'

∼

A prickly, dirty, dark cold crouched over Delhi like a fanged wolf gnawing at my ears as I stood waiting for my taxi. Headlights were blurry, human figures altered into shadowy, twisted forms and criminal intent seemed to be everywhere.

When my taxi arrived, I noted the small figure of Hanuman on the dashboard. The driver kept looking strangely at me in the rear-view mirror with his small, dark eyes. But maybe I was being paranoid as I usually was.

'Kalkaji no problem sir,' he said suddenly.

'Uh what?'

'Kalkaji no issues.'

'Oh, the riots?' I asked.

'Yes sir. Only that side, north side. Many poor people are there. No jobs. No work. That is why they fight,' he explained. 'This Hindu–Muslim nonsense doesn't matter.'

At least I won't be lynched, I thought as he began to hum a tune. One arm hung out of the car.

'Anyway I am not worried sir,' he said after a brief silence. 'Summer is coming. Too hot to do rioting.'

I smiled and realized I hadn't smiled in a few hours. My face felt strange and alien.

And the city felt alien, as most cities do, in the first few hours when you reach them. Then you get used to the filth and the noise and the hypocrisy.

At this time of the night the roads were empty. The taxi flew over narrow flyovers with plastic walls and past mansions with five cars parked outside, then past small, unpainted houses with blue tarpaulin sheets as roofs and a few people wandered about, who couldn't afford to sleep, or who didn't want to wake up in the morning.

The sky was a dirty orange. Man had even made light into pollution. He was responsible for this, the hirsute oaf who sparked the first flame with some stones and then danced about it stupidly. Wouldn't the world have been nicer if he had set himself on fire?

A PSA on the radio was telling people not to go to northeast Delhi.

'Ha, now they're telling,' said the weary taxi driver. 'Too late. Now riots are almost over. Anyone can go there now. Sir you want to go there and see? You can put on Facebook. I will take you.'

'Uh no, thank you,' I said quickly. 'I have to meet my parents.'

He shook his head understandingly. 'Yes sir. I always meet my parents at least once a week to get their blessings.'

But my parents were dead and I was glad.

∼

The taxi squeaked to a halt in front of a tall wood and metal gate and I gave the driver some money.

'Sir it is online payment on Uber app,' he said, looking confused.

'No, this is a tip for you.'

He shook his head and said with unexpected rudeness, 'No. Please see.'

He pointed to a sign at the back – 'no tips'.

I nodded and got out, a little shaken.

The guard at the gate had already taken my suitcase out of the boot. The taxi driver, frowning, sped away in his scratched, unwashed car.

'Mamaji is there?' I asked the security guard as I followed him into the house.

'Yes sir. Lots of people are there. There is meeting.'

Meeting? Perhaps there was a fundraiser. I dreaded to think it was connected to the riots. I just didn't have the capacity to deal with that kind of thing, so late at night.

'How are you Biswas bhai?' I asked, as I followed him down the cobbled driveway.

Agendas

'Fine only sir. What to do? It is difficult life,' he said. 'My family is fine sir. God's grace.'

'You're not fine?'

'My legs hurt sir. I have to go to doctor.'

He went quickly towards the house, torso tilted left to balance out the suitcase, legs doing a funny in-line shuffle.

He placed the suitcase down outside the large front door and rang the bell.

A round, fair face appeared at the barred window and smiled widely – Shamim didi.

'Alif bhaisaab has come,' said the guard tiredly and went back to the gate.

'Alif!' Shamim didi cried, unlatching the door from inside and stepping out. Then she began to weep loudly and wiped her face with the sleeve of her kurta.

'What a time to come back to Delhi beta,' she said, sobbing and trying pathetically to pick up the suitcase.

'Didi don't do that, I'll take it,' I said.

But she kept sobbing and then began to drag the suitcase into the house, muttering, crying out loud, sniffling.

When we reached the hall she left the suitcase and shouted, 'Here he is, your stupid nephew, see him, how thin he has become. And what a time to come back to Delhi! It's all your fault only!' And saying this she stormed off into the kitchen muttering and spitting.

The man she had directed all this towards sat legs crossed on a maroon velvet sofa. He was bearded, dressed in a spotless white kurta and pyjama. His face wore a look of calm intensity as if he was thinking of something very important and as if in fact he had never ever thought of anything trivial. He rose from the sofa and came towards me, smileless, tall, stern. His curved, sharp nose seemed to lead the way, his hands clasped behind his back.

'How are you Alif?' he said embracing me, left, right, left. His voice was calm and deep as ever.

'Why is didi so upset?' I asked.

He sighed deeply.

'Come upstairs. We will talk. The others also wait.'

~

On the stairs he stopped me. 'You obviously heard of the riots,' he said. I nodded. He took two steps and stopped again. 'How was your research trip?' he asked. 'Did you find anything? Any new discoveries? How long are you staying with us?'

He asked the questions quickly, uninterested in the answers. I had never seen my uncle do anything in a hurry.

'Who is upstairs?' I asked him.

'Friends, some family.'

We reached the first floor and my uncle opened the door.

~

Agendas

We were greeted with serious and concerned faces that looked up from their phones or looked away from their conversations. A television screamed silently at the back.

'My nephew has come,' Salim Uncle announced.

Grave faces turned away. Some smiled warmly and nodded their heads.

'Salim bhai, I think you must start the meeting,' someone said loudly. There was general agreement and an approving murmur.

My uncle sat down on a large, white leather sofa. All the others sat too and those who couldn't get a seat stood with their arms crossed, frowning.

There was a brief silence and then my uncle cleared his throat. 'I have decided that I will not call for violence from any of our friends,' he said. His voice was firm and loud and specially designed for a small crowd.

Again an approving murmur rippled through the room. But some shook their heads and turned to each other and said things.

'Before you interrupt me Afroze, Wahid,' Salim Uncle continued, 'all you people who have seen them burning houses and walking with the police, we must defend ourselves, there is no denying it. But I will not call for retaliatory violence.'

'Sometimes offence is the best defence,' said an angry voice.

'Wahid bhai please, we cannot use that logic here. What will you do? Kill all of them? Kill all the Hindus, all the policemen? You will burn every Hindu shop and house you can find? Think of the innocents.'

My uncle had raised his voice now and suddenly I realized he was standing.

Another man stood up. 'So what do we do? We cower in our homes and galis and wait for them to come? We are sitting ducks there. We must get on the streets and push them back,' he cried.

A brutal silence thickened in the room. Salim Uncle sat down and rubbed his temples with his large hands.

'We are peaceful people,' said a voice from the back. Again there was a murmur of approval.

And another answered, 'But we cannot be slaughtered any more. We must do something.'

'The police will not help us. The government wants us out of the country.'

'We are not Indians in their eyes.'

'We are peaceful Muslims.'

A clamour of voices all made themselves heard. And then all waited for Salim bhai to speak.

'Yes we are peaceful,' he said finally. 'We will not let people say that our religion is violent or that we are Salafi or terrorists or any such things. We are Indians. We are Muslims. We are peaceful.'

They agreed. They clapped. I clapped too to my own surprise. The dissenting voices were drowned out in humanity.

'But we must do something,' he continued. 'We cannot

just sit in our houses. That is for another time perhaps. We must march through the streets. All of us — as Muslims. We must march peacefully through this city till the seat of the government. And they will beat us and they will call us anti-nationals but we must do this if we don't want this pogrom to be forgotten.'

Salim Uncle's voice trembled. He sat down and his hands shook. He wiped his face with the white handkerchief that he always carried with him.

Everyone seemed to agree. Discussions on logistics followed. At one point Salim Uncle dismissed the idea that they wouldn't get votes unless they fought on the streets.

'I refuse to believe that,' he snapped at the small, nervous-looking man who suggested it.

'And even if they don't vote for me, I wouldn't want the vote of someone who thinks we ought to murder people.'

That was the end of that discussion. The nervous fellow slipped out shortly after, Wahid and Afroze behind him. Once they were gone the atmosphere lightened. Salim Uncle told another young man to keep an eye on the three who had left. The young man nodded and followed them quietly out of the door.

∼

When all the discussions that were meant to be had were had and the hugs and smiles and handshakes were complete, the group filtered down the stairs and out. Salim Uncle had shifted sofas and now sat on one, legs crossed and eyes closed at the far end of the room.

When the sounds of footsteps and slamming doors and the sounds of cars had faded away, he opened his eyes and looked at me. 'Will you join us tomorrow Alif?' he asked.

I hesitated. 'I thought it was only for Muslims.'

'No, no, it is for anyone who supports us,' he said. Then frowning, 'But you are a Muslim also right?'

'No. I'm an atheist.'

'Since when?'

'Since I learned to think.'

'But you must identify as a Muslim, especially now, and since your family is Muslim,' said Salim Uncle.

'But I don't believe in Islam.'

'You don't have to believe to be part of our community Alif,' he said.

'But I don't want to be part of any community that is identified by its religion.'

'Why not Alif? What is so bad about us Muslims?' he asked with a sad smile.

'Oh, please don't do that now. Don't make it seem like I'm being bigoted or something, like I don't like the people of your religion.'

'Isn't that what you're implying? That you don't like us as a group?'

Agendas

'That's because I don't like groups. I don't like groups of Muslims, or Hindus or Congies, or bhakts. Or even bankers. I know some really wonderful people who are bankers, but I wouldn't want to be part of a community of bankers.'

'We are not like bankers my dear Alif,' said Salim Uncle laughing. 'We are more like insurance salesmen. Islam is our insurance against the evils of this world.'

'Religion is the wrong kind of insurance then,' I said. 'The premiums are too high and the payoffs too late and customer service is impossible to reach.'

Now he really laughed in that way he always laughed, stamping his feet on the floor and almost falling off the chair.

When he had caught his breath he said, 'So you'll come then tomorrow?'

'Salim Uncle you don't understand what I'm saying. I don't want to have anything to do with groups of religious people under a religious banner. I genuinely think religion is a horrible and evil thing.'

'What is so evil about religion Alif?' he asked. He was beginning to sound stern now.

'I don't even want to get started Mamaji,' I said. 'It'll take the whole week.'

'No please, please continue,' he said. Now a sharp edge was beginning to form in his voice.

Unfazed and blissfully occupied by my own ideas and opinions, I continued, 'Okay just one example: what is religion's problem with women? Every religion makes it a point to treat women as inferior to men. Why is that? Why were there no women today in the meeting?'

Salim Uncle shook his head slowly. His face was serious. The laughter of just a few moments back seemed a distant memory.

'That has nothing to do with our religion,' he said. 'And you know I have no such problems with women. I welcome them everywhere. But my friends who were here, most of them, they ... they wouldn't want women in the same meeting.'

He was upset now and fidgeting. Then he said with irritation before I could argue the point, 'But also you think the other side is very egalitarian or something? You think the Hindus are having gender-equal meetings?'

'That's why I didn't convert to any other religion,' I said. 'That's why I *abandoned* religion.'

Then I saw Salim Uncle's eyes blaze and he took a deep breath to calm himself. 'My religion is very dear to me Alif,' he said presently, 'so I would advise against speaking so casually about abandoning it.'

'I am not speaking casually at all,' I replied. 'This is the most important thing in the world to me, that I am not put into any religious category. Hindu, Muslim, Sikh, Christian, I don't want or like or respect any of it.'

Salim Uncle rubbed his face with his hands restlessly as if deciding what to do next and then at once something seemed

Agendas

to snap inside him and he stood up and cried, 'But it gives people strength.' He towered over me, his large hands shaking with anger. 'You should bloody respect that at least! You don't have to believe but at least show some respect.'

I was taken aback. A great angry power seemed to radiate from him. This was not the Salim bhai I knew from when I was a child – the man who stood outside his gate and greeted his constituents; the man who adopted every dog on his street and named them all Sukeena after his dead wife; the man who flew every month to see his troubled, drunkard sister till one day he couldn't because she had killed herself and her husband driving back drunk from some gallery opening, having not spoken to their son for three years. This was something meaner, something driven to an extreme by unresolved internal arguments, something that had come from a lifetime of contradictions, hypocrisy and pain. That's what religion did: poisoned the good insides of regular people till they stumbled around with splitting headaches.

I recovered and braced myself against some furniture.

'Strength?' I shouted. 'Strength to do what? To burn other people's homes? To slaughter other people? From the beginning of the history of our miserable whimpering, splayed-out-like-a-corpse country, every fucking problem is because of this arbitrary us versus them. This made-up bullshit that rots people's brains and burns their bodies. The strength to hate, that is what religion gives people.'

Salim Uncle steadied himself on the arm of the sofa. 'Loving one's own religion is not hating another's!' he bellowed. I reeled backwards with the force of his words.

But I continued. A lifetime of suppressed anger at filthy, egotistical gods and arrogant, ignorant ideas came rushing out like a battalion of raving warriors, frothing at the mouth.

'No it is exactly the same thing sometimes,' I shouted. 'And "sometimes" is all you need to destroy civilization.'

Salim Uncle seemed to burst into flames. He took two hard steps forward then decided against any more and stopped in his tracks, vibrating, boiling, simmering and fuming.

'Get out! Get out of the house!' he screamed. 'Go back to the airport and go home. You don't need to stay the night. I should have just sent you a cheque. But no! I thought it might be nice to see you after many years. You haven't changed a bit. No wonder your parents threw you out. It was a mystery to them as it is to me what the hell you want.' Salim Uncle pointed threateningly at me. 'You learn some respect before coming back. God rest your mother's soul if her spirit has to witness such things. And don't forget to take the cheque from the table because I don't want to see you here again.'

Now that he had mentioned my mother all bets were off. Long ago we had made an unspoken pact to never talk about my mother again. But now he had forgotten that mutually beneficial agreement.

'Fine, I will,' I said, backing away to the door (picking up the cheque) and grabbing the handle, ready to spring out if things got out of hand. 'And let me just say, I hate your religion as much as I hate all other religions. But I'm not going to burn anything or kill anyone. I leave that to all you pathetic, weak, hypocritical assholes who think going to the temple or the mosque every day makes them better than everyone else; that they can bribe their stupid, insipid, lazy gods with false promises and eternal servitude so their kids get good marks in their exams, or their business turns over a profit. I hope all of you are thrown into one large room somewhere between heaven and hell and made to tolerate each other for an infinite amount of time and even then you bunch of morons wouldn't be able to do anything useful. Even monkeys do better with an infinite amount of time. And don't you talk about my parents. I knew them better than you. They were drunkards and assholes. And they knew very well what I wanted and what I always want – freedom from people. But of course you people enslaved to some medieval text, or some even more medieval philosophy, will never understand the idea of true freedom. Slaves to the past will never master the present or anticipate the future and that's why I want nothing to do with any of you.'

He shook, he spluttered, he quivered like those tall balloons outside car dealerships.

'Get out!' he screamed, 'get out!' And then his voice broke and became a squeak and I leaped out of the room and stumbled down the stairs.

The maid was on her way up with a mug of buttermilk and her face curdled as she saw me.

'Bye didi,' I said, racing past her as she muttered something weakly about coming back soon.

On the way out I grabbed my suitcase and stumbled out of the gate and on to the dark roads of Delhi.

~

I was in a taxi again, heading back to the airport. This driver was a young fellow with aggressively faded jeans and Tik-Tok hair. Auto-tuned bhangra played softly on the radio.

He noticed my agitation and the fearful look in my eyes.

'Are you okay bhaiya? Somebody attacked you?' he asked.

I shook my head and told him that I had argued with my family. Nothing else.

He smirked.

'Delhi is burning and you are upset because you argued with somebody,' he said. 'What a life you *bade log* live yaar.'

He laughed quietly to himself and then was silent, watching the road ahead with faraway eyes.

I wanted to be alone more than anything else. The godless jungles of Borneo, where you were isolated with yourself, and the spider monkeys in the canopy cackled and screamed at you. The sudden clearing. The unpeopled rush of a brown river. And away most importantly from the ones who thought they were unfalsifiable, who had nothing else to discover. The one-booked, the many-goded, the sanctimonious, the self-righteous – the murderous.

Agendas

I wanted to be alone. The religion-and-politics-ravaged streets of Delhi were too full of sickness.

'Can you take me to a hill?' I asked the driver, leaning forward with some automatic energy.

'A hill? This is Delhi sirji,' he said.

'But you don't know any hill?'

He thought for a second and then said, 'Yes there is one in Saket. There is Durga temple on top. You have to walk little bit.'

At this time of the night there probably wouldn't be anyone there. So I told the puzzled and irritated driver to take me there and he muttered something, stabbed at his phone and made a series of dangerous, rapid turns. Before long we reached the base of the hill.

'You have to get off here and walk,' said the driver.

I thanked him, got off, walked. A small gate with a sign that said 'Tempul' was half open ahead. I began to walk the gentle slope, dragging my suitcase, ruining the wheels in the rocky, sandy path. Dog and human shit, torn bags of Lays, the stray slipper of some child (parents in a hurry) were mercifully in the weeds by the side and not in the centre. Where the bulge of the hill fell away, Delhi lay spread out like the floor of some sadistic child's room – things thrown around, crushed, torn and ultimately forgotten. Only the Qutb Minar stood erect and brave in the smoky air.

The night was chilly and stifling but slowly, as I climbed, I felt better. The weight and anxiety of all the things left unsaid, and the weight of the dead, began to fall away. The wide open space of the sky relieved the throbbing in my forehead.

Finally, I could see the summit. There a small, broken, once-white structure with a twisted metal gate stood alone in a clearing. Inside some many-armed idol glared, faded pink paint, stripes.

A man slept on a bench.

'Bastard,' he said, opening his drunk, red eyes. 'You woke me up. Just let me sleep you bastard.'

11

I Have Faith in My People

Dr Usha Mehta and the Congress Underground Radio

Aanchal Malhotra

'The first slogan I shouted against the British was "Simon, Go Back!" That was in 1928 when I was only eight years old,' the noted Gandhian scholar Dr Usha Mehta recalled in an interview nearly seven decades after the event.

Born on 25 March 1920 in Saras near Surat in Gujarat, she was the daughter of a judge working under the Raj. Due to the nature of his work, her father was naturally uncomfortable with Usha taking part in the nationalist struggle, but she didn't let it deter her. As part of the manjar sena, or cat's brigade, her activities included daily prabhat pheris, holding flags and reciting nationalist slogans, the picketing of liquor shops and spinning.

'We young girls had formed a *manjar sena* just as the boys had formed the *vanar sena* [the monkey brigade]. We followed our elders who were against the Simon Commission's entry into India. Though we could hardly understand what it was, we were the front-runners in shouting the slogan . . . Our slogans were our only weapons.'[1]

Once during their daily procession the children faced a lathi-charge. One of the girls, Sarla, fell to the ground unconscious, and with her fell the Indian flag she had been holding. The next morning the children resumed their procession, only this time they held no flags. Instead, dressed in saffron, white and green, they marched to the police station and declared stridently, '*Ae policewallon, chalao lathi, chalao danda; jhukk na sakega apna jhanda!* You can wield your sticks and your batons, but you cannot bring down our flag.'

When she was nine Mehta met Gandhiji and immediately became an ardent follower, wearing only khadi thereon and vowing to practise the tenets of non-violence. 'The struggle,' she said, 'was not merely to win political freedom, but it was also a moral campaign.'[2]

Can ethical and moral principles serve as weapons in the fight against an imperial power? The psychologists Deleuze and Guattari wrote memorably in *Mille Plateaux*: 'a concept is a brick. It can be used to build a courthouse of reason. Or it can be thrown through the window.'[3] Usha Mehta's brick was her Gandhian principles, and she used them to build an institution of morality.

I Have Faith in My People

By the age of twelve, she was immersed in the freedom struggle, which was now less problematic as her father was no longer a judge. Her family had moved to Bombay and she was engaged in distributing bulletins, and making salt from the water at Chowpatty and selling it in small packets. Salt, namak, the most basic ingredient of any meal, was not only taxed by the British but they also claimed monopoly on its sale.

Inspired by Gandhi's Dandi March, the women of Bombay, led by the freedom fighter Kamaladevi Chattopadhyay, marched to Chowpatty and began making salt from the sea. Mehta thus learnt at a young age that revolution grew from the ground up: to claim the earth we had been born on – the earth that had been looted from us – one had to become amalgamated with that earth. Salt, drawn from the water of the Indian Ocean, wove Mehta into the land of her birth. She also learnt that the struggle for freedom belonged to all Indians of all ages and genders.

∼

By the early 1940s, India's freedom struggle had intensified. The declaration of the Quit India Movement in 1942 – the first time that the Congress asked for an immediate and complete end to the Raj – allowed the twenty-two-year-old her moment in the sun. It led to the creation of the underground Congress Radio, and of Usha becoming its voice. But to understand the establishment of the Congress

Radio, we must first understand the political situation in India at the time.

On 3 September 1939, the voice of Viceroy Lord Linlithgow rang through the frequencies of All India Radio, announcing that His Majesty's Government was at war with Germany. As a colony of the government, so was India. The leaders of the Indian National Congress were not pleased to hear this. India's involvement in the Second World War had begun, although the Viceroy had consulted neither his advisers, nor the Legislative Assembly, or Indian leaders. The anger against British rule grew incrementally, and almost three years into the war, on 8 August 1942, thousands of people gathered at the Golwalia Tank Maidan in Bombay to attend the meeting of the All India Congress Committee. It was here that the historic Quit India Resolution was passed and Mahatma Gandhi's mantra of *Karenge ya Marenge*, Do or Die, was proclaimed.

Usha Mehta, now a master's student at Wilson College, was present in the crowd that day and took Gandhi's motto to heart. Announcing that all the leaders of the Congress could soon be arrested, Gandhi exhorted everyone 'to act as his or her own leader, and find out activities which they can undertake on their own'.[4]

The British came down heavily on the Quit India Movement, jailing nearly 60,000 Indians, including Gandhi and Nehru and most of the Congress leadership, within twenty-four hours. Protests erupted across Bombay, with thousands taking to the street, targeting the railways, telegraphs, telephones, police stations, post offices and other government buildings, because inactivating the means of communication and transport would make the ruling British literally incommunicado and unseat the government.[5] Against the backdrop of famine, World War and imprisonment of the Congress leaders, if the Quit India Movement was going to survive, it would require new leadership. Young leadership.

The Congress also realized, having examined its past campaigns, that communication with the public was central to its success. Thus, the idea of an underground radio station was conceived, and Usha Mehta became its voice. Though it was known by many names – the Freedom Radio, the Ghost Radio, the Congress Radio – it was, very simply, the secret anti-imperialist voice of the Indian National Congress[6] and almost no one, apart from those involved, knew anything certain about its inner workings. *Where did it broadcast from? Who was behind it? And how long could it survive?*

'A transmitter of our own was perhaps one of the most important requirements for the success of the movement,' Mehta would later say.[7]

~

In India, radio broadcasting began in 1923 with the Radio Club of Bombay, followed by the Calcutta Radio Club, which was set up in the same year. Both went bankrupt after a few years. But it was not until 1936 that the Indian State Broadcasting Services (established in 1930), became the All India Radio (AIR) or Akashavni.

The Congress Radio, which began operations in August 1942, was set up to counter the British-controlled AIR, often tagged as 'anti-India Radio'.[8] Interestingly, the iconic AIR jingle based on raag Shivaranjini – violin played to the background notes of the tambura – was the work of a man who himself had fled a tyrannous regime. It was composed in 1936 by Walter Kaufmann, a Czech Jew who had fled Nazi persecution in Prague and arrived in India two years earlier.

Though the radio was a tremendous tool for propaganda, it was also an expensive one. A relative of Mehta offered her ornaments to buy the equipment, but ultimately one of her colleagues, Babubhai Khakhar, managed to procure the funds. Other members of the team included the prominent socialist leader Dr Ram Manohar Lohia, Chandrakant Jhaveri and Vithaldas K. Jhaveri. As chief organizer of the enterprise, Vithaldas Jhaveri approached Nariman Abarbad Printer, well trained in radio engineering, to construct the Congress Radio transmission set.

Nanik Motwani, the owner of Bombay's Chicago Radio, supplied the equipment. When the Congress Radio began broadcasting in August 1942, it was with the intention of telling people what was actually happening. And so it began.

At exactly 7.30 p.m., Mehta announced, 'This is the Congress Radio calling on 42.34 metres from *somewhere in India*.'

~

Correspondence between the Bombay station director of AIR and the Government of India's home department shows that the government became aware of the clandestine station on Sunday, 16 August, just three days after it was launched.[9]

It was not easy to remain hidden from the police. Claiming to be recorded from *somewhere in India*, the workers of the Congress Radio were careful to change their addresses very often, moving from flat to flat, often in the middle of the night. Code names were given for the key Congress members: Sucheta Kriplani, in charge of the Bombay Congress office, was known as *Bahanji*; Dr Ram Manohar Lohia as *doctor*; Achyut Patwardhan, founder of the Socialist Party of India, as *Kusum*.

At first, the station broadcast news bulletins and talks by prominent leaders of the freedom struggle. The news dispatches – ranging from merchants refusing to export certain goods to the arrests of leaders and civilians, were received by special messengers in remote corners of the country. Since newspapers often dared not touch on politically sensitive subjects, the Congress Radio became the sole means by which people knew what was actually happening. 'When the press is gagged and all news banned, our transmitter certainly helps a good deal in furnishing the public with the facts of the happenings and in spreading the message of rebellion in the remotest corners of the country.' These words by Mehta became emblematic of the freedom struggle.

The news was read in English by Dr Ram Manohar Lohia, Achyut Patwardhan, Moinuddin Harris and Coomi Dastur. Usha Mehta read in both English and Hindustani. They began each programme by playing Iqbal's '*Saare Jahaan se Achha*' and ended with Bankim Chandra Chatterjee's '*Bande Mataram*'. Their programmes gained momentum, connecting people from all across India, broadcasting first only once a day, and later twice, in the morning and evening, in English and Hindustani. Sure enough, in villages and cities, large groups would gather around a single radio and listen to the broadcast, whose content was often brazenly against imperial rule and Britain's plunder of India.

The words floated out of the frequency, resolute and unafraid. 'We used to relay news, speeches, instructions, appeals to different classes of people. For this, there was a batch of speakers and writers . . . The recording place was different from the broadcasting station. Thus, the risk was lessened considerably. The news item was a daily feature of the programme . . . We were the first to give the news of the Chittagong bomb raid, of the Jamshedpur strike and of the happenings in Balia. We broadcast the full description of the atrocities [against women] in Ashti and Chimur.

I Have Faith in My People

When the newspapers dared not touch these subjects under the prevailing conditions, only the Congress Radio could defy the orders and tell the people what was really happening. Our listeners helped us in spreading the news to the people at large.'[10]

As I read these speeches and listen to Mehta's voice on the recordings, it dawns on me that it was a twenty-two-year-old woman who led an underground revolution against a tyrannical rule, with the courage and decisiveness of a seasoned revolutionary. In later photographs, she is often seen in a white sari with a coloured border, her stance erect and proud, despite her short frame, her eyes calm and full of purpose. It is evident, both in her visage and in her words, that she was a woman unafraid. The word 'courage' is derived from the old French word *corage*, which comes from the Latin word *cor*, heart. *Where did Usha Mehta's courage come from?* It emanated from the absence of fear, which is only possible when the heart – the epicentre of a person's thoughts and emotions – is certain that it has embarked on the path of righteousness.

∼

The radio broadcasted for three months before it was disbanded. Ultimately, the betrayal came from within. For a few weeks, the police had tried to locate their whereabouts.

They drove a detection van around the city, which could make out the direction from where the broadcast message was transmitted, but couldn't pinpoint the exact location. Mehta recalled that the police would often have been within a radius of barely two or three miles, while the broadcasters escaped with the transmitter concealed in the back seat of a car, moving from flat to flat in the middle of the night.[11]

In the second week of November 1942, Printer, who had built their transmitter, arrived with the Crime Investigation Department (CID) to Babubhai's office. Usha was in the cabin, typing out the speech for the evening's broadcast and to alert her Babubhai shouted that he did not know anything about the Congress Radio and the police were free to search his office.

In a 1968 interview, she admits that even though she had taken the risk of hiring Printer to build that first transmitter, she never thought he would deceive them. Immediately, she began typing something else and Babubhai, employing their code names, asked her to go see the *doctor* about a prescription. From his office, she arrived at the recording station, where she told Dr Lohia of what had happened.

Regardless of the threat, they decided that the broadcast for the evening must continue, for they had not missed a single day in the last three months. People in Bombay and across the country would be waiting for the clock to strike 7.30 p.m., so that they could tune in. After that, she went home and told her mother that she would perhaps not return from the station that evening. There was no fear to be discerned in her actions.

On the night of 12 November 1942, the Congress Radio aired its final programme, while waiting for the police to show up. They did, at the end of the programme, while the anthem *'Bande Mataram'* was playing. There were knocks on the door as the deputy commissioner of police and his team of fifty policemen stood outside. Mehta recalls attempting to destroy two or three records in haste, but they entered, breaking down the strong door, before she could do that. *'Bande Mataram'* still played on in the background, and they asked to shut the record immediately. Only then, Mehta spoke.

'It will not be stopped,' she said, telling them to stand at attention, as it was the anthem of the country. And they did.

The unfolding of events could be heard across the length and breadth of Hindustan, transmitted through the frequencies of the radio. Mehta admits that she wanted to pick up the microphone there and then, and name Printer as the culprit who had outed them. But before she could, he grabbed the fuse that powered the transmitter, and shut it. The room was dark; the programme over.

∼

Usha Mehta and her colleagues, Babubhai Khakhar, Chandrakant Jhaveri, Vithaldas Jhaveri and Nanik Motwani, were meted out the same fate as their idol, Mahatma Gandhi.

Mehta was kept in an isolated cell and taken to the CID for interrogation, which continued for six months. A special court was set up for the Radio Conspiracy Case, as it came to be known.

Describing her life in police custody, she said, 'The lock-up period is perhaps the most trying time in the life of a prisoner ... it is humanly impossible to sleep in a cell full of filth, dirt and nauseating smell.'[12] Later she said, 'You know what solitary confinement can do to a prisoner ...'[13] But she didn't break during her interrogation, refusing to say anything to her captors.

She used the same strategy during the trial. When the judge asked her questions, she only offered a single phrase – 'Is it compulsory to answer your questions?' To which he replied, 'No,' and she told him then that she would not speak, for she preferred not to lie.

Usha Mehta was imprisoned for four years from 1942 to 1946, which swallowed the better part of her twenties. It was a sentence even longer than the Mahatma's himself, who was released in 1944. When she was finally released from Yerawada Jail in March 1946, she was the only female prisoner.

The memory of that day remained vivid in her mind, her eyes lighting up years later as she described the extraordinary reception that she was met with. 'There were crowds and crowds and crowds of people at the Victoria Terminus Station. People appreciated this work very, very much. We were very happy, and those were really... golden days and unforgettable days. The happiest days of our lives.'[14]

∼

When India gained independence in 1947, Usha Mehta was confined to her home with ill health, which prevented her from partaking both in the movement against partition and in the celebrations of independence in New Delhi.

Thereafter, she completed her PhD in Gandhian thought and taught at her alma mater, Wilson College, for thirty years, heading the political science department until 1980. She was president of the Gandhi Peace Foundation, New Delhi, and in 1998 received the Padma Vibhushan, the second highest civilian award of India. Each year, she unfailingly participated in the anniversary celebrations of the Quit India Movement at the Gowalia Tank Maidan, now renamed August Kranti Maidan in Mumbai, commemorating the day she rose to the need of her nation. On 11 August 2000, just days after the anniversary, she passed away at the age of eighty.

∼

Twenty years have now passed since Dr Usha Mehta's death, and as I read one of her final interviews[15] recorded three years before her passing, I am struck by the parallel she draws – not only to a past that she had lived but also to a future she would not see. She speaks of poverty and development, the tenets of democracy and equality, and I wonder how a decades-old dream could remain relevant even today.

'Our debt outweighs all our achievements. The division between the rich and poor is so vast that it seems impossible to bridge the gap. This is not the freedom for which we sacrificed our all.'[16] And then, most prophetically, she ends the interview with the same message that I will end my essay with, acknowledging that the following words apply to the revolutionaries not only of the 1930s and 1940s, but also of today and perhaps to all future revolutionaries, fighting for the cause of justice.

'The situation at present is grim. But it is for our youth to accept the challenge and go ahead . . . I have faith in my people and hope that our struggle will not go in vain, and India will once again emerge as a country to be proud of.'[17]

Notes

1. Chandrika Vyas, 'Dr. Usha Mehta', *Freedom Fighters Remember*, Publications Division, Ministry of Information and Broadcasting, Government of India, 1997, p. 173.
2. Haresh Pandya, 'Usha Mehta', *Guardian*, 25 August 2000.
3. Gilles Deleuze and Félix Guattari, *A Thousand Plateaus: Capitalism and Schizophrenia*, trans. Brian Massumi, A&C Black, 2004, p. xiii.

4. Neel Thakkar, *Congress Radio Calling: Underground Broadcasts during the Quit India Movement*, Stanford Storytelling Project, 21 March 2014.
5. Gautam Chatterjee, 'Quit India Movement and "Illegal" Congress Radio', *Mainstream*, 12 August 1989.
6. Neel Thakkar, *Congress Radio Calling: Underground Broadcasts during the Quit India Movement*, Stanford Storytelling Project, 21 March 2014.
7. T.K. Tope, *Bombay and the Congress Movement*, Maharashtra State Board for Literature and Culture, Bombay, September 1986.
8. Aruna Asaf Ali and G.N.S. Raghavan, *The Resurgence of Indian Women*, Nehru Memorial Museum and Library, 1991.
9. Neel Thakkar, *Congress Radio Calling: Underground Broadcasts during the Quit India Movement*, Stanford Storytelling Project, 21 March 2014.
10. T.K. Tope, *Bombay and the Congress Movement*, Maharashtra State Board for Literature and Culture, Bombay, September 1986, p. 104.
11. Neel Thakkar, *Congress Radio Calling: Underground Broadcasts during the Quit India Movement*, Stanford Storytelling Project, 21 March 2014.
12. Manmohan Kaur, *The Role of Women in the Freedom Movement (1857–1947)*, Sterling Publishers Private Limited, 1960, p. 231.

13. Chandrika Vyas, 'Dr. Usha Mehta', *Freedom Fighters Remember*, Publications Division, Ministry of Information and Broadcasting, Government of India, 1997, p. 174.
14. Neel Thakkar, *Congress Radio Calling: Underground Broadcasts during the Quit India Movement*, Stanford Storytelling Project, 21 March 2014.
15. Chandrika Vyas, 'Dr. Usha Mehta', *Freedom Fighters Remember*, Publications Division, Ministry of Information and Broadcasting, Government of India, 1997, p. 175.
16. Ibid.
17. Ibid.

12

Emergency and Freedom

Salil Tripathi

When liberty is taken away, someone with power over us usually tells us, always reassuringly, that it is for our own good. Each generation has someone like that, seeking to comfort us by invoking fear.

I remember Indira Gandhi's words in a radio speech as the Emergency was being declared in 1975. 'The President has proclaimed an emergency. There is nothing to panic about.'

I was thirteen at that time. I was surprised by the mutual contradiction. If the nation faced an emergency, surely we should panic? If there was no need to panic, how could we be in an emergency? Why then did we have this climate of fear, the excessive presence of police on the streets, the grim-sounding announcements on radio and television, the erection of billboards with tawdry slogans, the aura of suspicion and blank spaces in newspapers? The *Statesman* featured a telling photograph of a man pushing a cycle with two children on it and a woman walking behind and scores of policemen all around, with the caption 'Life is normal in Chandni Chowk'.

We learned to value liberty after we realized its absence.

Liberty allows us to do what we want, when we might want to do it and how we would like to do it. It enables us to wear what we like, eat what we desire, read what we think is interesting, say what comes to our mind, go where we would like to, and love, and sometimes marry, the person we want to spend our life with, assuming the one we love feels the same way. Liberty gives meaning to our being, a sense of our self, a purpose, creates our private space. It defines who we are.

For every generation, a moment comes when its political consciousness awakens. For my mother, it came early, in her childhood. At the age of seven, she joined other girls from her school in a town in Gujarat and marched with them singing songs as part of the prabhat pheri, a procession in the morning. It was August 1942. Gandhi had been imprisoned; a spark had been lit. Because Mohandas Gandhi had said so, my mother and her friends shouted, 'Quit India!' along with *Karenge ya Marenge*, Do or Die. My mother was too young to be arrested, too precocious to be disciplined and yet annoying enough so that she could not be ignored. Her father was a schoolteacher in the Baroda state. The police asked him to discipline his daughter; he threw his hands up in despair.

Emergency and Freedom

My moment of political awakening arrived in my teenage years. In 1975 I had the normal concerns of an adolescent – convincing my parents to buy me a pair of jeans, packing for my first summer trip to the Himalaya with my school friends. I was curious about the girls in my class. I wished that Sunil Gavaskar would recapture his magical 1971 form and start scoring those centuries again.

There were annoyances, like frequent strikes. George Fernandes had brought the railways to a standstill a year earlier. Restlessness swept the nation. Prices rose; the economy was stagnant. Indira Gandhi's popularity was beginning to dim. We cheered at the revolt against Chimanbhai Patel's government in Gujarat. It was a period of strife and violence. In January, the railway minister, Lalit Narayan Mishra, was assassinated in Samastipur, and Jayaprakash Narayan drew vast crowds when he spoke of a total revolution.

It was in that environment that Justice Jag Mohan Lal Sinha issued his judgement in the Allahabad High Court on 12 June 1975, voiding Prime Minister Indira Gandhi's election to Parliament because of electoral malpractices that today seem charmingly minor. But the law was clear; the prime minister was unseated. The same day, we were thrilled as the Janata Front, led by Babubhai Jashbhai Patel, defeated the Congress in the Gujarat Vidhan Sabha elections. It was a hot summer, and political demonstrations picked up, turning melodramatic. JP, as Jayaprakash Narayan was known, called upon the police and the military not to obey unconstitutional laws. Overwrought supporters flocked to Indira Gandhi's home, pleading with her not to resign, and Congress leaders queued up dutifully urging her to stay. Her crisis was personal and political, but it was termed a national one.

I was thirteen and didn't care too much about the nuances, but I sensed that it was an exciting time. My parents had been lifelong Opposition voters, their support veering between socialists and the Swatantra Party, depending on the calibre of the candidates. Everyone discussed politics – our neighbours, my parents and relatives, my schoolteachers.

I stopped reading Indrajal Comics. I started listening to the people around me.

At my school, New Era, in our history class, we were studying the French and American revolutions. At midnight on 25 June, the Emergency was declared.

I walked home from school the next evening with my friends Apurva and Kaushik. We shouted as loudly as we could, 'Liberty! Equality! Fraternity!' and 'No taxation without representation!' Those words were new to us but they were thrilling. We were teenagers, we did not pay taxes, but shouting those slogans near Kemp's Corner in the city then known as Bombay felt stimulating. As we neared my house, an elderly Parsi gentleman, my mother's philosophy professor at college, frowned at us. Be quiet and be careful, he told us. The Emergency was not a joke; the police could take us away. 'They will hit you with a danda.'

The newspapers were suitably cowed. The *Times of India*

Emergency and Freedom

was too coy; its headline would only say 'STATE OF EMERGENCY DECLARED: Several leaders arrested', not naming any of the jailed leaders – JP, Morarji Desai, Asoka Mehta or Atal Bihari Vajpayee – in the headlines. We relied on rumours, and new names got added to the list. But in the same newspaper, something astonishing happened.

Ashok Mahadevan was a young editor at the *Reader's Digest*. He went to the *Times* office to place an ad, mourning the death of 'D'OCRACY – D.E.M. husband of T. Ruth, loving father of L.I. Bertie, brother of Faith, Hope, Justicia expired on 26th June.'

The clerk protested, saying the ad was over the word limit. Mahadevan made a quick edit. The clerk asked if he was Bertie. Mahadevan at first didn't understand, but then said yes, he was. The next day the ad appeared. Mahadevan called the newspaper anonymously, alerting a reporter about the ad. It became the talk of the town and was featured in the foreign media.

The government was flustered. The police were called in to find out how the ad came to be published, but nobody could link it with Mahadevan. He outed himself a few years later, telling an interviewer: 'When I learnt the news on the morning of the 26th, I was incensed. India no longer a free country? As a citizen, even more as a journalist, it was intolerable. I had to do something. But what? Fear was spreading like an infection. When I asked a friend, who'd just flown in from the US, how it felt coming to a dictatorship, he told me to shush. People were too scared to jump queues at bus stops!'

It was what wasn't printed, what wasn't said, what was only hinted at or alluded to that was more credible. Years later, when I was a reporter in Singapore, an American colleague who had reported out of China told me what dissidents had told her: when you can't believe the printed word, you trust the spoken word.

Silences mattered. The *Indian Express* and the *Statesman* published blank editorials as a protest against censorship. The stark whiteness of that space in the newspaper told us, eloquently, why silence was the one way left for us to protest.

Nearly a decade later, when I returned to India after my graduate studies in the United States, it was my privilege to work at the *Indian Post* under S. Nihal Singh, the courageous former editor of the *Statesman*, who had published those blank editorials. He would later tell me how the Emergency forced editors to turn oblique, to allude to what was going on by using metaphors and examples from elsewhere, figuring out ways to confuse the censors.

Rumours gained currency. Students at a college were warned against gathering in groups; workers at offices were sternly ordered to start coming on time; humourless men had a quiet word with potential troublemakers; and people disappeared.

Slogans multiplied.

'Rumour-mongers are the enemies of the nation.'

Emergency and Freedom

'Work more, talk less.'

'There is no substitute for hard work.'

A 20-point economic programme was rammed down everyone's throats. '*Haunsla humara naya rang layega, / Ab andhera deshme hone na payega*', a dreary song ran endlessly on the state-run radio station. It meant that our determination would bring about a new dawn, that there would be no darkness in the nation. Another slogan promised in Marathi, '*Ekach jadoo – sapatun kam, deergh drishti*', meaning, there's only one magic – work hard, be far-sighted. Vinoba Bhave spoke of the Emergency as '*anushasan parva*' (the age of discipline) and the Rashtriya Swayamsevak Sangh (RSS) chief, Madhukar Deoras, wrote a letter to Indira Gandhi, pleading with her to remove the ban on the RSS. He offered to cooperate, saying the RSS would help promote the 20-point economic programme.

But we secretly treasured the many individual acts of defiance. The feisty writer Durga Bhagwat spoke truth to power at the annual meeting of the Marathi Sahitya Sammelan in Karad, wishing good health for the ailing JP, who was in jail, forcing everyone, including the cabinet minister Yeshwantrao Chavan, who was in the audience, to stand in solidarity. Her address was sharp and scathing, and the politicians squirmed.

Our school was inspired by Gandhi and Tagore and our medium of instruction was Gujarati. A vast mural created by our art teacher Dinesh Shah greeted us at the entrance wall with scenes from Gandhi's life. Our principal, a khadi-clad Gandhian called Kantibhai Vyas, spoke openly at our daily assembly about the sad times the country was facing. The readings our teachers chose at our school assembly each morning were from inspiring political tracts.

Kantibhai often met with parents informally after school. After one meeting, my mother told me, one of the parents, a businessman, argued that the Emergency was a golden era for industries, since labour was not permitted to strike. 'Production has increased so much,' he said, expecting praise. Kantibhai responded that the right to strike was important not only for workers; it was the right to dissent in action. What would the businessman do if his business was closed down arbitrarily? What rights would he have then, Kantibhai asked. To whom would he complain? The businessman was silenced, but my mother worried about Kantibhai. 'This is a very difficult time,' she said. 'Kantibhai is courageous. He should be careful.'

But most prominent businessmen unquestioningly supported the state. When George Fernandes became the minister for industries in the Janata Party government that followed the Emergency, he admonished India's business community. What makes men behave like rats, he asked. When I heard of that speech, I remembered that businessman and Kantibhai's gentle remonstrance.

Most of the media caved in. Lal Krishna Advani was jailed for much of the nineteen months of the Emergency. When he joined Morarji Desai's Janata Party government as the information and broadcasting minister, he said to newspaper editors: 'You were asked to bend, and you crawled.' Many did, though smaller magazines kept up the fight – Nikhil Chakravartty's *Mainstream*, Romesh Thapar's *Seminar*, Minoo Masani's *Freedom First*, Rajmohan Gandhi's *Himmat* and Astad Gorwala's *Opinion*.

The story of Gorwala's little magazine was truly remarkable. It came out as a pamphlet. Only a few issues were longer than 16 pages. Printed at the Mouj Printing Bureau in letterpress, it featured no illustrations or photographs, only sharp, scathing criticism of the Emergency. In retaliation, the government shut down Mouj Press.

Our school had a proud tradition of Gandhian dissent. The Quit India Movement of 1942 had been launched at the Gowalia Tank Maidan, opposite the school building. The khadi-clad Usha Mehta, who would later run the Gandhi Museum at Mani Bhavan in Mumbai for many years, was a feisty freedom fighter. She used the school to run a clandestine radio station which played hide-and-seek with the British authorities, operating from several locations to rouse the people against the evils of colonial rule.

Such habits die hard. Buildings, it seems, remember. In 1976 two members of the school staff – social sciences teacher Dinesh Buch, who had been part of the vanar sena (or monkey brigade) as a child during the Quit India Movement, and senior school administrator Bhagwandas Marker – quietly allowed some former students and their friends to come to the school late at night to cyclostyle literature against the Emergency. The teachers kept the material with them overnight. The next day, a few of us would slip those roughly printed sheets under the doors of nearby apartments – on Pedder Road, Carmichael Road, Breach Candy, Nepean Sea Road, and so on. We did this regularly. Nobody noticed, or if somebody did, nobody told us. That was how some issues of *Opinion* were distributed in south Bombay during the Emergency. It felt good to be doing that at that time; I felt I was only following in my mother's footsteps.

Many took far more valiant action and showed enormous courage in challenging the Emergency. They also suffered far more. My friend Prakash Shah, now the president of the Gujarati Sahitya Parishad, spent months in jail. Some leftist activists were tortured in prison. In northern India, hundreds of thousands of men were sterilized compulsorily, as part of the government's notorious population control programmes. Slums were razed and structures the government considered illegal were demolished. The police opened fire at Turkman Gate in Delhi, killing at least twenty. We learned about so many atrocities only after the Emergency was lifted.

Mainstream newspapers had other priorities. Discipline makes the nation great, one of the Emergency slogans said. The newspapers carried front-page stories about the rising star and heir apparent, Sanjay Gandhi, Indira Gandhi's second son, who was clearly being groomed to take over from her. It was a good time for sycophants. Khushwant Singh published fawning accounts extolling Sanjay and Indira in the *Illustrated Weekly of India*. One Piare Lal Sharma wrote a book called *World's Wisest Wizard: A Psychography of Sanjay Gandhi's Cosmic Mind*.

Contrast such pusillanimity with the courage showed by the actor Dev Anand. The veteran BBC correspondent Mark Tully recalls interviewing him and asking him what he thought of the Emergency. 'I deplore it in all its aspects,' Dev Anand said. Tully paused the recording to ask him if he was sure of what he was saying, because Tully was going to broadcast the interview. 'You asked me a question, I gave you an answer. What you do with it is up to you,' the dashing actor said. But few were as brave.

The state-run television and radio were full of abject propaganda. A particularly egregious instance of servility was when the playback singer Mahendra Kapoor took part in a concert to promote government policies that Sanjay Gandhi had organized. The concert was called *Geeton Bhari Shaam (*An evening filled with music), where Kapoor sang the popular patriotic song '*Mere desh ki dharti*' (which he had sung in Manoj Kumar's 1967 film *Upkar*). He replaced former prime minister Lal Bahadur Shastri's name in the lyrics with Indira Gandhi's.

There were other disappearances. In December 1976 I was in Baroda, staying with my aunt, and my cousin Neeraj and I went to visit an uncle who was a senior official in the state's wildlife department. We were talking of animals and sanctuaries when Neeraj lamented the ban of Kishore Kumar on national radio and television because he had refused to sing at *Geeton Bhari Shaam*. Our uncle didn't know that. 'Who is Indira Gandhi to decide whose songs we should listen to?' he asked, and brought out a long-playing record of Kishore Kumar's songs, put it on his turntable, turned up the volume. Kishore Kumar's sonorous voice surrounded us – '*Jeevan se bhari teri ankhen*' and then the mad yodelling in '*Main hun jhum jhum jhum jhum jhumroo*'.

News travelled slowly – the BBC World Service broadcast news only after they had verified it, and we heard of certain developments only over time. Uncles from Gujarat visiting us in Bombay would bring us copies of the plucky journal *Bhumiputra*, run by Gandhians and defying the Emergency in the state which was still headed by the Janata Front government (but not for much longer).

But through whispers, we learned that George Fernandes was trying to organize resistance, that Subramaniam Swamy, who was an Opposition parliamentarian who had eluded arrest, had turned up one day in Parliament and asked a question, embarrassed the government, and disappeared again.

We heard the worst stories only much later, stories of the disappearance (and subsequent death) of the engineering student Rajan, the arrest, torture and death of the actress Snehalata Reddy, the shackling of George Fernandes. Many went underground, working quietly to dismantle the

Emergency and Freedom

Emergency. In Bombay, Mrinal Gore and Pannalal Surana acquired a mythical reputation fighting for justice. They stayed incognito for some time at the home of the socialist activist Pushpa Bhave before they were eventually arrested. Pushpa Bhave told me the story as though what she had done was nothing special. I heard the story much after the Emergency, in the 1980s, when I married Bhave's brother's daughter.

In Maharashtra, Shankarrao Chavan, the chief minister, warned the opposition parties that they should be grateful that they hadn't faced bullets. That wasn't an empty threat. Niren De, the Attorney General, actually argued before the Supreme Court that the court was powerless to protect the right to life. This was in the ADM Jabalpur Case, better known as the habeas corpus case, where the Supreme Court made the disgraceful ruling that during an Emergency fundamental rights could be suspended. (The remarkable Justice H.R. Khanna dissented, and was passed over in retaliation when it was his turn to become India's chief justice.) A pliant Parliament passed the Forty-Second Amendment, which eroded rights further, by reducing judicial oversight over Parliament which could amend any part of the Constitution, reduced court authority to stay governmental actions, lengthened the duration of an emergency, increased the prime minister's authority, permitted suspension of fundamental rights and weakened the power of the states and strengthened the centre.

Many lawyers challenged these restrictions valiantly. The ones I knew were at the Bombay bar, Ashok Desai, Anil Divan, Atul Setalvad, Iqbal Chagla, Homi and Navroz Seervai, and jurists like V.M. Tarkunde, but many others too, and yet, there were many who complied with the new system.

Acquiescence has its benefits and rewards. India's institutions showed their weakness. Travelling through India at that time, V.S. Naipaul wrote: 'The turbulence in India this time hasn't come from foreign invasion or conquest; it has been generated from within ... The crisis of India is not only political or economic. The larger crisis is of a wounded old civilisation that has at last become aware of its inadequacies and is without the intellectual means to move ahead.'

In January 1977 Indira Gandhi announced elections, catching everyone by surprise. Maybe she felt confident. Maybe she had lost touch, and underestimated the ability of her opponents to unite. It might be that she remembered she was Jawaharlal Nehru's daughter and resented being called a dictator. The opposition parties united and their rallies drew large crowds. Some newspapers discovered their spine and began publishing all the news their reporters had already known but had not been allowed to report. Film stars stepped out and campaigned for the Janata Party. Jayaprakash Narayan campaigned for democracy from his wheelchair.

The results were sensational. In state after state in northern India, where the atrocities had been particularly brutal, the

Emergency and Freedom

Congress was wiped out, and deservedly so. We were in the middle of our school-leaving examinations, but we followed the election with great excitement.

All India Radio began by broadcasting results from the southern states, where the Congress held firm. But through the BBC we learned how Indira Gandhi had herself lost her seat in Rae Bareli, and Sanjay Gandhi was losing in Amethi. The enormity of the loss slowly began to sink in – Congress had lost all eighty-five seats in Uttar Pradesh, all fifty-four in Bihar.

Towards the end of *The New India*, Ved Mehta's short book about the Emergency, he writes of Leela, a young niece, listening as election results were announced: 'On the first counting day she had as many as three drives in the evening – to the various newspaper and party offices and scoreboards – and confidently declared, "*Pupup, main election se badi khush hoon* [Papa, I am very happy with the elections]."'

That child's happiness was shared by so many of us. We had grown up in those nineteen months, and we had become acutely conscious of what freedom meant. The country was forced to grow up, to not take for granted the freedoms for which Gandhi, Nehru and many others had fought for many decades.

Two and a half years later, when the Janata Party government collapsed and Indira Gandhi was set to return to power, I was seventeen, not yet eligible to vote. But I was out on the streets, campaigning for the Janata Party. I translated an appeal that Justice Tarkunde, Dharmavir Bharati, Durga

Bhagwat, Nissim Ezekiel, Suresh Dalal and other luminaries had drafted. They asked the people to vote, and vote wisely, to punish the potential dictators and those who had defected, and to support those who would uphold democracy. We travelled through all parts of Bombay. I stood on a wooden box at the entrance of Churchgate station, speaking from a megaphone, canvassing votes for candidates who upheld liberty. It's the only time I've ever campaigned in an election. Indira Gandhi returned to power but, as Arun Shourie said when he received the Magsaysay Award, there are some causes worth failing for.

Emergencies do not occur in an identical fashion; history never repeats itself exactly as in the past. It returns in newer, different forms. But recognizing those forms is the first step. Challenging arbitrariness is the next step. The worst outcome of the Emergency was the grievous harm done to India's institutions. The press, the Parliament, the judiciary – every one of the institutions intended to protect citizens buckled under pressure.

Other institutions emerged – the People's Union for Civil Liberties, the People's Union for Democratic Rights, the Committee for the Protection of Democratic Rights, the Editors' Guild of India – all autonomous, all vigilant. Today, tragically, those calling for such vigilance, those who dissent, those who oppose are being vilified, humiliated or vociferously condemned as being anti-national, as the erosion of protection of rights continues.

Emergency and Freedom

When he was produced at the court, George Fernandes said the chains that handcuffed him were shackling the country. Emancipating oneself from those chains and embracing the spirit of the foundational idea of India is the way out of darkness. The Emergency taught us to learn how to defend freedom because it taught us its real value.

As Umberto Eco said in his essay *Ur-Fascism* in 1995: 'We must keep alert, so that the sense of these words will not be forgotten again. Ur-Fascism is still around us, sometimes in plainclothes... Freedom and liberation are an unending task.' Authoritarianism is not the monopoly of one party. Power corrodes and corrupts. And tyranny returns in other forms. To stare back at power, to stand firm against onslaughts, to sway and bend if necessary but not to break and succumb, and to challenge falsehoods, is not easy. But Indians have done it in the past – before Independence, by marching with Gandhi to Dandi, by spinning the wheels of satyagraha, braving assaults during the Quit India Movement; and then during the Emergency, spending months in jail, facing torture, whispering the truth from one ear to another, distributing literature the state didn't want read, and voting out tyranny.

Indians can do it again.

13

Exile in the Age of Modi

Aatish Taseer

'You realize,' a friend wrote to me from Kolkata earlier this year, 'that, without the exalted secular "idea" of India . . . the whole place falls apart.'

India had been on the boil for weeks. On December 11, Prime Minister Narendra Modi's Hindu nationalist government had passed its Citizenship (Amendment) Act (CAA), which gave immigrants from three neighboring countries (Afghanistan, Pakistan, and Bangladesh) a path to citizenship on one condition: that they were not Muslim. For the first time in India's long history of secularism, a religious test had been enacted. If some commentators described the CAA as 'India's first Nuremberg Law,' it was because the law did not stand alone. It worked in tandem, Indian Home Minister Amit Shah menacingly implied – in remarks he has recently tried to walk back – with a slew of other new laws that cast the citizenship of many of India's own people into doubt. Shah, who has referred to Muslim immigrants as 'termites,' spoke of a process by which the government would survey India's large agrarian population, a significant portion of which is undocumented, and designate the status of millions as 'doubtful.' The CAA would then kick into action, providing non-Muslims with relief and leaving Indian Muslims in a position where they could face disenfranchisement, statelessness, or internment. India's Muslim population of almost 200 million, which had been provoked by Modi's government for six years, finally erupted in protest. They were joined by many non-Muslims, who were appalled by so brazen an attack on the Indian ethos. The constitutional expert Madhav Khosla recently described the effect of the new laws as a swift movement toward 'an arrangement where citizenship is centered on the idea of blood and soil, rather than on the idea of birth.' In short, an arrangement in which being Indian meant accepting Hindu dominance and actively eschewing Indian Muslims.

India was seething, but I could not go back to the country where I had grown up. I was deep in my own citizenship drama. On November 7, the Indian government had stripped me of my Overseas Citizenship of India and blacklisted me from the country where my mother and grandmother live. The pretext the government used was that I had concealed the Pakistani origins of my father, from whom I had been estranged for most of my life, and whom I had not met until the age of 21. It was an odd accusation. I had written a book, *Stranger to History*, and published many articles about my absent father. The story of our relationship was well known because my father, Salmaan Taseer, had been the governor of Punjab, in Pakistan, and had been assassinated by his bodyguard in 2011 for daring to defend a Christian woman accused of blasphemy.

None of this had affected my status in India, where I had lived for 30 of my 40 years. I became 'Pakistani' in the eyes of Modi's government – and, more important, 'Muslim,' because religious identity in India is mostly patrilineal and more a matter of blood than faith – only after I wrote a story for *Time* titled 'India's Divider in Chief.' The article enraged the prime minister. '*Time* magazine is foreign,' he responded. 'The writer has also said he comes from a Pakistani political family. That is enough for his credibility.' From that moment on, my days as an Indian citizen were numbered.

In August, I received a letter from the Home Ministry threatening me with the cancellation of my OCI. Then, in November, an Indian news site leaked what the government was planning to do. Within hours, the Home Ministry's spokesperson was on Twitter, canceling my citizenship before I had been officially informed. In one stroke, Modi's government cut me off from the country I had written and thought about my whole life, and where all the people I had grown up with still lived.

To lose one's country is to know a feeling akin to shame, almost as if one has been disowned by a parent, or turned out of one's home. Your country is so intimately bound up with your sense of self that you do not realize what a ballast it has been until it is gone. The relationship is fundamental. It is one of the few things we are allowed to take for granted, and it is the basis of our curiosity about other places. Without a country we are adrift, like people whose inability to love another is linked to an inability to love themselves.

For me, the loss was literal – I could not go back to India – but also abstract: the loss of an idea, that 'exalted' idea of a secular India. India, as its first prime minister, Jawaharlal Nehru, vowed, was not meant to be a 'Hindu Pakistan.' Rather, it was to be a place that cherished the array of religions, languages, ethnicities, and cultures that had taken root over 50 centuries.

Nehru's idea of India as a palimpsest, where 'layer upon layer of thought and reverie had been inscribed, and yet no succeeding layer has completely hidden or erased what has been written previously,' served as the foundation for the modern republic, born of British colonial rule in 1947. The new country gave secularism a distinctly Indian meaning. As the parliamentarian Shashi Tharoor told me recently, '*Secular* in India merely meant the existence of a profusion of religions, all of which were allowed and encouraged by the state to flourish.' The idea of India was a historical recognition that over time – and not always peacefully – a great diversity had collected on the Indian subcontinent. The modern republic, as a reflection of that history, would belong not to any one group, but to all groups in equal measure.

But beneath the topsoil of this modern country, a mere seven decades old, lies an older reality, embodied in the word *Bharat*, which can evoke the idea of India as the holy land, specifically of the Hindus. *India* and *Bharat* – these two words for the same place represent a central tension within the nation, the most dangerous and urgent one of our time. *Bharat* is Sanskrit, and the name by which India knows herself in her own languages, free of the gaze of outsiders. *India* is Latin, and its etymology alone – the Sanskrit *sindhu* for 'river,' turning into *hind* in Persian, and then into *indos* in Greek, meaning the Indus – reveals a long history of being under Western eyes. India is a land; Bharat is a people – the Hindus. India is historical; Bharat is mythical. India is an overarching and inclusionary idea; Bharat is atavistic, emotional, exclusionary.

It was this tension between two distinct ways of looking at the same place – modern country or holy land – that the founder of Hindu nationalism, Vinayak Damodar Savarkar, took aim at in the early 20th century. As he wrote in his 1923 book, *Hindutva: Who Is a Hindu?*, 'To be a Hindu means a person who sees this land, from the Indus River to the sea, as his country but also as his Holy Land.' This Hindu person was, in Savarkar's view, the paramount Indian citizen. Everyone else was at best a guest, and at worst the bastard child of foreign invasion. Savarkar was, as Octavio Paz writes in *In Light of India*, 'intellectually responsible for the assassination of Gandhi,' in 1948, at the hands of Nathuram Godse, now a hero of the Hindu right. Modern Hindu nationalism is represented by the Rashtriya Swayamsevak Sangh (RSS), the cultural organization in which Narendra Modi was reared, and of which his party – the Bharatiya Janata Party – is the political face.

As much as people in India bridle against the binary distinction of India and Bharat, it recurs again and again in the country's discourse – Bharat as a pure, timeless country, unassailable and authentic; India as the embodiment of modernity and all its ills and dislocations. When a medical student was raped and murdered in Delhi in 2012, the head of the RSS had this to say: 'Such crimes hardly take place in Bharat, but they occur frequently in India ... Where "Bharat" becomes "India," with the influence of Western culture, these types of incidents happen.'

Growing up in 1980s India, in a Westernized enclave where, to quote Edward Said, the 'main tenet' of my world 'was that everything of consequence either had happened or would happen in the West,' I had no idea of this other wholeness called Bharat. That ignorance of Hindu ways and beliefs was not mine alone, but symptomatic of the English-speaking elite, which, in imitation of the British colonial classes, lived in isolation from the country around them. Mohandas Gandhi, at the 1916 opening of Banaras Hindu University, a project that was designed to bridge the distance between Hindu tradition and Western-style modernity, worried that India's 'educated men' were becoming 'foreigners in their own land,' unable to speak to the 'heart of the nation.' Working closely with Nehru, Gandhi had been a great explainer, continually translating what came from outside into Indian idiom and tradition.

By the time I was an adult, the urban elites and the 'heart of the nation' had lost the means to communicate. The elites lived in a state of gated comfort, oblivious to the hard realities of Indian life – poverty and unemployment, of course, but also urban ruin and environmental degradation. The schools their children went to set them at a great remove from India, on the levels of language, religion, and culture. Every feature of their life was designed, to quote Robert Byron on the English in India, to blunt their 'natural interest in the country and sympathy with its people.' Their life was, culturally speaking, an adjunct to Western Europe and America; their values were a hybrid, in which India was served nominally while the West was reduced to a source of permissiveness and materialism. They thought they lived in a world where the 'idea of India' reigned supreme – but all the while, the constituency for this idea was being steadily eroded. It was Bharat that was ascendant. India's leaders today speak with contempt of the principles on which this young nation was founded. They look back instead to the timeless glories of the Hindu past. They scorn the 'Khan Market gang' – a reference to a fashionable market near where I grew up that has become a metonym for the Indian elite. Hindu nationalists trace a direct line between the foreign occupiers who destroyed the Hindu past – first Muslims, then the British – and India's Westernized elite (and India's Muslims), whom they see as heirs to foreign occupation, still enjoying the privileges of plunder.

Almost 30 years ago, in the preface to his book *Imaginary Homelands*, Salman Rushdie, fearful of the 'religious militancy' threatening 'the foundations of the secular state,' had expressed alarm that 'there is no commonly used Hindustani word for "secularism"; the importance of the secular ideal in India has simply been assumed, in a rather unexamined way.' As it happens, the exalted idea of India has no commonly used translation either. Rushdie was saying that this is not merely a failure of language, but an expression of the isolation of an elite that thought its power was inviolable. 'And yet,' Rushdie wrote, 'if the secularist principle were abandoned, India could simply explode.'

India is now exploding. Even the visit of an American president in February was not enough to contain the rage. As Modi and Donald Trump bear-hugged each other, Hindu nationalist mobs roamed the streets of New Delhi a few miles away, murdering Muslims and attacking their businesses and places of worship. The two leaders did not acknowledge these events, in which Hindus and Muslims alike were killed. India is approaching an especially dangerous point: the right quantity of unemployed young men, the right kind of populist strongman, and the right level of ignorance and heightened expectations, emanating from an imaginary past. Who knows what elements of modern nation-building and democracy might conveniently be sacrificed on the altar of a vengeful and revivalist politics?

I was not Muslim, and not Pakistani, but, as the writer Saadat Hasan Manto once noted, I was Muslim enough to risk getting killed. It was game over for my sort of person in India. We had been so blithe, so unknowing, so insulated from a wider Indian reality that it was as if we had prepared the conditions for our own destruction. If I became attuned to the danger, it was because I had seen what had happened to my father in Pakistan, where the shape of society is identical to that of India. He had died like a dog in the street for his high Western ideals. They mourned him in the drawing rooms of Lahore, and in the universities, think tanks, and newsrooms of the West. But in Pakistan, his killer was showered with rose petals; his killer's funeral drew more than 100,000 mourners into the streets.

All over the old non-West, as well as in Western Europe and America, the symbols of belonging – race, religion, language – are being repurposed for a confrontation between what David Goodhart has referred to as the 'somewheres' and the 'anywheres,' the rooted and the rootless. I, with no tribe or caste, no religion or country, have had nowhere to go but to the cities of the West, where I hoped to wait out the storm. But, as my break with India acquired a cold new finality, exile turning into asylum, I could not help but ask whether any harbor would survive the destructive wrath of what may be coming for us all.

14

Vaishnava Jana to Kone Kahiye? Reclaiming Gujarati Identity from the Haters

Suketu Mehta

One of the most beautiful poems ever written happens to be in my mother tongue, Gujarati. It's a bhajan called *'Vaishnava jana to tene kahiye'*, written by the great fifteenth-century saint-poet Narsi Mehta, who was instrumental in forming the Gujarati language. It was also Gandhiji's favorite bhajan. The first stanza is:

> vaiṣṇava jana to tene kahiye
> je pīḍa parāyī jāṇe re,
> para duḥkhe upakāra kare to ye
> mana abhimāna na āṇe re

sakaḷa loka māṁsahune vande,
nindā na kare kenī re,

The Vaishnavas are those who
Feel the pain of others,
Help those who are in misery,
But are never conceited.

They respect the whole world,
Never speak ill of anyone . . .

Narsi was thrown out of his community, the Nagars, which is also my community, because he would sit down and eat with anyone, Dalits, Muslims. His Vaishnavism had room for all humanity; it was *all* about humanity. Narsi was the true Gujarati. His disciple Mohandas Gandhi was also a true Gujarati. But the tradition of Narsi is being perverted today, because there's another image of Gujarat, and Gujaratis, that the world sees today. It's the Gujarat of Narendra Modi, not Narsi Mehta. And I belong to the Gujarat of Narsi, not Naren.

The 2002 massacres in Ahmedabad, in which children saw their parents set on fire and their mothers raped, made me ashamed to be Gujarati. The CAA [Citizenship (Amendment) Act] and the NRC (National Register of Citizens), with its eventual goal of a nationwide system of gulags for Muslims, now make me ashamed to be Gujarati, because they were propagated by a pair of Gujaratis. There's

Vaishnava Jana to Kone Kahiye?

another Gujarati, Gautam Adani, who's opening the largest coal mine in Australia, an existential threat to the planet. There are Gujarati industrialists that say nothing as all the nation's institutions are corrupted and corroded by other Gujaratis. I want to tell the world: please don't judge all Gujaratis by their actions. These people do not represent me, or millions of other Gujaratis. We are kinder than them, we are more open than them, we are better than them.

But it's true that my homeland has, in recent times, a bloody history. I grew up going to Ahmedabad. My grandfather's house in Maninagar was right next to a Muslim locality. In peaceful times the Muslims shopped in the Hindu-owned markets; the Hindus went to Muslim tailors. During the 'toofan', the border suddenly became visible, tangible. You were not to step across this line; there were always the boys standing guard, armed with hockey sticks, knives, kerosene.

The same people who would willingly throw kerosene on a man and burn him alive would then go home and eat a strictly vegetarian lunch. The Gujaratis who lead the country today are vegetarian, because they don't want to hurt animals. I'm vegetarian too. So was Hitler. My vegetarianism is a very personal decision; it does not allow for lynching a man just because he doesn't follow my religion, and eats beef. My Gujarati thali has room for all kinds of foods, all kinds of flavors: some sweet, some salty, some spicy. The BJP thali has only two flavors: sour and bitter. Where is the famous Gujarati sweetness, the gadpan? And just to be clear: I'm no fan of the

Congress party either. I don't think India should be run like a family business, another kind of Tata–Birla dynasty.

The Gujaratis who lead the country now want to turn India into a national Ahmedabad. All are welcome in their India, they say, except Muslims – and also Christians, once they're done with the Muslims. And gays, once they're done with the Christians. And women, once they're done with the gays. There are people in their party who admire not Gandhiji but Godse. They openly praise the murderer of the man who defined the best of Gujarat.

Vaishnava jana to kone kahiye? What kind of Gujaratis are these? These are certainly not the Gujaratis of Narsi; these are not Vaishnava Jan, because they do not feel the pain of others – they actively cause pain to others, as we have seen in the messaging they are giving to Muslims that they do not belong in India. They do not respect the whole world – they believe everything was invented in India first, and India is superior to all others. They constantly speak ill of others – Pakistanis, journalists, writers, NGOs – and they are full of conceit about their 56-inch chests. A Vaishnava is not filled with pride, 'garva' or 'asmita' as the Hindutvadis define it. *Mana abhimana na ane re,* as Narsi sings. For the true Vaishnava, there is only humility, acceptance, welcome, empathy with those who are suffering. Any wanderer who comes to his house will be given water, shade, rest.

There was an earlier Gujarat, which had to rely on an openness to other cultures, religions, if nothing else than for

Vaishnava Jana to Kone Kahiye?

purely mercantile reasons. In order to be a good businessman, in order to have the widest possible market, you have to trade with many people who may be very different from you. You have to put aside your hatred, and you have to be pragmatic. *Dhandho karvo che.*

The Gujaratis now in charge of the country's business have failed in the first duty of a Gujarati businessman: to make a profit. They are running India as a loss-making unit. The unemployment rate is the highest in forty-five years. Consumer prices are 7.3 percent higher than last year; onions cost 328 percent more than they did. India now has the slowest growth of all the emerging economies, at 4.8 percent and falling. According to *The Economist*, it would have been 3.1 percent if the government hadn't gone on a spending spree to boost numbers. For decades, the Indian growth rate was so steady at 3.5 percent that it used to be known as the Hindu rate of growth. Under Modi, we're now experiencing an even lower rate: the Hindutva rate of growth. He promised to build millions of toilets but it's the economy that he's dragged into the toilet. *Dhandho karta aavde che?*

And so, to divert attention from its failures, the government is encouraging everyone to focus on hating Pakistan, hating Muslims, keeping an imaginary Bangladeshi horde out. It's the politics of mass diversion. Trump does it with Mexicans; the Brexiteers do it with Eastern Europeans; Modi and Shah do it with Bangladeshis.

Any real Gujarati would be concerned about the

incalculable harm these nativist, Islamophobic policies are having on the country's international image, and its business prospects. Satya Nadella, Microsoft's CEO, recently had the guts to take on the CAA directly: 'I think what is happening is sad... It's just bad,' he said. 'I would love to see a Bangladeshi immigrant who comes to India and creates the next unicorn in India or becomes the next CEO of Infosys.'

So far, few other industrialists, except Rahul Bajaj – and certainly none of our Gujarati mill-maliks – have had the guts to say openly what many think privately. But many countries and companies like to trade with India because we are better than, say, China. We are an open society, we are not Pakistan. We don't have a state religion, we are not a Hindu country. But if that image changes – if you yank someone's OCI card because of what he writes; or if you use the tax authorities to browbeat media houses into submission; or if you use the machinery of the state to beat up students in their dorms – then we become a kela republic just like all the other banana republics. Then our companies will be the targets of boycotts in the West, and they will stay away from India.

Already, there are official bodies, like the US Commission on Religious Freedom, that are recommending sanctions on Indian ministers. Young South Asians on university campuses abroad are outraged by what India is doing in Kashmir – depriving twelve million Indian citizens of access to the Internet, which has become a matter of life and death these days, for months on end. There is talk of boycotts against India, like the BDS movement against Israel.

Some time ago, *The Economist*'s cover featured the slogan 'Intolerant India'. The *New York Times*, the *New Yorker*, and *Time* Magazine have all featured long cover stories about what we're going through, the greatest crisis in our democracy since the founding of the Republic. When Amazon's Jeff Bezos visited India in January 2020, bringing with him a billion dollars of investment, he was given the cold shoulder by the government, because he owns the *Washington Post*, which has also run caustic editorials about India. Whether we like it or not, the world now thinks of India in the same league as other corrupt and repressive regimes such as Brazil – whose leader was the chief guest at the 2020 Republic Day parade – and Turkey. We have lost our good name. This is going to cost us money.

Gujaratis are, above all, a pragmatic people. It is pragmatic to make accommodation with everyone, even your enemies. Today, India is the world's second largest Muslim country, right behind Indonesia. By 2060 India will be the biggest Muslim country on earth. The Muslim population will go from 15 percent to 20 percent of the country, and nothing short of an outright genocide is going to change that. So far, Indian Muslims have not been radicalized; no Indian Muslim joined ISIS and the women of Shaheen Bagh wave the tricolor even as they protest government policy. These are people who voted with their feet to stay in the country after Partition. But if Indian Muslims are constantly otherized, if they are told over and over again, you don't belong here, you are not truly Indian, then some segment of them is sure to become radicalized. Even if it's one percent of Indian Muslims, that's still four million people. And then what? We'll have the mother of all civil wars, something that will make Partition look like a fight in the schoolyard.

We can't afford not to work together, or be diverted by fighting each other. Because the next few decades are going to be challenging, even apocalyptic. Take just one issue: water. By 2030, 40 percent of Indians will have no drinking water, and demand for water will be twice the available supply. India will have run out of groundwater. I saw this every time I went back to Gujarat as a child. My grand-aunt could recite the names of the five rivers that flowed through her part of Gujarat. All of them are dry now, or mere trickles in the monsoon. Dhoodiyu desh, they call it, 'the dust country'. All of India's going to be a dust country. June 2019 was the hottest in India's history, as you well know. Thousands of people died in heatwaves. If global emissions continue at the current rate, temperatures will rise 4.5 degrees by the end of the century, and large parts of northern India and Bangladesh will be, quite literally, unsurvivable. Human beings will roast to death if they step outside.

We have to fight all these problems together, Hindu, Muslim, and all the other religions. United, we survive;

Vaishnava Jana to Kone Kahiye?

divided, we die of thirst. And in Gujarat, we have a long tradition of living with the other, even when we don't like their politics.

One of my mother's uncles was a famous lawyer in Bharuch, a communist, and a member of the Gujarat legislature in the 1950s. I grew up going to Bharuch, and some of my happiest memories are of sitting on the roof of the house at the end of a hot summer evening, as my fua drank beer with the local bootlegger, who was his client, and the local police inspector, whom the bootlegger was bribing. Sometimes I would go for a walk with his son, my cousin Raju, who was also a lawyer. Raju's best friend was a Muslim man named Shaikh. Every evening, they would go for a walk by the river, and then to the Bharuch railway station, arguing ferociously over politics. Then they would share a cup of chai. My cousin is a staunch bhakt, and his best friend is a staunch Muslim. 'Shaikh you are a communalist,' my cousin lambasted him. As the bootlegger shared a beer with the cop; the Hindutvadi and the kattar Mussalman shared a cup of chai. After all, they're both Gujarati, why get a whole cup all for yourself? One by two, they say. One by two, the bootlegger says to the cop; one by two, the Hindu communalist says to the Muslim communalist. I find it an endearing formula. The joke is that five Gujaratis come into a tea shop and ask for 'two by five' – two cups of chai split into five. 'And while you're at it,' they instruct the boy, 'put the fan on and dust off my scooter outside.'

One by two. Two by five. Three by eight. We Gujjus are

used to sharing, economizing. We may not be inclined to spend, but we know how to share. But these new Gujjus don't believe in one by two anymore. It's all one by one, one for one, one and only one.

We are one people, many-splendored. The British divided us, made us two. One by two. Let us not believe in this rubbish. Western logic rests on a fundamental binary: the Aristotelian law of the excluded middle. Something is true, or false. You believe in my God, or you are an unbeliever. There is no gray area. You're with us or against us, as George Bush declared.

Indian philosophy is very different. The Jain system of logic has no fewer than seven possible states of being: something can be true, false, both, neither. It's the most exquisitely developed system of conditional logic the world has ever known. And you know what it's called? 'Syadvada' – the science of maybeness.

The BJP is now saying, you are either Hindu, or you're not. And if you're not, you can't be Indian. Let's get back to syadvada. Let's admit doubt. Let's not be so damned sure about everything – who is an Indian and who's not.

There's always been a tradition of openness, hospitality, coexistence in Gujarat, no less than in any other part of this marvelous land. This was the Gujarat that welcomed all kinds of outsiders, including the Zoroastrians fleeing from Iran. When they landed near Udwada, the ruler, Jadi Rana, came out to greet them, but said that Gujarat was already full, pointing to a pot of milk filled to the brim. The newcomers

Vaishnava Jana to Kone Kahiye?

stirred some sugar into the milk and presented it to Jadi Rana. 'We will live here like this; we will sweeten your life without displacing you.' And the Parsis took up the Gujarati language, and their women wore sarees. Later, the Bohras, Khojas, Memons did the same. They eat, pray, and love in the same language that I do. The great filmmaker Ismail Merchant was Gujarati, and I spoke to him in Gujarati. The great historian Mehmood Mamdani is Gujarati, and when we meet in New York we crack off-color jokes in Gujarati with an East African accent. The great writer Adil Mansoori was a family friend who encouraged me early in my writing career.

The Palanpuri diamond merchants I grew up amongst were not big fans of Muslims; many of them financed the Jana Sangh and are now financing the BJP. Yet the older Palanpuris could recite ghazals in Urdu. The Nawab of Palanpur had excellent relations with his Hindu and Jain subjects, whom he appointed as his ministers. We are next door to Pakistan, but for seventy years the door has been firmly shut. But if we put our ears close to the door, we can hear the same bhasha.

Now we have Gujaratis speaking in bad Hindi telling 200 million people of this land that they need to prove that they're Indian. They are demanding papers to prove their citizenship. In *Maximum City* I wrote that government bureaucracy had made India 'The Country of the No'. I'm writing this partly on board an Air India flight from New York. Nothing works. The TV controls are broken, many of the seats are broken. The headphones are broken, the blankets and eye masks have all been stolen, and when I ask for something, the answer is generally, 'No'. To trust such a government machinery to perform such a mammoth task as assign birth certificates or citizenship papers fairly is to expect the impossible. As a result, millions of Indian citizens are going to be classified as illegal, and put in camps.

The CAA and the NRC will tear apart this land, this beautiful idea of India, which is that it does not belong to any one community – not Hindu, not Muslim, not anybody else. It belongs to all of us. This is supposed to be a country where the mind is free from fear. The mind is not free from fear these days. Very far from it. The mind is full of fear.

Gujaratis are global citizens par excellence. We approach the world with confidence. One out of every three overseas Indians is Gujarati. We Gujaratis are wanderers. When Neil Armstrong stepped off Apollo 11 and took his first step on the moon, he was greeted by a Gujarati chaiwalla who said, *'Neilbhai, aavo aavo.* What took you so long?' My own family has been in and out of Gujarat for over a century now, and is spread all over the earth: in Kenya, Dubai, America, England, Australia. We do not lose anything by wandering; we respect the countries we wander to and contribute to them.

But Gujaratis also know what it feels like to be hated, hunted. During the 1960 riots in Bombay, when the state was being broken in two and Gujarat and Maharashtra were both claiming the city, Maharashtrian mobs ran after Gujaratis

Vaishnava Jana to Kone Kahiye?

in the streets with sticks shouting, '*Soo che, saaru che, danda le ke maru che!*' Yes, we too were called termites once: illegal immigrants, told to go back to where we came from.

What explains this anger, this insecurity, this hatred? How could Gandhiji and Amit Shah come from the same land?

Gujaratis are, by legend, supposed to be frugal, thrifty. Nehru referred to us in *Discovery of India* as 'a small-boned, mercantile people'. Would that he could see our 56-inch chests! Throughout my childhood, I was mocked because I was Gujarati, and therefore thought to be weaker than, for example, Punjabis or Kashmiris. The joke goes: Do you know why there isn't a Gujarati Regiment in the Indian Army, a First Gujarat Rifles? There used to be one, but they were all shot for trading with the enemy.

In recent times, there's been a curious sexual insecurity, a crisis of masculinity, among Gujarati men. The whole 'love jihad' thing – what is it but a fear of Muslim men being more sexually attractive to our gullible women? And then along came Modi with his 56-inch chest, and all over Gujarat, and in New Jersey and in Wembley, Gujarati hearts started fluttering at the Gujarati Elvis. Here was Krishna, and here were his gopis, rescued from the lascivious topiwala. Modi, with his bombast, his aggression, reclaimed an idea of Gujarati virility. The RSS, the organization that he came from and that now controls him, is an entirely male body. That tells you everything you need to know about their ethos, and their insecurities. Gandhiji had another idea of masculinity, which was closer to a form of androgyny. But today's Gujaratis have enough of Gandhi, enough of nonviolence, of satyagraha. They believe only in graha, not satya. '*Dekho dekho kaun aaya, Gujarat ka sher aaya,*' they said in Gujarat at Modi's rallies. A lion, not a pussy.

It is a family fight, among Gujaratis. Most of my relatives vote for the BJP, as they did for the Jana Sangh before that. But many children of Gujarati immigrants in the US and the UK want nothing to do with this politics of hate. They identify as South Asian, or desi, rather than Indian. They don't understand how their parents could oppose Donald Trump – 87 percent of Indian-Americans voted Democratic in the 2016 election – and also support Modi. They don't understand how we can demand tolerance for Indian immigrants abroad while being intolerant to Bangladeshi immigrants at home.

We need to respect the whole world, like Narsi says; we need to let good thoughts come to us from all sides, like the Rigveda says. When my uncle Vasantkaka came to visit us in New York soon after we immigrated, he gave me a bit of advice which I'll always follow: 'Take the best from the East, and the best from the West.' He was not privileging one over the other. The Vedas don't have a corner on truth, and neither does the Koran or the Bible. But each one has some of it.

I am an overseas citizen of India. I was born in India. There's a little-noticed clause in the CAA under which the government can stop me from entering India for any violation of any notified law, like a parking ticket. They might go after writers like me for saying things they don't like. Let them try. They can never stop me from entering India unless they rip out my heart, because India is not an external entity for me, it is who I am. I carry my India within me. There's a line in a poem by Ardeshir Khabardar: '*Jya jya vase ek Gujarati, tya tya sadakal Gujarat.*' Where there is a Gujarati, there's always a Gujarat. We can wander the earth without losing ourselves, without wondering who we are, because we carry our Gujarat with us, like our thepla-chundo. I have eaten my thepla-chundo in the favelas of Brazil, in the palaces of Europe, in the ryokans of Japan. I appreciate all cultures, but I do not lose myself to any of them. They add to who I am, they never take away from me. We are Gujjus, we are globo-Gujjus.

Every Gujarati home I have gone to has been welcoming, with a glass of water first brought to you, then ganthia, farsan, and an invitation: come eat with us. When you part from a Gujarati, he will not say, 'Goodbye.' He will say, '*Aavjo.*' Come again. That is the true spirit of Gujarat. We do not erect doors, fences, walls, detention camps. Our home is open to all. *Aavjo. Ghare aavjo.* Come home. *Chokkas aavjo.*

January 2020

15

The Actual Shafi Shauq

Amit Chaudhuri

The lobby had been appropriated. Writers sat on sofas, talking. Any reminder of the purpose of their visit was met with resentment. Indian musicians hate sharing their repertoire with students. They eke out what they know with reluctance. It looked like the writers were no different. They were content to be 'Indian writers' as if the category were a caste. They *appeared* – the word is emphasised as a caveat against taking appearances at face value – uninterested in writing. Periodically, they burst into laughter. If you overheard a snatch of the conversation, you'd realise that the subject of mirth was writers who weren't in their company. Their anecdotes proved the truism that every second writer is a fool.

I must say two things here. First, this story is from a

The Actual Shafi Shauq

long time ago. Twelve years have passed since the sixtieth anniversary of Independence brought us together in a strange foreign city. I'm using both adjectives despite the fact that a foreign city is bound to be strange because Frankfurt is stranger than most. If it had city-like characteristics (the poor; the working class; cafes; bus shelters), we – made to gather in the lobby, then herded off in groups to do readings – were kept from them. I saw little of Frankfurt and a lot of the writers.

The other thing is that the story is fictional. There may be a skeletal correspondence with an event that's elapsed, but the tissue is fiction. The writers in it don't exist. Their namesakes might, but they're as independent of the 'characters' I'm about to introduce as they are from their other namesakes. For instance, there may be many Javed Akhtars in the universe. They're not to be confused with the one I spotted in the lobby, who shouldn't be confused with the lyricist of the same name.

I say 'long time ago' because twelve years is a long time in the life of a nation. Our country's achievements at the time, its stupidity, its misguided ventures (of which the railway platform-like congregation in the hotel lobby could be counted as one), its generosity, its self-serving disagreements – all these seem as unreal now as frictions and friendships developed over a holiday. Some of the writers – Mushirul Hasan, Girish Karnad, Ananthamurthy, Dilip Chitre – are dead. Others may be in a state of siege.

The long-standing tension that simmered in the lobby – between those who wrote in Indian languages and the ones who wrote in English – still rankles, but – like people and misunderstandings that belong to a vanished world – also makes me smile. There was mutual contempt between the camps, and inequality – but no violence. Barring a few national figures, I preferred the bhasha writers. They comprised the old artistic order; we, the new social order, for which there was no 'art' – only 'nation'. We had breakfast together; one camp paid obeisance to the other, then moved on, since there was nothing to be gained by being in their company.

Among those I met was a small, suited Kashmiri poet called Shafi Shauq. The term 'Kashmiri poet' carried a mild voltage. I was speechless for an instant, then said, 'Hello!' Not that a Kashmiri poet is an impossibility, but that Shafi Shauq represented a concatenation of impossibilities, to do with his presence here, with a resolution to the problem being found, and peace ever being regained. I wanted to study him closely and ask him for forgiveness. He was diffident, as non-Anglophone writers – especially poets – are. Kafka-like, he'd adopted the guise of normalcy – I mean his twentieth-century appearance, the black suit, meant to sidestep attention. He was fair; his eyes shone gently. He had lost hair, like a Jewish intellectual. Keep in mind that he is a character in a story. There *is* a Kashmiri poet called Shafi Shauq, who's very different, as this photo bears out.

The Actual Shafi Shauq

We spent some time in proximity to each other, as writers were driven in vans to buildings to read in different rooms. The Germans had developed a taste for chaotic self-regard; they sat in unprotesting groups. Anyway, even if Mr Shauq and I had liked each other (which we did), what could we have talked about? I had examined him for signs of past explosions (any telltale residue on his jacket) and was relieved he was more intact than I was. I was also disabled by my sense that he'd lived, while I hadn't; that writers in English, to make up for not having lived, must be relentless spokespersons. My love for Shafi Shauq was real, but we exchanged few words. Still, I went discreetly to one of his readings. He was mumbling into the mike, and then every few seconds the lines were repeated in German translation. The small audience was cowed into silence, either by the theme or the Frankfurt Book Fair. I still have the handouts with the English versions of the poems he read out.

Carthage

If there's a paradise on earth, this is it.
He repeated 'this is it'
three times, because once wasn't enough
to dispel doubt. The first time he muttered
to himself, the second
and third declamations were to the world.
The exhortation reached Roman ears.
Carthage no longer stands.

The second poem is from the same page, just under 'Carthage'.

Crossing a Street

Crossing a street, I lower my head
in case of danger. Sometimes, it's something's
absence I sense – nothing as tangible
as rocket or gun. I must be careful.

The Actual Shafi Shauq

I cross the street, to find the house
where I'd expected it to be not there. I look
around in case I'm in a new neighbourhood.
Easy to lose your way.

It's easy to lose your way at home,
to cross the street and never look back.
I lower my head instinctively
to protect myself from what I can't see.

What struck me weren't individual phrases – I couldn't judge the translation – but the absence of overt politics, the lack of specific contemporary references or of protest. What's stayed with me – reconfirmed as I revisit the page – is the poet's lostness, his unsureness about the world.

Something happened the next day which became a matter of discussion in the lobby. We heard Shafi Shauq had gone out for a walk; he'd discovered a bridge. When he was on it, he saw a man in uniform approach him from the opposite direction. The man asked to see Mr Shauq's papers, and then demanded to have a look at his wallet. Once he had the wallet, he made off with it.

We were scandalised. Is there no free country for a Kashmiri? To be ambushed *here* of all places! Might the terrors of home have a familiarity that you feel safer negotiating than an encounter with a stranger? Shafi Shauq seemed out of sorts, but he smiled. He looked like he wanted to go back. Liberty had begun to feel inimical. But go back to what?

No more was achieved at the Frankfurt Book Fair than at a family wedding. There was the same unfocussed jubilation and aimlessness. As in a phased mass migration, we were put on trains to Brussels. Some people arrived earlier, some later. It depended on when your panel was scheduled. Brussels had decided to take advantage of the large contingent at Frankfurt and, in the Book Fair's aftermath, host its own extravaganza. Western Europe was showing signs of an 'Indian culture' contagion. Who were we to argue with our role in the epidemic?

My panel was the next morning, with writer and diplomat Pavan Varma, poet and lyricist Nida Fazli, and another well-known Hindi poet whose name I have forgotten. We were supposed to start at eleven, but heard that Nida Fazli and the other poet hadn't reached Brussels. At 11.30 a.m., Pavan Varma and I were told to hold the fort, and we embarked on a variant of the debate – common to festivals at the time – to do with whether or not writing in English was a betrayal.

At 12.30 p.m., Nida Fazli and the other poet walked in, heads bent, silent, like escapees from a calamity. Pavan, who was also a translator au fait with Hindi and Urdu literature, leapt up when he saw them. They greeted him gravely, and occupied the chairs left empty for them. Nida Fazli, in a patient, wounded voice, informed us of the reason for the delay. He and the other poet had been received at the station

The Actual Shafi Shauq

by festival volunteers. They'd been taken to a car, their luggage loaded in the back. Just as they were about to be driven off, a man knocked on Nida Fazli's window and told him that there was something wrong with the rear bumper. Nida Fazli got out to have a look. The driver urged him to get back in immediately: the station was full of pickpockets. A little while after they'd finally set out, Nida Fazli found that his passport, money, and a notebook of unpublished poems had vanished from his overcoat pocket.

'I don't care about the money,' he told us. 'Money will come and money will go. It's the loss of the notebook I can't get over.'

People made consoling remarks.

'They have no use for the notebook. You may get it back.'

'A passport was once found in a garbage bin.'

Without preamble, Nida Fazli plunged into a poem – interrupting himself only to say: 'Those were dark days in Bambai! Human being had turned on human being'; we knew he was speaking of the riots at the end of 1993, when Muslims, terrified by the toppling of the Babri Masjid (*'ab gira!'* Uma Bharti had shouted as she'd struck a blow), were punished in Bombay for being terrified – 'Dark days had descended and there was no light! And then one morning in the midst of that violence I saw a child getting ready as usual for school and I thought: There *is* still light! There *is* a tomorrow!' So addressing the audience, he resumed:

Amit Chaudhuri

> हुआ सवेरा
> ज़मीन पर फिर अदब से आकाश
> अपने सर को झुका रहा है
> कि बच्चे स्कूल जा रहे हैं

> morning comes –
> again, the sky
> lowers its head
> towards the earth in salutation
> because the children are going to school

Rising from his chair and looming over us in his long kurta, he repeated the verse, in the slightly irritating looping manner of Urdu and Hindi shairi, where tension is built up by retracing a path.

> in order to bathe in the river, the sun,
> wearing a turban
> of gold malmal,
> is standing
> on one side of the road, smiling
> that the children are going to school

Each verse was doubled, trebled, its span expanded, and money, notebook, and passport were placed in abeyance. Great bereavement and optimism converged. Is it the lot of those who have been besieged to recurrently relive their past? Is it worse to be a visitor without a passport or in a home

The Actual Shafi Shauq

where you have no status? Do we falter terribly without the birthplace that threatens us?

Coda

All this is from a long time ago. I was reminded again of the theft of Shafi Shauq's wallet in 2014 or 2015, while I was teaching a creative writing workshop in Calcutta. Among the participants was a young Kashmiri writer called Asiya. She'd come from Baramulla on the recommendation of a well-known novelist. She was shy and, when she thought she was out of my sight, effervescent. She composed vivid accounts of her small town.

The participants, of course, went off exploring the city in their spare time. On one of these excursions, a tiny misadventure was averted. The details have become hazy: I had to get them corroborated by Asiya. In itself, the anecdote may not be worth repeating. It was reported to me by Flavius, a French participant, before one of the classes began. 'We almost lost Asiya yesterday!' he said. 'Lost?' I asked. 'What do you mean?' Asiya was standing next to him, diminutive, dramatic, shaking her head in denial. 'We were in the metro going to Park Street. We wanted to walk from there to Victoria Memorial. We'd got off the metro when, suddenly, the doors closed before Asiya could get off.' 'Is that right?' I asked Asiya. 'Oh but,' she exclaimed, 'then the doors opened again! He's exaggerating, sir. You should know Flavius by now! It was a temporary technical fault.' Asiya tells me that

I then said (I don't recall my exact words, but I know I said something of the kind): 'You Kashmiris tend to get into trouble outside Kashmir.' She laughed loudly, as if at an observation that was not only absurd but incontrovertible. I then told her that Shafi Shauq had had his wallet taken from him in Frankfurt. 'Do you know him?' I asked. She said she did: after all, she'd already written a book of poems in English – Asiya is part of Kashmir's literary terrain.

She attended two workshops, returning to Calcutta in 2015. Maybe she liked the experience. I later met up with her in Delhi, when I told her of my long-standing plan to write a story about the depredations Kashmiris face when they're placed in an environment in which unhindered movement can take place. 'It will be about Shafi Shauq,' I said, 'but not the actual Shafi Shauq.' 'You *must*!' she cried passionately: I wonder if she had doubts in retrospect.

I had a chat with her on the phone when she was in Delhi last month, to ask after things that have no direct relation to this story, but which had to do with unfolding events. Communicating with her – on Messenger or by email – has become out of the question when she's back in Baramulla. My sketch isn't reliable as there are several facts I can't check up on. Nida Fazli died about four years ago of a heart attack. Shafi Shauq, like most Kashmiris, is out of reach.

Note: *The poems by Shafi Shauq have no existence outside this narrative.*

2 December 2019

16

Arachnophilia

Amitabha Bagchi

juda jab tak teri zulfon se pech-o-kham nahin honge
sitam duniya mein badhte hi rahenge kam nahin honge

till the day the knots in your hair untangle
injustice will not decrease in this world, it will only deepen

It had begun a few weeks ago at the Durga Puja pandal. Rudraprasad Roychowdhury, founder and president of the Mayur Vihar Bengali Arachnologists Association, well known for his knowledge of spiders in all of Mayur Vihar Phase I and some parts of Phase II – Phase III had not yet been built in

---

All couplets in this story are by Kaleem Ajiz. All translations are by Amitabha Bagchi.

the early nineties – had been invited to give an illustrated talk. There was something irresistible about Rudraprasad when he took to the stage with his pointer. His eyes gleamed with knowledge, his mousy hair, combed carefully across his bald spot, gave him a debonair look, his photographs of spiders with their long legs – eight in number, spindly, curved – aglow on the screen. The atmosphere would become electric, the women in the audience breathless.

They had come up to talk to him together, Mrinmoyee Talukdar and her mother, Jyotirmoyee Talukdar.

'Oh Professor Roychowdhury, your spiders are so strong, so supple ... so ... so virile,' one of them had said. The other one just kept her eyes, her large, round, dark eyes, locked with his.

'Virile, you say,' he had rejoined. 'That is surprising because according to certain native American myths the Spider Woman is the creator of the universe. She is also Thought Woman or Creation Thinker Woman. As she thinks, so are we.'

'Oh Professor,' the one whose eyes he had been looking into had said, 'that is so ... profound.'

One thing had led to another. Meeting them together at Satyam Drycleaners or at Nine O Nine the Departmental Store with only one observable department, running into one or the other at the Thursday Bazaar, meeting for ice cream at the Kool Kat ice cream parlour or for aloo tikkis, with real pomegranate seeds in the sweet chutney, at the guy who stood across the road from Aggarwal Sweets; one thing had basically led to another. And today he had promised to meet both of them separately at seven-thirty at Haowin, the seafood restaurant.

Rudraprasad Roychowdhury was in a mess.

What better time to go looking for the Egg-Backed Cockroach than seven-thirty on an early winter evening, thought Rudraprasad. It had not been spotted near the Yamuna since 1936, when McDiarmid had reported seeing two magnificent mother-of-pearl-domed specimens at a point across the Yamuna, south of Bhairon Mandir. The Egg-Backed Cockroach is, of course, not a cockroach at all. It is a spider: *Arachnida blancova*. It is found only on the eastern banks of subcontinental rivers – not all subcontinental rivers, only those with eastern banks. The miscarriage of nomenclature that led to cockroach status being conferred on this spider is often attributed to a simple filing error by a clerk down in the musty archives of the Zoological Society's office. But there are some who hold to this day that it was the revenge of the Empire, a residue of deliberately created zoological confusion the natives would argue about for years to come.

The Egg-Backed was a spider that Rudraprasad had always wanted to find. The unlikelihood of actually running across it had discouraged him every time. Every time but today. He picked up his flashlight and set out.

When the light first shone on the little round hump Rudraprasad thought it was another stone, another false lead. But then he noticed the smooth texture, the perfectly round shape. Could this be it? he thought. Could it be that I have hit upon the first sighting of the Egg-Backed Cockroach on the banks of the Yamuna in the last sixty years? He put down the torch and started dusting the sides of the hump, careful not to press down on the shell, which was reportedly very fragile. The spider did not move. Maybe it was dead, he thought.

He brushed and brushed and tried to prise the shell out but it would not move. It seemed to be attached to something. He brushed further, excited at the thought that he had run into some strange mutant or perhaps a previously unknown nesting practice of the Egg-Backed. The shell was connected to an oblong, white, seemingly hollow cavity. Very strange, he thought, that a small creature like this could make such a large shell, almost the size of a human arm. Then he came across the finger bones. Ma Kali, it is a human arm!

~

agarche ishq mein marne ka khatra hi ziyaada hai
magar marne ke dar se marnewaale kam nahin honge

the fear of dying is prime amongst the fears that come with passion
despite the fear of dying the numbers of martyrs do not lessen

The board outside the shopfront proclaimed the office of the MVBAA. Inside, behind a single desk under a naked bulb sat a man with a newspaper open in front of him. Or, rather, there was the possibility of a man sitting there behind a spread newspaper because, after all, women rarely spread their newspapers so carelessly in this part of the world. To one side, on another chair, sat a person who was most definitely a man except that he was engaged in the rather unmasculine act of hiding his face in his hands.

The paper moved to reveal Sharadendranath Sanyal, the secretary of the Mayur Vihar Bengali Arachnologists Association.

'Rudra, have you heard this?'

'Gmph,' said Rudraprasad Roychowdhury.

'Madanmohan Makhija, the head of a prominent Hindu organization, today felicitated Rudraprasad Roychowdhury for uncovering a site of surpassing importance to Hindus worldwide. According to Mr Makhija, the ancient shrine to Parvati and Ganesh established by Maharaja Agrasen was a part of the lost heritage that had been neglected by the anti-majority policies of Indian governments until now.

'The discovery of the two skeletons of a mother and son locked in divine embrace clearly marks the spot where our scriptures had proclaimed such a shrine, he said. We plan to erect a magnificent temple complex that will extend from Okhla in the south to Seelampur in the north and will serve as one of the most important pilgrimages for all Hindus, he added.'

'Grmph,' said Rudraprasad.

'I agree,' said Sharadendranath, folding the paper. He began to hum a line from Lalon Fakir, replacing the words 'how many days before I meet the man of my heart' with a series of metre-appropriate elaborations of Rudraprasad's 'grmph'.

'They are out of control,' said Rudraprasad, righting himself with some effort.

'Very true,' said Sharadendranath, falling out of tune in order to pick up the end of the conversation that was rightly his. 'It makes no sense to dig up the river's entire flood plain to build a massive temple.'

'I mean Jyotirmoyee and Mrinmoyee. They read about my little escapade in the fields and put two and two together. Worse still, they discussed the matter. They both know. And they are furious.'

'Know what?'

'That I was wooing both of them at the same time. Now I only hope that Tarashankar Talukdar doesn't find out that I have been running after both his wife and his daughter. He doesn't like me to begin with.'

'I don't blame him,' said Sharadendranath, picking up the tune again, this time with the words Lalon Fakir had written.

~

Arachnophilia

agar badhta raha yuun hi ye sauda-e-sitamgaari
tumhi ruswa sar-e-baazaar hoge ham nahin honge

if it keeps increasing in this way, this frenzied tyranny
it's you who'll be publicly disgraced, it certainly won't be me

There was a knock on the door and a man with a beard, wearing a khadi kurta and Kolhapuri chappals, came in.

'Hello,' he said, effusively shaking the two mystified men by the hand one at a time. 'I am Rajendra Rawat.'

It was only out of politeness that the two men, the entire quorum of the MVBAA, did not point out that this meant nothing to them.

'I am the founder of *Fighting Fundamentalism*, the fortnightly that exposes the fascist forces fighting to take over the country.'

'Well, well,' said Sharadendranath. 'A pseudosecularist. My first. Glad to make your acquaintance, sir.'

'You flatter me, Mr . . .?'

'Sanyal.'

'You are not the discoverer,' said Rajendra Rawat.

'He is,' said Sharadendranath out loud, adding an indignant 'but I am a person worth greeting too' under his breath.

'Your discovery, Mr Roychowdhury, has provided the divisive forces that threaten our country with another opportunity to shamelessly buttress the edifice of Hindu nationalism. It is our duty as responsible citizens to stop this misappropriation of our heritage.'

'They were just a couple of skeletons, Mr Rawat,' cut in Sharadendranath. 'There are many possible explanations.'

'Exactly, my dear friend of Roychowdhury,' said Rawat, his eyes glowing with the fire of a practised polemic. 'That's how they work, cascades of confusion, multitudes of malapropisms, flocks of falsehoods, herds of half-truths.'

'Herds of half-truths?' said Sharadendranath. 'I thought half-truths came alone, sneaking in like thieves in the night.'

'Have you ever been mixed up with two women, Mr Rawat?' asked Rudraprasad, breaking in before bickering could break out. 'One the daughter of the other. Have you ever told Mrinmoyee that her walk was as graceful as a tarantula's and then looked up to find that you were talking to Jyotirmoyee? Have you ever looked into a girl's eyes and thought of her mother? Have you ever mistaken the slightly wrinkled lines of one face for the fresh spider web gossamer of another? Have you ever been caught in the conflicting chatter of two generations you cannot even distinguish between? Have you ever called a spider a cockroach?'

'Mr Roychowdhury, you don't understand.' Rawat could sense he was losing his audience. 'These people will make pants out of our nation's secular fabric.'

'Mr Rawat, I will have to ask you to leave now.'

∽

Arachnophilia

idhar aao tumhaari zulf ham aaraasta kar dein
jo gesu ham sanvaareinge kabhi barham nahin honge

come to me, come here, let me groom your hair
a lock that I have combed will never ever stray

As Rudraprasad drove along the approach to the Nizamuddin bridge he felt the curve in the road. He waited for the point at which Humayun's tomb would come into view. The tomb was in the dark but the shiny new gurdwara that stood to one side of it was lit. From the reflected light of that tiled dome it was possible to make out the dark, graceful, brooding silhouette of the tomb.

If you had been sitting up near the tomb's dome on that day in 1803 you could have seen the guns boom here, east of the river, as the British and French generals fought it out for their Indian employers. Perhaps that was when those two unfortunate souls had fallen, caught in a battle they did not understand, clutching each other as the shots tore through them. They had been lovers, it was possible, fated to be found by him near the end of the millennium, embracing like the hunchback and the gypsy girl in Victor Hugo's novel. Or maybe they had been mother and daughter. Maybe they had wrestled each other to death for the love of one man.

He gunned the scooter and felt the air rush into the space between his large, ungainly helmet and his small, oval head. He was heading across the river to meet someone for dinner.

Amitabha Bagchi

It was either Mrinmoyee Talukdar or Jyotirmoyee Talukdar. Rudraprasad Roychowdhury could not, for the life of him, remember which one.

yahaan to umr hi shamsheer ke saaye mein guzri hai
jo bhaagenge vo koi aur honge ham nahin honge

I have lived my entire life in the shadow of the sword
there may be others who will run away, I will never go

17

Freedom and the Idea of India

Romila Thapar

Those of my generation, who were teenagers in the 1940s, will doubtless recall that we were all obsessed with these two interrelated concepts: freedom and the idea of India. Freedom meant two things: one was the obvious freedom from colonial rule, encapsulated in the slogan of '*azadi*', and the other which was inherent in this, namely, the freedom to speak and give expression to what one thought. Freedom from colonial rule meant exploring the ways to achieve it. The forms stretched from satyagraha, or non-violent non-cooperation, to violent peasant protests, to organizing militant protest such as Subhas Chandra Bose's Indian National Army. It was the first of these that had the maximum impact.

Having acquired freedom, the next step was the form that the Indian nation and its society should take as a free nation.

In this, freedom of speech was a continuing component. So obsessive were these concerns that even as a fifteen-year-old in my last year of school when I was asked to make a small speech on 15 August 1947, this is roughly what I spoke about, and in the context of great optimism I quoted the poet in saying that 'Bliss it was in that dawn to be alive, but to be young was very heaven'.

Then we proceeded to try to define what we meant by the idea of India. Nationalism defined it as the inherited territory of British India and Indians referred to all its people with no differentiations. Both these were new historical features and therefore needed far more emphasis than we gave them.

So when did the idea of India take form? History reveals vast differences in the shape and size of the territory that referred to parts of the subcontinent, at different times, and the variance in names has its own interest. We do not know what the Harappans called the land where they were settled. Mesopotamian sources refer to the distant land to the east as Meluhha. Could this have been the name of the Indus civilization?

Vedic texts of the first millennium BCE mention *aryavarta* – literally the land of the *arya*s, where *arya* refers to those socially respected and whose language was Indo-Aryan. Language was a primary factor of identity. Iranian Aryans, whose culture ran parallel to the Indian Aryans', refer in the *Avesta* to the Airiianam Vaeja, as the land of the *airiia*s/*arya*s.

It is much more extensive than *aryavarta* as it stretches from Central Asia to the Hapta-Hendu (Iranian for Sapta-Sindhu). This appears to have been the earlier land of the *arya*s before they settled in northern India.

In Indian texts the boundaries of *aryavarta* expanded with settlements moving further afield. Early texts locate it in the Doab area, but the Buddhist and Jaina texts take it eastwards as well. Finally Manu at the turn of the Common Era included virtually all of northern India from sea to sea and from the Himalaya to the Vindhya. The peninsula seems to have been excluded.

Other names used in Sanskrit texts were Bharatavarsha and Jambudvipa. The first was derived from the name of a clan and a raja although it was also said to symbolize the four directions and the centre. Jambudvipa is a poetic reference to the island/space of the rose apple tree or of the jambu tree. Its geography tends to be vague with an early reference in an Ashokan edict and many later references in the Puranas. It is also featured as a segment in the representation of the cosmos.

The Greeks were familiar with the north-west, which they referred to as Indos, their rendering of the Iranian Hendu, and by extension the name Indica came into use.

In the early second millennium CE there is mention of Al-Hind, as being the land on the other side of the Sindhu river when viewed from West Asia. The people living here are referred to as Hendu/Hindu, originally a geographic label derived from the place name al-Hind, but used a few centuries later for their religion. Al-Hind was a precursor of Hindustan. The British familiar with the Greek name called it India.

The names refer either to geography and mainly the Indus, or to people of a specific descent, or else are fanciful. The territory is not mentioned with precision. Names focusing on the Indus are largely used by those outside the subcontinent, familiar with its north-west.

The British used the old name for the Indus region although they were first established in eastern India. However, with each colonial advance the boundaries of British India changed until by the end of the nineteenth century maps of the subcontinent were coloured pink. The old name continued perhaps to provide legitimacy from the past since the British saw themselves as inheritors of the empires of Alexander and the Romans.

It was an age when European powers were battling for colonies. This required a careful demarcation of territory with boundaries marked on maps. Cartography became a tool in registering colonial control, coinciding with the demarcation of territory being a required definition of a nation state. The India of 1946 was what the British had conquered and consolidated into a territory. Territories thus joined had either never known any proximity or else had been closely intertwined. To create a single culture from this divergence of communities with diverse identities was problematic for colonial authority. But if it could be a narrative of two large monolithic conflicting religious communities it would be more manageable and conducive to colonial control. The two nations/cultures were worked out and provided the basis of understanding Indian society and culture.

The coming of a nation state with its ideology of nationalism is a moment of immense historical change. The configuration of society and politics alters with this new concept emerging from the changes. The era of kingdoms and their subjects was fading out replaced by nation states and their citizens. The rights and obligations of each to the other was what was surfacing and is still doing so. The nationalism of ex-colonies was expressed as anti-colonial nationalism. This could have been the historical moment when the idea of a free India was not just a nationalist slogan but a reality for Indians. In creating a nation the diverse and visible cultures required integration.

Anti-colonial secular nationalism was confronted by the two religious nationalisms that surfaced in the early twentieth century. Whether they can be called nationalisms at all is debatable because they alter the meaning of the term. Their nationalism was for those of a specific religious community who would be given primacy in citizenship, and it was therefore not inclusive of all the people, and this latter was what was meant by nationalism. Religious nationalisms fused territory with religion and argued for separate states each based on the religion of the majority in the areas that constituted these states. The All India Muslim League was successful with the creation of Pakistan. The Hindu

Mahasabha and its various mutations ending up with the RSS has as its end purpose the conversion of India into a Hindu Rashtra.

The ideology of Hindutva exploits this combination to an unviable extreme. The Hindu is defined by his ancestry being from the territory of India, which territory was also the place of origin of Hinduism – *pitribhumi* and *punyabhuni*. By equating religion and biological descent it excludes those who follow a religion that originated outside this territory and argues that the ancestry of the followers of other religions is also foreign. This theory, rooted in the colonial construct of India, was less concerned with Hinduism but was essential to the political exploitation of religion as religious nationalism and to establishing majoritarianism.

If territory was one component of the nation, the other was a shared history that contributed to creating a common culture. Legitimation from history being essential to nationalism, historians have to be aware of the manipulation of history for purely political ends. In writing the history and culture of the nation colonial interpretations provided the legitimation for religious nationalism, by underlining an unshared history. The colonial interpretation posited two irreconcilable cultures of what were called the Hindu and Muslim nations constantly in conflict. This interpretation was internalized by a section of the Indian middle class in the context of ideologies of nationalism that were taking shape. For Hindu religious nationalists the idea of India was and is the Hindu Rashtra.

Culture evolves and changes in step with historical change. The colonial interpretation of pre-modern Indian history was the forerunner of the construction of what has come to be envisaged as our culture. I would like to mention two examples of how this reading of history continues to have an impact on our self-perception as a nation and our idea of India. The first is a reading that most secular historians accept but it is strongly opposed by Hindutva-vadins, and is concerned with the origin of the Aryans. The second reading was that religion was the major causative factor of historical events during what was defined as Muslim rule. This created two conflicting nations and resulted in the victimization of Hindus.

Colonial scholarship argued that a people known as the Aryans conquered northern India where they settled and created the Vedic culture, a pure unalloyed 'high' culture which became the foundation of the Hindu religion. This argument came to be questioned on two grounds. One was the discovery of the Indus civilization that not only pre-dated the Vedic culture but was an entirely different urban culture having little in common with the agro-pastoralist Aryan culture. The latter therefore was not the foundation of Indian culture and the Hindu religion.

Secondly, the linguistic analysis of Vedic Sanskrit indicates the presence of elements from non-Aryan languages, suggesting some interaction and mixture in the creating of the Aryan culture. This is supported by the Vedic texts differentiating between *arya* and *dasa* cultures. For the historian this was an exciting intellectual challenge in understanding the sources of Vedic culture, but not so for the claims of Hindutva. More recently genetic studies using DNA evidence posit a possible Central Asian strain in the population at around the approximate date that other sources suggest for the presence of Aryan speakers.

Most scholars of the subject agree on the basis of all the evidence we have now that a slow migration of Aryan speakers into north India was likely. The theory of an invasion was discarded many decades ago. Invasion and migration are distinctly different procedures and should not be equated.

Such a theory of cultural evolution upsets the Hindutva format according to which everything Hindu has to be indigenous. There is a desperate search to prove that the Aryan speakers and their religion were entirely indigenous, namely, from within the territory of British India; and if the roots of Hindu civilization go back to the Indus civilization then the Harappans have also to be taken as Aryans, paucity of evidence notwithstanding. Similarly, Hindutva has little problem in shifting chronologies back a few thousand years to accommodate its view. History is malleable. What used to be called the Aryan question in Indian history, and which has now taken on challenging dimensions with new evidence that enriches Indian history, has become for Hindutva the kind of research that is better shredded and replaced by the fantasy of their ideologues.

The second central subject is the two-nation theory that

has had a long innings. Here again we have to separate invasions from migrations. There were invasions but there were substantial migrations that created new communities, new ways of worship and many forms of cultural articulation. Commercial centres and small principalities in coastal areas attracted migrants, among them Arab traders. Their intermarriage with local women and finding a niche as traders and administrators resulted in the emergence of new communities of considerable economic significance, such as the Khojas, Mapillas and others. We only speak of the Arab conquest of Sind, not of these interfaces that created many new vibrant cultures in India.

Every religion changes with historical change. Such changes tend to be either explorations of what is acceptable or a rejection of what is unacceptable, or a modification of either. Hinduism was no exception. But it was not a monolithic religion unified by creed and catechism. Its acceptable openness, unique in some ways, allowed for a multiplicity of sects of varying beliefs to coexist. This may have resulted in part from the intertwining of caste and religion. Thus the Hindu was recognized by his belief and rituals but also by his observance of social distancing. The problem with the latter is that it can be set aside when required – as it frequently was in various occupations and in many devotional and reform movements – but it can also be emphasized by those that choose to do so. The victimization throughout the centuries of those outside caste – the *avarna* – by the upper castes, irrespective of their religion, has largely been ignored in constructing the past of Indian society, and even more so in what is defined as our cultural heritage.

The invasion of the Turushkas/Turks introduced a new political element into northern India. It also hastened the arrival of the Sufis, teaching a different kind of Islam. The dialogue between the Sufis and some of the Bhakti sants and Yogi sects gave a new dimension to evocative forms of devotional religion. Each of these groups fostered new cultures entirely unconnected from the kinds of cultures envisaged in the two-nation theory. Should we not recognize in greater detail the identity of what was accepted and what rejected and their nuances, and why, instead of using blanket terms such as Indo-Muslim to describe the whole lot and ascribing everything to Hindu–Muslim differences? Should we not concede that neither the Hindu nor the Muslim came from a single source and that ultimately this was the strength of the ensuing culture. This is of significance to the idea of India.

One comes back repeatedly to the question of what is the idea of India. To define it means that we start by ejecting the questionable colonial imprint such as in distorted history, or laws that support authoritarianism such as sedition, that we discard that which has helped legalize violence from various agencies, or that which tries to impose explanations of Indian culture that are rooted in colonial thinking but are defended as supposedly being indigenous. Does Indian pluralism lie in the juxtaposition of a range of cultures that washed up in the subcontinent? This was not accidental as history can explain them. We surely have to go a step further and analyse this plurality and ask ourselves what it requires to be sustained. It is not just a juxtaposition. It is not just a slogan. It is not arrived at by conformity to a single identity. Some of it has even come out of conflict such as that between some Shaiva and Buddhist sects, between Vaishnava Bairagis and Shaiva Dashnamis, between Sunnis and Shi'as, or of some others that had problems with Hindu or Islamic authority. But much more came out of many levels of interfaces between this and the other, between you and me, between the high and the low. This was creative for all concerned.

The idea of India has to address the citizens of the nation state, all those that create visible cultures and also those whose cultures we have treated as substratum but which have to be made visible in the shaping of this state. Citizens have rights and, as has been said, we have the right to have rights: rights that will bring some quality into the lives of all, and the guarantee of this has to come from the state and through the Constitution. We have the right to knowledge, and to alternative knowledge that may better answer our questions than the knowledge that is imposed on us. This implies an openness of dialogue and the legitimacy of dissent both of which played such a vital role in the past in moulding Indian thought and patterns of life. It implies the need to discuss the idea of India openly and with freedom.

18

Freedom in a Different Key: The Bhuinyas of Bihar

Gyan Prakash

Systemic inequality is the subject of a global conversation today. Across the world, marginalized groups are asking for real, not just formal, equality. Those subjected historically to class, caste, racial and gender discrimination are asserting that freedom must mean more than constitutional guarantees of equal citizenship; it requires dismantling the systemic basis of inequality.

It is in this context that I returned to B.R. Ambedkar and Frantz Fanon to think afresh about the historical ideas of freedom. Looking back on my research on the Dalit community of Bhuinya bonded labourers in Bihar, the question that I ask is: What was the meaning of freedom for them? Did it only suggest a change in legal status from bonded to free, or something else?

In January 1982 I was six months into my PhD dissertation research on bonded labourers in colonial India, focusing on Bihar.[1] Called kamias, the bonded labourers almost always belonged to Dalit communities and were landless. They were paid daily wages for their labour, but land and caste relations bound them to serve their upper-caste masters. It was essentially a relationship of dependence that went on for generations. To understand the history of this system, I began by consulting documents at the Bihar State Archives and the Gaya District record room, and read the available published reports and monographs on the subject. Bondage was a live public issue. Indira Gandhi's Emergency regime had passed the Bonded Labour System (Abolition) Act in 1976. Yet, there were reports of the existence of bondage all over the country. Social scientists were documenting the brutal exploitation of labourers by powerful landlords and rich peasants. In this atmosphere, when I told people about my research, they would observe sympathetically: 'Of course, Bihar is so backward.'

The assumption was that modernity ought to have freed labourers from bondage and restored them to the state of freedom to which all human beings are born. Bihar was backward, still stuck in its feudal past, and had failed to keep pace with the march of modern progress. The task was to jump-start Bihar on the road to modernity, releasing the bonded labourers into a state of what Marx called the freedom of wage slavery.

This was the discourse in the archival documents and the social science treatises on the contemporary situation. It left me dissatisfied. How could one accept as universal a concept of freedom that traced its roots to the Enlightenment and was disseminated by the British colonizers to legitimize their power? Did the bonded labourers understand their lives in terms of this master narrative of modernity and freedom? What were their own ideas of freedom?

The archives provided little help, for they all reflected official thinking. This is when I set out for Bodh Gaya. I knew from the records it was historically home to a substantial population of kamias. At a tea shop near the Mahabodhi Buddhist temple, I got lucky. Actually, the luck had a name: Anhach Manjhi.

After I explained my research interest on the history of kamias to the local CPI legislator and his entourage, he introduced me to Anhach. A young man in his early twenties, Anhach was a Bhuinya. He was educated and clearly wanted to make something of his education to climb out of his family's history as kamias. He was also very familiar with the Bhuinya community, almost all of whom in the region were kamias. Accompanied by him, I began visiting villages surrounding Bodh Gaya, speaking with the Bhuinya labourers, and collecting their stories and testimonies.

One day, Anhach led me to Shivan Manjhi in Bakraur, a

village you reached from Bodh Gaya by wading across a shallow river. Shivan was in his early forties, and lived with his wife, son and mother in Bakraur's Bhuinya basti, which was separated from the upper- and middle-caste quarters. He worked as a kamia on the fields of an upper-caste owner while living in a small thatched hut with a pigpen beside it. Shivan was also a bard of the Bhuinyas. Although many in his community knew parts of the Bhuinya oral traditions, Shivan was widely recognized as the master storyteller. Over the months that I spent in the village, I heard Shivan perform these oral epics to the throbbing beat of his mandar drum at Bhuinya weddings. As Shivan sang the epics with abandon, his audience would listen with rapt attention to his rendition of the stories of the Bhuinya heroes, their birs. Chief among them was Tulsi Bir, who was magically brought to life by the epic's performance to consecrate weddings in the Bhuinya community.

The genre of bir stories and their core plots and images are drawn from and are part of a larger repertoire of low-caste and Dalit epic poetry in Bihar and Uttar Pradesh. Structured as origin stories, these traditions narrate the history of subaltern castes. The recorded existence of such traditions goes back to at least the early nineteenth century, but they have been dismissed as myths and legends of no historical value.

In Bakraur, the Brahman village teacher insisted I was wasting my time with the Bhuinyas. 'What do they know? They are illiterate and know nothing of value to you,' he told me. The contempt for subaltern knowledge was common

Shivan Manjhi and his family. Anhach Manjhi is in the background. Bakraur, 1982.

among upper castes. But as I heard Shivan narrate these epics, it became clear that these origin stories contained a critical imagination of the past and a vision of freedom different from the universalist narrative of bondage-to-freedom.

In all of his performances, the protagonist at the centre of Shivan's narrative was Tulsi Bir, the legendary Bhuinya ancestor endowed with immense physical prowess and spiritual power. At its core, the plot involved an upper-caste landlord coming to Tulsi Bir's door, with folded hands, beseeching his help to seal the breach in an embankment.[2] Tulsi Bir agrees to help but first he sets out to seek the blessings of several warriors and gods and goddesses.

He then proceeds to the site of the breach to accomplish the daunting task. Hundreds of thousands of labourers and elephants are assembled, vainly attempting to fill the breach. Tulsi Bir asks them to stop their efforts and gets prepared to perform the task all by himself. To spur him on, the gods award him land grants of hundreds of villages. Then, with one swift movement, Tulsi Bir heaves a huge block of earth and hurls it into place at the breach. Everyone is stunned by Tulsi Bir's amazing feat.

But when he goes to survey the villages granted to him by the gods, the landlords laugh derisively. How could a poor labourer without ploughs and animals cultivate such vast tracts of land? But Tulsi Bir's wife comes to the rescue. With her inner power, she magically produces thousands of ploughs and bulls. Seeing Tulsi Bir, who is the god Brahma's kamia, now endowed with hundreds of villages and the means to cultivate the land, the gods become jealous. Basudev (Krishna's father) is particularly incensed to see a poor kamia suddenly gifted with such material and spiritual fortune.

Resolved to break Tulsi Bir's power, Basudev puts him to the test. He asks Tulsi Bir to bring him the flesh of an animal that is neither dead nor alive. Tulsi Bir is in despair until a cowherd comes to his aid. He points to the placenta of a cow that had recently given birth, which is the flesh of an animal that is neither dead nor alive. When Tulsi Bir presents the placenta to Basudev, the god becomes even more determined to destroy his power.

To carry out their plot, the gods invite Tulsi Bir to a feast ostensibly to celebrate his feat. After plying him with drink, they serve him a meal with the placenta mixed in. As soon as he takes the first bite, Tulsi Bir vomits. But it is too late. He is defiled, and his community is forever stigmatized as untouchable.

Such stories of origin abound among subaltern castes. What is important is not the mythic character of these traditions, but their remembrance as authentic representations of their past. The oral epic interprets the Bhuinyas' Dalit status not as divinely ordained but historically produced. The culprit is the Hindu divine order, jealous of Tulsi Bir's power.

The Bhuinya hero derives his power not from landed wealth or from Hindu gods. In a world of kings and warriors, he too is a warrior. But his warrior status indicates physical prowess and spiritual strength, not worldly wealth and power. In fact, he is a kamia without ploughs or animals. He is already a subaltern, but not ritually inferior. His miraculous feat in filling a breach in the embankment and the award of land grants, which he can cultivate with ploughs and animals that his wife magically produced, however, threaten the social and divine order. This is what provokes the gods to plot his downfall, which explains the subsequent incorporation of the

Bhuinyas as untouchable outcastes in the caste order. The basis of the Bhuinyas' subaltern position as Dalit bonded labourers, then, is the trickery of the Hindu divine order.

The Tulsi Bir epic mounts a fundamental critique of power relations, one more far-reaching than those centred on the analysis of unequal land relations or on the juridical status of kamias as indebted labourers. The epic identifies the devaluation of Tulsi Bir's labouring body as the foundational source of both his and his community's subordination. For once polluted by consuming a meal containing a cow's placenta, the Bhuinya ancestor becomes what Gopal Guru calls 'walking carrion, a concentrated expression of untouchability'.[3]

The Bhuinya body is forever marked as impure, fit only to serve as dependent labourers of their upper-caste landed lords. The Bhuinya impurity infects their basti, which is consequently separated from the village. At its core, then, the Tulsi Bir epic spotlights the stigmatization of Bhuinya bodies as an essential element of their history as kamias.[4]

Whatever we may think about the historical 'truth' in these traditions, what is important is that such a remembered past was collectively shared. This remembrance repudiates the present in which the subordination of the Bhuinyas as kamias and as Dalits goes hand in hand. It is at odds with the official discourse of freedom that viewed the kamia system as a residue of the backward past and projected their liberation by declaring long labour contracts as illegal.

In fact, there was nothing new about the 1976 legislation. The colonial government had already enacted the Bihar and Orissa Kamiauti Agreement Act in 1920, declaring all labour engagements longer than a year illegal. The colonial and the postcolonial governments envisioned freedom as a juridical matter. They believed that freeing labourers from the debt agreements they had made with landlords would liberate them. In fact, it was not the small loans the kamias took from their landlords on the occasion of the marriage of their sons that bound them to their masters. The 'loan' only symbolically expressed the power of land and caste. It was this condition of class and caste domination that the Bhuinya oral epics registered and contested.

Having identified the stigmatization of their bodies as the root cause of their subordination, the Bhuinyas paid little attention to the 1976 act. I didn't encounter any discussion of the legislation in Bakraur or in other villages. Of little attraction was the law's promise to liberate them from their debts and restore them as 'free' individuals capable of negotiating their work as wage labourers.

In any case, their daily lives involved demanding better wages and securing land to cultivate for themselves. What they valued was the dignity of their community, which they asserted by remembering their history. Their oral traditions articulated an idea of freedom that the juridical discourse could not – an assertion that their bodies were not untouchable but had been rendered so by the Hindu caste order. The new legislation did not overturn their Dalit status, and thus to them had no significance.

Ambedkar famously wrote that democracy exists only on the thin topsoil of India.[5] He meant that hierarchy and inequality were so deeply embedded in Indian society and culture that only their annihilation would provide a fertile soil for democracy. Ambedkar's identification of the systemic nature of caste inequality calls to mind Frantz Fanon's analysis of race in his *Black Skin, White Masks*. The book's title encapsulates Fanon's argument that racial inequality left the Blacks with no alternative but to grow 'white skin' in order to advance under colonial racism.[6]

This was akin to the 'Sanskritization' option under the caste system. According to Fanon, only Black political solidarity and revolutionary politics, not submission to white norms, could dismantle racial inequality. Ambedkar called for the annihilation of the caste system, and looked for an ethical order of equality, signified in his turn to Buddhism towards the end of his life.

The Bhuinya epic does not articulate a fully developed alternative in modern ideological terms to caste inequality. But one cannot but hear a yearning for an equality of bodies. And just as Fanon's critique was aimed not at racism as such but enslavement under colonial racism, the Bhuinyas critique the devaluation of the kamia body produced by land and caste domination.

For when Shivan performed the Tulsi Bir epics, he

narrated Bhuinya history in the contemporary context of the community's subordination as bonded labourers. In the present, these narrations were not just such stories, not mere folklore, not only origin myths. Instead, they recognized that land and caste combined to subordinate them, that their exploitation as kamias and as untouchables was intertwined.

While critiquing their condition through a telling of their history, the Bhuinyas also asserted dignity and respect for their bodies. This was not a demand for freedom in terms of legal status, but for freedom that came from equality. Is it any wonder that recent Dalit movements have steadfastly struggled for equality by demanding respect and dignity for their persons? And the upper-caste backlash has come in the form of humiliating Dalits and violating their bodies?

So, if freedom requires an ethical order of equality, if democracy is not to exist only on the topsoil but also deep in the ground, the Dalit body must win equality. Ambedkar identified a culture of equality as a necessary foundation for freedom. The subaltern culture of the Bhuinyas is one of the places where you might find it.

Shivan Manjhi passed away in the early 2000s, holding dearly to the Bhuinya oral epics. By then, the power of upper-caste landlords had waned. Now, equally important are backward caste (OBC) rich farmers who employ Bhuinyas as labourers. Shivan's surviving grandchildren are no longer kamias but work as agricultural wage labourers. But their Dalit bodies are still marked as untouchable by the caste order. They await the realization of the desire for equality and freedom embedded in their grandfather's oral epics.

Notes

1. My revised dissertation was eventually published as *Bonded Histories: Genealogies of Labor Servitude in Colonial India* (Cambridge: Cambridge University Press, 1990).
2. For a fuller description and analysis of these epics, see my *Bonded Histories*, 34–58.
3. Gopal Guru, 'Archaeology of Untouchability', in *The Cracked Mirror: An Indian Debate on Experience and Theory*, Gopal Guru and Sundar Sarukkai eds. (Delhi: Oxford University Press, 2012), 212.
4. The essays by Gopal Guru and Sundar Sarukkai in their book *The Cracked Mirror: An Indian Debate on Experience and Theory* contain fascinating and insightful philosophical and historical discussions on untouchability.
5. *CAD*, vol. 7, 4 November 1948.
6. Frantz Fanon, *Black Skin, White Masks*, Tr. Richard Philcox (New York: Grove Press, 2008).

19

Hasdeo Arand: Mine Is the Voice

Karthika Naïr

        Rajaji   Keladevi   Thottappally   Deomali
     Darlaghat   Narayan Sarovar   Jamwa   Ramgarh
     Dehing Patkai   Anamalai   Gir   Bhagwan Mahavir

Rajaji   *Keladevi*
     Mine is the voice, brothers, that few seem to hear.
    Ours the names, my sisters, people seldom hold dear.
Rajaji   *Keladevi*
     Hear my breath. It shaped ravines, rivers, even gods.
   My skin births tribes and trees, mammals, birds, arthropods.
Thottappally   *Deomali*
       Larger than Dilli, Nayi, Purani, and more.
       To be quartered for fuel, metal or some ore.
Darlaghat   *Narayan Sarovar*
   Now, they state, my children must all go. Our death-knoll.
      My belly ripped, for a few million veins of coal.
Jamwa   *Ramgarh*
    For open-pit mines with thirty-odd years of life,
  three hundred and seventy thousand trees face the knife.
Dehing Patkai   *Anamalai*
      Sal, tendu, mahua, aam, bamboo. And add River
    Hasdeo, sweet god Baba Dev, rice crops, then tiger,
Gir   *Bhagwan Mahavir*
    leopard, jackal, elephant, legions more . . . Creatures
   great and small, feral, mild, all torn from their futures.
Gir   *Bhagwan Mahavir*
   My lungs bleed black, besmirch the green of tomorrow.
  Humans, beware: Fear your deeds, their greedy white glow.
Dehing Patkai   *Anamalai*
    No god will save those that destroy beyond their fill.
     We'll remember, I promise. The earth always will.
Jamwa   *Ramgarh*

     Dehing Patkai   Anamalai   Gir   Bhagwan Mahavir
     Darlaghat   Narayan Sarovar   Jamwa   Ramgarh
        Rajaji   Keladevi   Thottappally   Deomali

20

Raga Swaraj

T.M. Krishna

We love freedom: ours. We fear freedom: that of others. We do not know whether to unconditionally embrace it or keep it on a leash like a pet dog. There are moments when expressing ourselves seems paramount to our very existence and living life as we deem it uncompromisable. Yet there are times when we fear freedom for the 'other'. And we wonder: will her or his freedom upset my apple cart? Then we proclaim in Indian English, 'Too much freedom is not good.' So while we lament about the restrictions that are overtly and surreptitiously imposed by the state and the lack of freedom in today's India, we need to step back and reflect on our own negotiations with freedom because at the foundation of the excesses that we are witnessing is a collective failure.

Most of what we treasure as intrinsic to our being is understood emotionally. Ideas such as freedom are difficult to articulate in their entirety. Every time we speak of them, we only express one aspect, condition or interpretation. Yet everyone, including those who have been suppressed and pushed to the edge of life, knows the ecstasy in it. It has been felt at some point of time, in a song or just a shared laugh. But it is this profundity that makes us want to own, manipulate and tailor its nature to serve only a few. To this end, we construct a society that allows this to happen with ease, unquestioningly. The socially powerful define freedom in ways that allow them to twist it in any direction they wish. The rest just have to accept their position in this constructed pyramid and obey. At times, in order to keep the rest in line, largesse and charity are offered. Don't be fooled, these are acts of control. The receiver knows this and plays by the rules so that the powerful feel ennobled. Freedom is, indeed, an ugly game. Therefore, I am uncomfortable speaking of it in abstract, poetic terms. And I wonder whether that utopia is just a fabricated fraud. Maybe even the experience of freedom that we all share is a simulation.

But what do I truly know about freedom? I am a privileged man, born into a brahmin family, who has lived a life of economic comfort. I have got everything I sought. Hardships have been few and far between. They were irritants, not debilitating injuries. We rarely discussed freedom at home or school because it was always there. The only time freedom became scarce was when my mother put a curfew on my playtime.

Am I even fit to write about freedom?

We use the term caste blind when referring to people of caste privilege with no realization of caste. Caste was never an impediment to normal life. But maybe we should add that being blind to the complex traumas associated with caste, gender, race or colour actually means you are free. This sounds wrong, doesn't it? Let us think about it. Every layer of privilege makes our lives that much more removed from dusty reality. We build our own clusters with restricted membership. And, in this microcosmic world, we live with boundless freedom. It is, of course, another matter that even those clusters were constructed and are served by those who have to fight for their seasonal showers of freedom. We could inverse this and say freedom is compounded by the erasure of every layer of stigma. As long as an individual is tainted by markers of discrimination, freedom is unattainable. And that taint, I must remember, is my work. Therefore, when I pontificate about freedom being this feeling, emotion, I am being disingenuous because I have never really felt free in all its glory, I have only always controlled it. When a Safai Karmachari is relieved of the torture of needing to sink himself into that deep dark hole of human excreta, he feels freedom – not me.

The soul of our Constitution lies in its understanding that freedom cannot be independently realized. That freedom only emerges in an environment that nurtures justice, equality, liberty and fraternity. And by enshrining these values in the Preamble, the founders challenged every social mechanism that, in various degrees, tramples upon freedom. The Preamble never uses the word, but informs us that freedom will be archived in a society that enables the values that it extols. Freedom is a fundamental right that comes to fruition if we ensure a fair, just and equal society. But human beings are conniving creatures and we have applied restrictions on citizens' freedoms through amendments and by introducing acts such as the National Security Act (1980), Unlawful Activities Prevention Act (1967), Jammu and Kashmir Public Safety Act (1978) and Armed Forces Special Powers Act (1958). We have successfully reverse-engineered an assault on the guiding principles of our Constitution. The manner in which these laws are enforced breaks every promise made to ourselves: 'We, the people of India'. The members of the Constituent Assembly too faltered by letting laws such as the colonial era Sedition Law (1860) remain. Quite astonishing, considering that M.K. Gandhi was jailed under that very provision.

But the Constitution is only words in a book. It comes to life when people act upon its advice, instructions and directions. The problem seems to come from the disconnect between the hopes and yearnings for our people as etched in our Constitution and the reality that surrounded us then and envelops us today. The Constitution is a letter of hope, an aspirational address to the people of India. But did the people of India believe in what it said? Were they even made aware of it?

We are a feudal country, entrenched in patriarchy and casteism, but the Constitution hopes that by following its spirit we will move beyond these demonic practices. But this does not happen unless we hold people's hand and take them along this path. Regrettably, we created an education system that doesn't care about ethics, equality, liberty, freedom, empathy, secularism or love. We have not taught our children about the grandeur of our Constitution. The independence struggle has been reduced to a battle between good (Indians) and evil (British), much like our epics, the Ramayana and the Mahabharata, have been. Our children do not learn about the sociological battles between Ambedkar and Gandhi, that this republic was given shape amid debate and discussions and by paying attention to diverse voices. There has been no nuance, intellectual rigour or emotional depth in the way we have understood our own coming of existence. Schools and colleges have functioned as employment agencies, not places of enlightenment. How students go on with their lives, share space, respect, learn, listen and grow have been immaterial to us. And we have done this unfailingly for over seven decades. We have created generations of citizens who believe the Constitution is a book of laws. Not just the common person, but also people who have held important judicial posts, occupied high constitutional chairs and have been repeatedly elected as our representatives. It is in such a country that we are seeking an understanding of freedom.

Our police force is a fine example of this insensitivity. They have been groomed to only worry about law and order. People are viewed as impediments to keeping law and order under control. A senior police officer once told me, and I paraphrase, 'Why do you want to have music, dance and theatre in public spaces?' He was least concerned about our rights as citizens, or the fact that he was there to make sure that every citizen could celebrate life, unafraid.

'But we need laws; you cannot have everyone doing whatever they want.' Don't we hear this said often? Using this as a pretence, we spank our children and don't really mind if the teacher uses the wooden ruler. Right from our childhood, violence is programmed into our lives, and if it is delivered from a position of authority, the benefit of doubt is always given to the person wielding the stick.

As a musician, I hear a similar refrain on form and freedom. They are seen as being in conflict, constantly tugging and pulling at each other. The other view is that their togetherness is proof of the need to place limits on freedom. Form is viewed as that 'rulebook' which keeps freedom in check.

But is that really form?

Form does not fall down from the sky. It is a product of cultures, time, people, contexts and nature. It comes into being from the exercise of freedom. The freedom to observe, reflect and act allows for ideas to be nuanced, turned, questioned, adapted and reimagined, bringing together diverse voices. Form is, therefore, not a homogenizing process but a way of giving aesthetic unity to multiplicity. This aesthetic coming together does not smother interpretations, rather it allows for space and interaction. The marvel is in how variations remain together intertwined. A single raga has so many interpretations, one note added here, another removed, one skipped and another doubled. The same phrase handled by different musicians has so many colours. This is form, a liberating possibility. The purpose of form is to ensure that every voice is heard. But when this is maligned and form is strangulated, only the loudest is heard.

It is with the freedom that thrives within form that the musician elopes. She then roams with the unsung melodies, the unstruck rhythms and unheard movements of that freedom-in-form. These then remind her that whatever she is experiencing, creating, offering can only live in harmony. For puritans who are unfree, this is unthinkable and blasphemous. They scream from the rooftops about the music being destroyed, corrupted, impurities being allowed in and demand vigilance. Form and freedom remain silent, smiling and watching all this go by. And as they do so, music breathes. This is my dream for India.

21

Fear and Belonging: Fraternity in the Time of Covid-19

Menaka Guruswamy

The Lockdown

23 March 2020. Delhi is unusually quiet. It's a Monday and in the middle of the day the streets are desolate. Birds with brightly coloured beaks I had never seen before perched on the tall trees in the leafy park across from my home. Against an unusually blue sky, I could also see a pair of kites building a nest. They were old residents of the tall trees in the park. The new bird species that I did not recognize kept a respectful distance from the kites. Even the birds knew the rules of the pecking order: keep a watchful distance from the predator.

The temple on the other side of my silent street wore a deserted look, a far cry from the usual cacophony of bells ringing and expensive cars blocking the street, as uniformed drivers let out well-heeled devotees coming to offer prayers. The temple is opposite the gate I use to enter my colony. Delhi is a city of gated colonies, with guards that look into your cars to decide whether to let you in, and whether you belong in the neighbourhood.

Yesterday, Delhi like much of India was 'locked down'.

Would Covid-19, like my avian neighbours, respect the pecking order of Indian society?

Pandemics have a way of laying bare the equities and inequities, truths and falsehoods of nation states, especially in societies like India with the country's history of spectacular inequality.

My Neighbourhood and Citizenship

I can look out on to my South Delhi street. The parallel street is a large, crowded, unruly marketplace, which houses both small kirana stores for essentials and large supermarkets with foreign cheeses and American peanut butter, alongside little eateries that make only delicious kebabs. When I was a child, my father would walk me across to the market to eat a few kebabs wrapped in hot rumali rotis.

This market separates the temple side of the neighbourhood from the 'other side' – the Jamia Millia Islamia university and Zakir Nagar, predominantly Muslim areas. The infamous 'Batla House encounter' took place in Jamia Nagar, the

Fear and Belonging

neighbourhood adjoining the university. On 19 September 2008 police stormed a house in the area and killed two persons they alleged were part of a terror group – the Indian Mujahideen. One police officer was also killed. However, civil society activists allege that the two civilians killed were students and not terrorists. What was common to my side of the tracks, which is Hindu majority and has more expensive real estate, and the 'other side' was that we all fall within the legislative constituency of Okhla. I knew we were the Hindu majority part of the constituency thanks to the neighbourhood WhatsApp groups, which had very few non-Hindu names on the temple side of the neighbourhood.

On most days, when I came home after a day in court, as the sun set amid the grey, smog-filled skies, I would hear the lovely ringing of temple bells and the familiar rise and fall of the azan being read out from the mosques beyond.

This was my neighbourhood. I had grown up here. When I moved away from Delhi for a few years, what I missed most were these sounds that defined my neighbourhood and created my sense of home. Smell, sound, taste: one of the key symptoms of Covid-19 is the loss of smell and taste.

∼

Almost three months before Covid-19 struck Delhi, my street had fallen silent with fear of a different kind. The early evening of 15 December 2019 was unremarkable. It was a

Sunday and I was preparing for a busy Monday in court. I glanced up from my terrace. A column of smoke rose from the street. I saw buses burning, students running away as columns of policemen thrashed them with steel-tipped lathis. The next day, a picture of the bus burning in front of the temple was circulated on WhatsApp with messages of how 'they' were rioting. No one in India needs to be told who 'they' are – blaming Muslims has become an inescapable part of our political and social life.

Jamia Millia was shut down. Varying accounts emerged of the police storming the university, and neighbouring Zakir Nagar stayed under curfew for weeks. Then too the street was quiet. But it was a different kind of quiet. There was a fraught quality to it, caused by whispers of division, and fear of the 'other'.

That December and January, the students had marched in protest against the then Citizenship Amendment Bill, 2019 (CAB), which has now been passed into law by India's Parliament. This law connects citizenship to the religion of asylum seekers from Afghanistan, Pakistan and Bangladesh. Essentially, Muslims cannot apply for citizenship. Many feared that this was the precedent to excluding Muslims in general from Indian citizenship, since the CAB was to be supplemented with a planned National Register of Citizens and a National Population Register. Both exercises would solicit, apart from other information, the religion of each inhabitant.

Fear and Belonging

The protests and counter-protests by supporters of the CAB halted in February when widespread riots swept north-east Delhi, leading to the death of over fifty people, most of them Muslim, and displacement of thousands from their homes – again, most of them Muslim. But riots, fear, empty streets, assessing one's status – do you belong, are you an outsider? – has a painfully long history in India. Delhi is familiar with widespread fear created by shifts in the history of the city and the nation. When undivided India was partitioned, refugees flowed into Delhi from newly created Pakistan between 1946 and 1949. They came in search of a new nation to belong to. Then too fear gripped the city and the country. In both India and Pakistan, neighbours turned on each other, torn apart by a different kind of virus – hate and distrust spread like a pandemic, a fear of the other infected ordinary people like a plague.

Partition displaced twenty million people, and historians estimate that it took two million lives in the subcontinent. Those figures match the number of people epidemiologists suggest India will be expected to provide critical care for in the wake of Covid-19. Partition and Covid-19 are the two singular non-war crises of independent India, setting off mass displacement, economic and social upheaval. And both are accompanied by widespread chaos – and fear.

Menaka Guruswamy

Fear: Our Partition's Constitution

Once fear manifests itself, it overwhelms those who suffer in its grip. As the American political theorist Corey Robin writes, fear 'prevents adults from exercising their reason and enjoying their freedom'. Fear comes in different shades. For instance, there is political fear, 'a shared apprehension that people have' of crime or terrorism or intimidation by the government or from other citizens or sections of citizens. The political philosopher Judith Shklar compared political fear to brute force, as a 'physiological reaction . . . involuntary and far too imperious to be controlled'.

The fears that have swept through India at different periods are distinct from each other and yet they overlap. The 'political fear', imagined or real, that minorities and majorities harbour towards each other, the fear felt by those on one side of the temple on my street and those on the other side of the market in my neighbourhood don't just stay in the realm of the political. It's corrosive. It flows into all aspects of being. This fear manifests in different ways in a pandemic – as racism surfacing against Chinese people and citizens from North-East India, or hateful acts against members of religious minorities in the garb of protecting one's neighbourhood from disease spread by the 'other'. Political fears prevent citizens from fully trusting the government and the police.

India's founders responded to Partition with a constitution that was inspired by the need to belong, and the desire to mitigate fears around divisions. The Constitution was enacted on 26 November 1949, but it was drafted through the Partition years of 1946–49.

India's antidote to a deeply divided society is beautifully expressed in the Preamble, where we promised to secure for all of India's citizens:

> Justice, social, economic and political;
> Liberty of thought, expression, belief, faith and worship;
> Equality of status and of opportunity; and
> Fraternity, assuring the dignity of the individual and the
>   unity and integrity of the country.

With a strong non-discrimination clause that prohibited any form of discrimination on grounds of race, religion, sex, caste and other comparable grounds, India's Constitution welcomed to its partitioned land all, irrespective of faith, and promised a better life to those previously excluded on grounds of sex, caste, etc.

As an eighteen-year-old first-year law student, I had read the Constitution for the first time sitting in a corner of the single large airy room that was the library of the National Law School. The library copy was a nondescript one, nothing elegant or fancy about it, and you could have mistaken it for any other statute or 'bare act' as we lawyers like to refer to them. But I knew that it wasn't like any other book I had ever read.

The words of the Preamble just flew off the page; justice, liberty, equality and fraternity – I remember thinking that this book held something that was larger and truly meaningful. Perhaps it described a way of life? For a nation or every citizen or me? India's Constitution is a long text, with hundreds of articles, multiple schedules and lists of legislative powers. I remember thinking the book was like an elaborate road map of a multidimensional dream. Yet it wasn't a dream.

The Constitution was a vision for the new nation that was created, out of the enormous loss of Partition and the joys of a new independence. It was freedom that was tinged with loss. Our founders did not pick the easier way of a homogeneous society defined by the religion of the majority of citizens. Instead, we opted for a way for all to belong. This was a more equitable and just way of dealing with political and social fears that resulted from Partition and its discontents. This was a country that promised justice for all – Muslims and Hindus, upper castes and lower castes, women and men – all on my street, and in the neighbourhoods on both sides of the marketplace.

Fear and Fraternity

Of all the promises in the Preamble, the one that might mean the most in these times of fear, induced by the pandemic or by politics, is the constitutional value of fraternity. The Supreme Court in *Raghunathrao* v. *Union of India*, 1993, tells us that 'fraternity is a sense of common brotherhood of all Indians . . . with so many disruptive forces of regionalism, communalism and linguism . . . it is necessary to emphasise . . . that the unity and integrity of India can be preserved only by a spirit of brotherhood. India has only one common citizenship and every citizen should feel that he is Indian first irrespective of other basis.'

The idea of our India has been divided by so much – by centuries of the dehumanization and 'non-belonging' of 'lower caste' Indians, by the fears arising from Partition that were passed on across generations of religious majorities and minorities, among other divisions. Dr B.R. Ambedkar, chairman of the Drafting Committee of the Constitution, was clear that fraternity was a critical constitutional value, given the tensions due to religious, linguistic and caste-based differences. He believed that fraternity was significant since it would be crucial in creating unity among Indian citizens.

It is not that common for constitution-makers to settle on the spirit of brotherhood, the promise of fraternity between all people in a nation. For instance, the Constitution of the United States is located in an understanding of individual rights being protected against intrusion by the state. That is the heart of American constitutionalism. 'Brotherhood' and 'dignity' of each individual came slowly and as an afterthought, through the contemporary amendments to the US Constitution that abolished slavery and eventually recognized the dignity of African Americans and women.

However, in India, the idea of a fraternal country through protection of the dignity of the individual shores up the unity and integrity of the country. Fraternity is the justification for equality, freedom and justice (political, social and economic). For instance, in *Indra Sawhney* v. *Union of India*, 1992, the Supreme Court used fraternity to justify reservation for backward classes. This meant that to enable a brotherhood and sisterhood that was based on dignity (not paternalism), the courts and the framers of the Constitution recognize that we need to make reparations for the injustice suffered for hundreds of years of caste-based discrimination. Brotherhood and sisterhood means that we must make amends for our past, so that our present will be an equitable one.

A Nation of Cruel Long Walks

In the aftermath of the north-east Delhi riots, relief camps were set up for thousands, mostly Muslims, whose homes had been destroyed in the communal violence. One such was Delhi's Eidgah relief camp, located in Old Mustafabad and housing over 600 riot victims. In the state's anxiety to implement a hastily announced, poorly planned lockdown, the camp was dispersed by force. The residents who had just survived a murderous riot were asked to go elsewhere in order to enforce social distancing, the aim of the lockdown. They had lost their homes; this hasty dispersal is the opposite of the fraternity that the nation's founders had hoped would be the guiding light of any future government after Independence.

This battle against the Covid-19 pandemic will also show us the nature of our government. The government can turn authoritarian and exploit the opportunity that a health pandemic affords – of a fearful citizenry willingly accepting lockdowns and curfews. In times such as these, citizens are most constitutionally vulnerable, for the measures taken ostensibly to protect their health enable an assortment of atrocities.

Perpendicular to my street is one that houses a gurdwara. On any morning, you can find a long line of young men sitting by the gurdwara. They are daily wage labourers. Most of them are from Uttar Pradesh or Bihar, India's most populated and poorest states. Some are from other, more remote parts of Delhi. For a few hundred rupees, you can hire their services for tasks including construction, moving home or even cleaning your yard. A few with more skills to ply earn a higher wage as painters or carpenters. What is common to all of them is this – on the days they work, they eat.

On 24 March 2020, Prime Minister Narendra Modi addressed the nation in a televised broadcast at 8 p.m. He announced that from midnight of the same day there would be a national lockdown that prohibited all forms of public transport and public movement of all citizens in the country, who were ordered to stay indoors. Only essential services such as hospitals and grocery stores could function. All non-essential economic activity was to come to an abrupt halt. The daily wagers had disappeared by the next morning, making their way back to the remote parts of outer Delhi, or faraway homes in villages left behind. They joined millions like them in the unorganized sector, who account for over 70 per cent of India's labour force, whose livelihood had effectively ceased, who had no state support or assured salary to fall back on.

With just four hours' notice, the labourers near my street saw their livelihood disappear, without which they had no means of surviving the prime minister's social isolation diktat in the biggest of Indian cities. As at Partition, these 'migrants' would be forced to walk home, some of them over a thousand kilometres from Delhi to villages in east Bihar. This time around, however, none would face the ire of the forced exodus of the 'other'. They would be brutalized by the police, who had orders to make them stay put in Delhi. No provisions would be made for food or water or shelter for these labourers, carrying whatever possessions they could on the long, long march home.

Even at Partition, the state had ensured that trains ran between India and Pakistan to help ensure movement of those migrating. No such facilities were planned or offered seventy-five years later for what became the largest post-Partition migration in India. Even the chaos of Partition had been announced well in advance, enabling migrating people to organize by village and town, and walk in long columns of humanity with the aim of staying safe. Many of them succeeded, making it across borders, building new lives.

In 2020 locked-down India, no such planning was permitted to the most vulnerable section of the workforce. It was as if the Indian government had either forgotten its working poor or simply had contempt for them. Even as India's poor marched, ministers posted pictures of themselves in pyjamas, socially isolating at home, relaxing and watching the *Ramayan* serial on TV.

It's not just the untold misery inflicted on the millions of migrant poor who work and fuel India that is a sign of a thoughtless state. There is also the manifestation of the old colonial state in independent India. For instance, the immediate imposition of Section 144 of the Code of Criminal Procedure all over the country means that no one can gather, either to celebrate or protest or even simply move from one place to another. It may be warranted in response to a virus that demands social isolation and distancing as a national response. Yet the suppression of criticism in the times of a pandemic has a long history.

In 1898 Bal Gangadhar Tilak became the first person in India convicted for sedition. The charge against him was that he had engendered disaffection against the British colonial government by critiquing their handling of the bubonic plague. The 1896 Epidemic Disease Act and the 2005 National Disaster Management Act allow for prosecution to critique state responses to disease. Only time will tell if our government will follow a more thoughtful policy or utilize this as an opportunity to be authoritarian. After all, a state's response to a pandemic is as much about mitigating fears and encouraging a fraternal response as it is about health policy and economic support packages.

Conclusion: The Quiet Street

What Covid-19 is doing is taking away the most effective response to fear, of physically gathering in solidarity to calm one another. What it demands is a different solidarity – that of a sense of fraternity, a recognition that my neighbour's well-being depends on me. What it also demands is a citizenry that will not countenance the use of a pandemic to enable the crushing of a free, constitutional fraternity. A citizenry that recognizes that its collective well-being is located in the dignity of each and every individual, in lockdown, in isolation, in poverty and in despair.

22

Grief and the Freedom of Forgiving

Priyanka Dubey

I was born in a conservative, patriarchal northern Indian household. And as fate would have it, I ended up spending all of my adult life reporting on social justice and human rights across the length and breadth of India. I wonder then, what should I write about when I write about freedom? Should I write about my own personal domestic battles with patriarchy and explain how I fought each day to claim every inch of freedom that I 'seem' to have acquired today? Or should I write about those hundreds of ordinary Indians whom I saw surviving excruciatingly tiring battles every day to reclaim their bit of democratic skies?

 The reporter's life traces the many fault lines of our democracy – I've covered violence against women, crimes against Dalits, collapsing health infrastructure, farmer suicides, atrocities against minorities, trafficking of women and children, rape, child labour, hunger, malnutrition, tribal rights, excessive use of power by police, impact of conflict on children, citizenship-related crises and so on.

Over the years, while reporting, I discovered that perhaps the most fundamental form of freedom is the freedom of seeking forgiveness and the freedom to forgive. What drives me and so many women outside the tiny and often privileged world of the big cities to become journalists is often so deeply personal that it is hard to write about it, but to write it is also a kind of freedom and reclamation.

I earned one of the deepest wounds of my life when in late 2005 I told my parents that I wanted to be a journalist. I had just passed out of school as a science student with distinction and had also done reasonably well in engineering entrance exams. Reading and writing of any 'general' kind were alien concepts for my family. There were no books or bookstores close by. It was only later when I discovered the Swami Vivekananda Library situated in the heart of Bhopal that things slowly started to change for me.

All that my family knew about journalism was that it was a bad profession for girls. 'A profession which requires a girl to meet unknown men, go to bad places like police station, courts, jails and requires her to travel at odd hours is unsuitable not just for her but for the whole family. She will be scrubbing her torn slippers on roads [*chappal ghiste hue firegi*] and will bring only disgrace to us,' my uncle would tell my father on

Grief and the Freedom of Forgiving

the phone. '*Ladki haath se nikal jaayegi bhaiya,*' he would insist – the girl will slip out of your hands. Was I a kite or an object that could be kept in someone's hands, I wondered.

My family was dead against me taking up journalism. I have reported on so much violence, but *this* is the most delicate and the most wounded part of my life. It is not easy to share. What I can say is that they used extreme verbal and emotional violence to try to stop me. In their minds, my parents felt justified that the harm they were doing would protect me from the further harm of being 'exposed' to the world. '*Shareef gharon ki ladkiyan subah se raat tak bahar nahin fira karti,*' they would often repeat – girls from 'respectable families' don't stay out at odd hours. Their approach was filled with so much disgust and ferociousness that it dug a crater in my heart. That crater was so deep, so wide that I was not able to mend it for years.

I was only seventeen and I can't count the number of nights I spent howling alone. 'Why are they beating me?' I'd think as I sobbed myself to sleep. I now know that I was fighting patriarchy. But at that age, I felt the denial twice over – the denial of my choice of career and also the denial of my desire to shape my life. The wound ran deep because it was inflicted by my family, by the people I loved most. Those who should have trusted me in every situation demonstrated the deepest mistrust in my capabilities and character, in my integrity as a person. Later, I did manage to attend a journalism school. After surviving a long, persistent fight, my parents permitted me to enrol into a journalism course, unwillingly though. But the damage that my early domestic battles did to my soul was irreparable.

All my life, I was fuelled by this feverish desire to excel and succeed. Even though I did not like success very much. The poet Sahir Ludhianvi's words *'yeh duniya agar mil bhi jaaye toh kya hai'* are close to my heart – what does it matter even if you gain the whole world? I am a natural drifter. My instinctive sympathies are always with backbenchers and losers, humans who are labelled 'failures' by society.

But I wanted to succeed. So that I could convince my parents that I am a human – and not a bag of shame that deserves to be thrown out. I wanted to succeed so that other girls in my family could get a chance without suffering through the violence that I survived. Because my eternally nervous, impossibly lower-middle-class family only understood the language of success.

So I did succeed – whatever that means in the worldly ways of this material world. But I was never able to 'enjoy' any of it. I won medals for topping the university exams, national and international awards for my reporting. But I never invited my parents to the award ceremonies.

When my father asked if he could come, I lied to him that there was no seating available for parents. I would go to events alone, pick up the award, and later find a quiet corner to cry in, sometimes for hours.

Grief and the Freedom of Forgiving

One memory stays with me all through. I returned from my first day of work as an intern at the *Pioneer* at around 9.30 p.m. My mother was outside on the veranda, tears in her eyes, such hurt on her face that I have never forgotten it. I had brought immense shame on the family, she told me, by becoming the first girl in generations who stayed out so late. These basic freedoms – to have a say in your life, to go to work, to be out late like a man whose late working hours never risk bringing 'shame' on the family – some stubbornness drove me to claim them, no matter what I faced. I was not even nineteen. If my struggles and everything I was doing had brought shame to my family then, just because I was a woman, how could medals and the dozen awards I received over the years bring them joy?

∼

I swam in the sea of my own sorrows for years. My work took me to remote corners of India. I was reporting on caste atrocities, gender crimes, police excesses, human trafficking, crime against children and on rape, from one ocean of poisonous darkness to another. Reporting helped me see beyond my own suffering. It put me on the path of not only standing up with but also understanding, empathizing and expressing solidarity with the grief of others.

I witnessed infants dying in front of my eyes in semi-rural government hospitals, frozen bodies ridden with bullets, people killed in riots, girls burned alive after rape. A stark memory – I was interviewing survivors of child trafficking in upper Assam during the rains of 2013. A few of them took my hand in theirs and shared their nightmares, where they are still working as bonded labour. Their palms and hands were mutilated due to extreme physical labour of years.

For years, my first response to injustice and violence has been anger – that anger drives my writing. Injustice, violation of constitutional rights, patriarchy, rape, caste-based violence – all still make me angry and push me to jump on to the next story again. But the grief I was witnessing on an everyday basis was overwhelming and it added to my internal wounds.

To be a reporter in this country is to collect scars, both personal and on the work front, a collection that rivals any number of award certificates or medals. But as you travel, as you speak to people whose sufferings sometimes match your own, it sometimes dwarfs your own life experience – these deep scars can transform you once they enter your heart and your realm of lived experience.

Slowly, I began to locate my parents in the map of their own past. My mother and father have battled abject poverty and misery, growing up in nondescript villages of Bihar and later struggling to make a life in the suburbs of Bhopal. The opportunities I reached for in my own life were not available to either of them. My mother is unlettered, but she worked very hard to provide me with the education which gave me dreams that had been an unthinkable luxury for her. She single-handedly raised my two younger siblings and handled a whirlpool of tedious household chores, cooked, washed and mopped the whole day but never asked me to leave my reading desk. She allowed me to study and never forced me to assist her in domestic work like all girls of my family are mandatorily made to do. My father had lived in a cowshed for some years; he had given tuitions and sold milk to pay the fees for his school exams. The lives of my parents had been marked and scarred by poverty; they had weathered cycles of brutality, hardship and violence. The world has mostly been cruel and unkind to them, and that might have made it difficult for them to show me the understanding and support I'd craved. The moment I could see them through this prism, the anger I'd carried in my heart for so long began to dissolve. Through the cracks, compassion and forgiveness surged into my heart, and these are powerful emotions. I believe that if we are ever to break the cycles of violence and devastation around us, we must teach and learn forgiveness as a necessary practice – I have seen in my own life how much it can transform.

Thirteen years after I first dreamed of becoming a journalist, I invited my parents and my family to the launch of my first book, *No Nation for Women: Reportage on Rape from India, the World's Largest Democracy.*

It was a first for all of us. They have still not changed much, and they still ask me to do something more 'secure'. But instead of getting angry, I can smile at their suggestions.

One of my favourite ghazals by Mirza Ghalib has this

remarkable line: *Kabhi neki bhi uske jee mein gar aa jaaye hai mujhse, jafaayein kar ke apni yaad sharma jaaye hai mujhse* – Perhaps some day a sense of goodness and humanity might yet germinate in the heart of his persecutor, the poet wrote, and at that moment, he might feel ashamed of the hurt he had caused. You cannot ask someone to set aside their quest for revenge or vengeance, but you can hope that goodness and compassion might arise in the heart of the oppressor.

For breaking the cycle of unending violence and cruelty that we all are entangled in in our public and private lives, to be able to forgive is as important as seeking forgiveness.

This question of forgiveness again entered my life during the execution of the Nirbhaya convicts. I am not an academic, but I have lived through gender discrimination for a significant part of my life, reported on gender for eleven years and spent seven of those researching rape for my book. I have gained a little understanding of the degree of pain and suffering that unpardonable crimes like rape cause to those who survive them.

My heart was with the mother of the young woman who died of that terrible gang rape in December 2012; it will always be with her. Also, I am no one to question her right to ask for death penalty for the murderers of her child. And I dare not ask any because these are complicated, layered and knotted emotional human spaces. I do understand that the burden of violence that one lives through can be unbearable.

But the violence of hanging convicts also scars my soul.

Grief and the Freedom of Forgiving

I cannot speak for others as everyone has a right to decide for themselves. But I have seen enough bloodshed in my small life to know one more death will not eradicate the root of evil from our lives.

On the night of the execution of the Jyoti Singh gang rape convicts, trembling with horror, I woke up earlier than usual and called my mother. My work has sometimes taken me into situations of risk, in remote villages where no help is available, or where the community is hostile to reporters. For example, once while reporting undercover on women trafficking on the Neemuch–Mandsor highway in Madhya Pradesh, I was threatened by two middlemen involved in trafficking minor girls and forcing them into prostitution. Many women reporting in this field face the same risks. So I told my mother that if I ever met some unfortunate end, she should know that I would not want my killers to be hanged. That I forgive them.

Then with tears in my eyes, I wrote an email to a writer friend who has followed my work over the years. I repeated what I had told my mother. If I die due to a gender crime or any other crime, then please inform the courts that I would want forgiveness for my killers.

Because as Oscar Schindler has said, the one who saves one life saves the entire world.

I have burned myself for a decade on and off field to make myself think beyond my own immediate existence. Because I have learned that the moment you become willing to save another person's life at the cost of your own, you internalize forgiveness which not only elevates and forgives the other person, but also liberates you in unimaginable ways.

Because forgiveness is the only way through which we can reclaim our own humanity and compassion, which is otherwise decaying at an exponential rate in this cruel, brutal world.

Because forgiveness is the only answer through which we can protect, define and reclaim the meaning of being a human.

As my beloved author Caesar Pavese wrote in his last letter before leaving the world forever, 'I forgive everyone and ask for everyone's forgiveness. OK? Don't gossip too much . . .'

23

Afterword: A Brief History of Freedom

Pratap Bhanu Mehta

I

Freedom, like most good things in life – kindness, love, beauty, divinity, happiness – is perhaps a mystery that should not be rationalized beyond a point. I love my freedom; I resent it being taken away from me. But then I am reminded that the 'I' whose freedom I want to defend is itself an obstacle to freedom.

This 'I' – what in less polite times was called Ego – is my unfreedom. It is, as so many traditions from Sankara to the Buddha would have suggested, the source of delusion. To think of oneself as an 'I' is to be immediately bounded. Where is freedom if its horizons are limited to the admittedly upright pronoun 'I'? If the Self is bounded what kind of a freedom is this? It is freedom within a larger prison. How does one break its boundaries? By annihilating the 'I' that is the constraint, so many great thinkers intone. If we can overcome the Self – by pouring it into the Boundless Self (Brahman) or by annihilating it altogether – we will be set free.

But then immediately we are drawn back: If Freedom is the dissolution of *my* Self, how am *I* free? Perhaps I need a freedom with more finite horizons; my bounded Self is not the constraint on freedom, it is a precondition. 'I' constrain my own freedom seems like a cop-out, a metaphysical version of blaming the victim. Is dissolving the Self granting *me* freedom? Or is it simply changing the question? Taking me to a place where the question of freedom becomes irrelevant. Freedom speaking the language of escape, dissolving the Self that demands freedom in the first place. Perhaps freedom requires accepting our finitude and boundaries, not dissolving ourselves into oceanic consciousness.

Perhaps we come down a notch. My liberation is not in rescuing the Self from the chain of causation. My freedom is that 'I' can insert myself as a cause in the world. We like doing things. We make a difference by acting. We *make* the world. We *imagine* it differently. Our freedom is the fact that we are agents. The world is different because we act. It is sometimes made beautiful because we create lovely things. It is sometimes more dangerous because we ruin it by our actions – our freedom gives us the power to put the whole of earth into peril.

Afterword: A Brief History of Freedom

But as everyone who has been trapped by the free will and determinism paradox knows, I feel free because I think I am a 'cause'. But what if I am really an 'effect'? What if I am simply my genes, or my upbringing?

The world is nothing but a series of effects, and we are just that. We were reassuringly told by philosophers like Kant that we can act *as if* we are a cause. We assign blame and responsibility, resent and repent, as if we were *free* to act. We can never know the truth of whether we are free, but we can *pretend*. Or better, we cannot help pretending we are, whenever convenient, free. We can ascribe freedom to ourselves. That is good enough. But somewhere the thought still haunts you: Is freedom real?

But an even deeper thought haunts you. Freedom for whom? Historically freedom was simply an aristocratic hankering only a few could have. Indian thinkers called escaping the cycle of causation freedom, simply because the cycle of causation was such an unremitting tale of woe and suffering. Freedom was escape from the cycle of existence itself, since existence itself was a burden. Freedom as the negation of finite existence.

Even this is an escape reserved for only a few, for the virtuosos and the adept. Most remained condemned to the cycle of birth and rebirth. Perhaps only a society in which quotidian life was so regulated by the burden of caste identity could think of freedom as escaping all identity altogether, including the identity of the 'I'.

The Greeks were obsessed with freedom because it was the opposite of slavery: the cruel subjugation to someone else's will. But in this view freedom was not a right, or a condition, or the sweet elixir of existential lightness. It was a privilege. To defend freedom was to defend a privilege. And what is the privilege? Defining the boundaries of humanity: who is a barbarian, who can be made subordinate to our will?

The American promise of freedom, articulated in the language of rights, endowed by the creator, was similarly a privilege: a privilege to define who might count as human, or three-fourths human. Freedom was simply the assertion of privilege in a hierarchical society. This was how freedom also worked in the nineteenth century. Freedom was a pretext to colonize. The 'free' nations would subjugate the 'unfree' nations, ostensibly to emancipate them. Like with the Greeks freedom was about policing the boundaries of civilization.

Of course freedom was always a marker of boundaries. The great Republican freedoms, or all freedom, was freedom largely for men. 'Free labour' performed a similar function. It ostensibly liberated human beings from the bondage of serfdom, only to hand them over to another empire of necessity: free labour simply meant the freedom to sanctify our chains. We had no option but to sell our labour, on terms that we did not choose, for purposes we did not set. So, you see, freedom has historically always come with hierarchy; it has legitimized it, reproduced it, and not negated it.

There are those who have told us that we can always be

Afterword: A Brief History of Freedom

free. No hierarchy can really trap us. The Stoics told us even slavery could not take away our freedom. No matter what the external circumstances, we could shape our Self, steel it against any misfortunes. We were free to be an 'Inner Citadel'. The Romantics told us we were always free – free to imagine, free to create, free to sing. Artistic liberty had no essential connection with social or political liberty. It was, in fact, proof that no social or political subjugation can tame the empire of the imagination, the true location of freedom. Existentialists told us we are always free. To even think that we are constrained, by material necessity of external circumstances, is to give over to bad faith – to deny our freedom. We can always *choose* a different course. Indian thinkers tell us we are always free. All we need to do is reflect on our consciousness, or rather reflect on consciousness reflecting on consciousness. The chains of the external world will disappear; the Inner Eye will take us to a boundlessness that is always available. You simply have to assert it. It is really as simple. Existence is Freedom, if you simply care to look. In that case, why is it not easy to look? Why is it not easy to claim this freedom?

II

But we know what stands in the way of freedom. There was the tyranny of priests, in every religion, we said. Those who would use the authority of God's word or some esoteric knowledge to confine us. Those who would scare us that deviating from existing social forms would create disorder. Stay in your appointed place – your caste, your gender role – or hell will break loose.

Then we said there were tyrannical states, where the arbitrary will of some men was exercised over others through the power of the sword. Then we said there was the domination of those who controlled economic life: who expressed freedom through luxury, while keeping others in penury. Occasionally there was the foreigner, the alien power, subjugating our will for their own purposes. Get rid of the priests, and the kings and the aristocrats, and the foreign yoke, and freedom would come.

Freedom is not a philosophical idea. It is a social and political achievement. It has to be fought for daily. Power never yields freedom to others – it has to be snatched away from them.

In this dream of a social freedom revolutions were born. We discovered a few more things about freedom. Instead of priests, a new intellectual clerisy of the gifted could dominate us. The arbitrary power of kings could be replaced by the will of people; less arbitrary perhaps, but more demanding in its subjugation of the individual. The aristocrat could be replaced, but it turned out that he who controls capital controls power. We sought to shake off the foreign yoke, by uniting as a people.

But who is the people? That stunningly simple question seemed to create a new foreignness amidst us. Who gets included and who gets excluded? So the nation state – that

Afterword: A Brief History of Freedom

political form that might embody liberty, equality and fraternity – has also invented ethnic cleansing and genocide. The *process* of creating freedom turned out to be Janus-faced: excluding and killing, even as it prepared the conditions for freedom and democracy.

But new charters of hope were created. One was even called the Constitution of India. This Constitution had a Preamble. The Indian Preamble is spare and elegant because it is, somewhat unusually for preambles, not burdened with God, history or identity. Its pulsating heart and unredeemed promise is liberty, equality, fraternity and justice. This is not because God and history are not important. But it is because our Constitution liberates us to imagine them in whichever way we choose.

The Constitution presented a new source of hope. It created a new social contract. It promised those who had been socially ostracized, ritually excluded, materially deprived and politically marginalized a new freedom. It protected individual freedoms. But it also offered a new collective form of politics: where we relate to each other as equal citizens not enemies. The ties that bind us are not the ties of sameness but of reciprocity. It promised an India that would, to use Aurobindo's phrase, not belong 'to past dawns but noons of the future'. After all, can freedom mean anything if it is not oriented to a new, different, better future? If it is tied by the dead weight of the past, if it looks back not forward, can it be freedom?

Everyone understood this was not going to be easy. That slayer of all gods, and the scourge of all pretension, Dr B.R. Ambedkar, repeatedly told us as much. Power will not bow to new dreams so easily. We will have the exhilaration of making and unmaking our own government – which remains a most emphatic assertion of freedom. But without fraternity, that minimum bond of common sympathy, this freedom will always be what it has been: a marker of the privilege of the few, not the deliverance of the many. Unless the material basis of freedom – the minimum condition for social respect – is brought to all, freedom remains truly an illusion.

The opposite of freedom is not, as philosophers like to think, determinism. It is necessity: being confined to an existence where there is literally no choice if one has to survive. Yes, we can console ourselves that freedom from want has diminished.

There was a time when India's growth at 8 per cent created a new dream: tomorrow will be better than the present. That growth did expand opportunities for many, but it seemed to give more freedom to the plutocrats than comfort to the precariat. But, as the plight of millions of migrant workers reminded us, this is bare comfort.

In what form is freedom going to come? The material struggles to hold on to shards of freedom continue. They have, in some senses, always been the stuff of history. Freedom is tested in the struggle between those who have and those who are unfairly excluded: in the claims of agricultural workers,

Afterword: A Brief History of Freedom

Adivasis, domestic help, labour, small entrepreneurs and informal workers. Our Constitution was supposed to be the framework in which these claims could, with some modicum of justice, be addressed. It is at one level an expansion of freedom that no citizen is now seeking someone else's mercy or benevolence. They are claiming their rights, based on a sense of their own dignity.

Perhaps we underestimate the significance that the promise of a gas cylinder, sanitation, piped water and electricity holds out for freedom. Perhaps this is the freedom those who have been previously deprived now see in Prime Minister Modi. Will this freedom come in the form of better jobs, the sine qua non of freedom? After all what is freedom if not control over the circumstances of your work? Or will it require a basic income: a guarantee that no one has to ever experience deprivation, a floor that gives greater bargaining power to everyone to ensure they are not at the mercy of necessity? Or will economic mismanagement once again convert freedom from a material reality to a metaphysical obscurity?

III

There is extraordinary energy all around us. In democracies voters are still turning out. A bewildering variety of voices can be heard around us. We are seeing new levels of human inventiveness. Knowledge has been democratized like never before. But freedom turns out to be more paradoxical than we thought.

When we traditionally thought of freedom, we thought of the freedom to collectively remake the social world. The exhilaration of working with fellow citizens, on terms of reciprocity, to remake the contours of social existence, was a new kind of freedom we imagined. After all society was, to use Hobbes's word, 'artifice'. It was not Nature, whose contours were relatively fixed.

But it turned out that we acted as if we had more freedom over nature than we did over social arrangements. Humans have always tried to master nature – we have exercised, as part of our freedoms, a species privilege. But in doing so we transformed it beyond recognition, as if it was not a fragile system with laws of its own, but a plaything in our hands. The pandemic and climate change are perhaps ways in which nature reminds us of where our freedom transgressed its boundaries.

On the other hand, social arrangements turned out to be much less plastic, much less amenable to collective control than we imagined. Freedom as a political category is not just about the protection of individual rights; it is the experience that the collective terms of our existence are ones we could agree to and shape. But there seems to be an air of inevitability about the social forms we inhabit. Capitalism, the nation state: these circumscribe the horizons of freedom. We find it hard to think beyond them. Perhaps freedom will require the recognition of limits in the face of nature, and greater imagination in the face of social forms. For now, we seem to have things upside down.

Afterword: A Brief History of Freedom

Then there is this paradox. Does the very effort to have our desires fulfilled introduce new chains, new shackles? The power of states, in the literal sense of their control over their citizens, has grown. The Chinese are showing what a rival model of state control might look like, and liberal democracies like ours in India are enviously eyeing the possibility of emulating it.

Have we given up the freedom to define ourselves? We will be defined not as we choose to, but as the state and private entities decode us through our metadata. We also became more vicarious, intruding on moments in other people's lives. And a deeper concern: as everything about us is potentially colonized by the imperatives of state power or commercial needs, what we are left with is a wholesale instrumentalization of the self, where every action, every gesture, every thought ends up serving the logic of mammon or the state.

But the paradox is this. This power is acquired in our name. The state acquires power over us, in the name of protecting us, pre-empting threats to us. Private companies acquire power over us in the name of our own desires. They claim to fulfil our desires before we know them. The fears of their power may be overblown, but we are still left with a fissure in our sense of freedom. Many will see in this construction of us by state and capital a fulfilment of our freedom: our own desires being efficiently serviced. However, this triggers the old anxiety: if we render ourselves too transparent to others, if we constantly need to justify ourselves, we lose our freedom.

Perhaps freedom will require us to withdraw. Privacy is not about the wish to hide; it is about having a space which is truly one's own, where we are not instruments of someone else's purposes. Where will such a space be found?

The two most precious freedoms we have is the power to imagine and the power to define ourselves. The seat of freedom is not reason or truth, it is the imagination. Freedom resides in the imagination. Through the imagination we expand the boundaries of the Self, we overcome any quotidian limitations, and we imagine other worlds and other lives.

Reason is too coercive. Its conclusions are too authoritative. Its diktat inescapable. Two plus two equals four: I cannot get myself to deny that truth. Truth is too constraining. You have to adjust to the truth. Some exalted souls tell us that freedom is ultimately found only in Truth. But it feels more like that Truth might bludgeon Freedom. What kind of a freedom is this, if truth is my only choice?

My imagined Self is far more interesting, and often I think it is more me than my 'real' Self. The imagination seems less coercive, more expansive. Perhaps more fickle, but also more novel: more about invention than truth. Reasonable people believe in reason and truth; true pioneers imagine different worlds. There is a thrilling freedom in being able to deny the truth. We love this state of denial; and we increasingly love leaders who can enact that for us.

As the imagination expands freedom, so it can also constrict it. It allows us to live vicariously: through other

Afterword: A Brief History of Freedom

lives. But it can also create vicarious connections. In our imagination our life and the life of the nation can be fused. The vicarious thrill I get when Virat Kohli hits a six is a feat of the imagination – as if his six was my six. It allows that identification with a larger collectivity. The 'I' and the 'We' fuse together. I am lifted out of my insignificance. The glories of this 'We' become my glories. What an alchemy of the imagination.

This alchemy can also be a trap. It allows me to leave an 'I', only to lose myself in a 'We'. Instead of the narcissism of the Self (not pretty but harmless), I am now part of a collective narcissism (thrilling but potentially deadly).

Through the freedom to imagine, I also have the freedom to identify. This identification is thrilling; it is liberating; it can enjoin me to do good deeds.

And yet, as my teacher George Kateb used to remind us, in very strong attachments to groups, individuals acquire abstract passions. On the one hand, they alienate their own individuality. They are determined by something outside of themselves. This at once elevates them, makes them part of a larger and more enduring whole. On the other hand, their identities become abstract. They become one thing rather than another. Both this abstraction and self-surrender render individuals invisible even to themselves, curtailing their own sense of multitude and possibility. And they comprehend others only through abstract identifications. The very imagination that was meant to liberate us, by producing this identification, also limits us. It is as if the imagination takes us out of a small prison only to dump us in a larger one.

Freedom chafes at the limits of this prison. This prison has a name: identity. Identities matter to people. They have to be recognized because often people are targeted simply for being who they are. But identity is also a foe of freedom. The mere act of naming itself is a loss of freedom in two ways. On the one hand, it constricts us. It makes us one thing rather than another. On the other hand, in this world, the mere act of naming takes away the power of self-definition from you.

As an act of freedom I might want to say 'I am Indian', 'I am Hindu', 'I am Muslim'. I identify with these categories. By some act of imagination those others who identify with me also become mine. I can identify with different categories; I can have multiple allegiances. But each act of naming seems to bind me to a script. What behaviour will entitle me to use that name? As identities abound, so do scripts. Who is a good Indian? Who is a good Hindu? Who is a good Muslim? What set of expectations are associated with those terms? Our imagination creates these identities, and the identity in turn limits the reach of our imagination, and often our empathy.

IV

This potted history of freedom – the different concepts, the different sites in which it is articulated, and the threats to it

Afterword: A Brief History of Freedom

– is meant as a reminder of the complexity of freedom. It is also a bit tragic in cast: a gain in one dimension of freedom may entail a loss in another dimension. The several essays, poems, short stories, ruminations that you have read in this volume chart the contemporary struggle for freedom in vivid and telling detail.

Without using these terms they traverse over the four freedoms that Roosevelt talked about: freedom of speech, freedom of worship, freedom from want, but most importantly freedom from fear. But what marks this moment of struggles over freedom, in their brave, courageous, poetic voices, is the sense of heaviness in this struggle. They are speaking to a contemporary moment in India when the twin spectres of communalism and authoritarianism seem to be haunting Indian politics. Why India has come to such a pass is a question that requires systematic analysis.

This book offers something more valuable. These essays document and enact the acts of resistance: the small constitutional victories, the acts of protest, the clinging on to truth in the face of lies, the expansion of empathy in moments of hate.

What makes this moment paradoxical is that the very expressions of freedom, the very institutions that were meant to protect it, have become its enemies. When democracy becomes majoritarian democracy, which power higher than the people do we appeal to? When the institutions that provided checks and balances now act as instruments in the armoury of repression, who do we appeal to? When the work of the imagination is now devoted to constricting our identities, expanding the circle of enemies rather than the ambit of empathy, which faculty do we turn to? When love becomes a crime because it transgresses the script of identity, what other sentiment do we draw on? When the economic future looks less promising, does our fulfilment come from the comforts of reimagining the past? When truth is seen as boring, isn't there a performative attraction to those who can situate themselves above truth? When the process of coming together in a public sphere simply deepens partisan rancour and diminishes our ability to work together, what will change our politics?

These are disquieting questions. But India has a long history of wrestling with these questions, and the intellectual depth to take them on again. And these essays, stories and poems draw our attention to one simple fact: the only way to claim freedom is to start practising it.

24

Ghazal: India's Season of Dissent

Karthika Naïr

This year, this night, this hour, rise to salute the season of dissent.
Sikhs, Hindus, Muslims – *Indians*, all – seek their nation of dissent.

We the people of . . . they chant: the mantra that birthed a republic.
Even my distant eyes echo flares from this beacon of dissent.

Kolkata, Kasargod, Kanpur, Nagpur, Tripura . . . watch it spread,
tip to tricoloured tip, then soar: the winged horizon of dissent.

Dibrugarh: five hundred students face the CAA and lathi-
wielding cops with Tagore's song – an age-old tradition of dissent.

Kaagaz nahin dikhayenge . . . *Sab Kuch Yaad Rakha Jayega* . . .
Poetry, once more, stands tall, the Grand Central Station of dissent.

Karthika Naïr

Aamir Aziz, Kausar Munir, Varun Grover, Bisaralli ...
Your words, in many tongues, score the sky: first citizens of dissent.

We shall see / Surely, we too shall see. Faiz-saab, we see your greatness
scanned for 'anti-Hindu sentiment', for the treason of dissent.

Delhi, North-East: death flanks the anthem of a once-secular land
where police now maim Muslims with *Sing and die, poison of dissent.*

A government of the people, by the people, for the people,
has let slip the dogs of carnage for swift excision of dissent.

Name her, Ka, name her. Umme Habeeba, mere-weeks-old, braves frost and
fascism from Shaheen Bagh: our oldest, finest reason for dissent.

for #TurbineBagh

Copyright Acknowledgements

'The Actual Shafi Shauq', Amit Chaudhuri, first published in the *Indian Express*, 15 March 2020, Copyright © Amit Chaudhuri 2020.

'An Evening Walk', Akhil Katyal, first published in *Shimmer Spring*, edited by Kiriti Sengupta (Hawakal: 2020), Copyright © Akhil Katyal 2020.

'Exile in the Age of Modi', Aatish Taseer, first published as 'India Is No Longer India', *The Atlantic*, May 2020, Copyright © Aatish Taseer 2020.

'Ghazal: India's Season of Dissent', Karthika Naïr, was written for #Turbinebagh, the movement visual artist Sofia Karim initiated in support of Shaheen Bagh and the anti-CAA protests, which was to culminate in a platform in the Turbine Hall of Tate Modern on 28 March 2020. It was postponed due to the Covid-19 pandemic. First published in SAMAJ, France (December 2020), Copyright © Karthika Naïr 2020.

A Note on the Contributors

Roshan Ali is a writer; his first novel, *Ib's Endless Search for Satisfaction*, was shortlisted for the 2019 Shakti Bhatt First Book Prize and the 2019 JCB Prize for Literature.

Rana Ayyub is an award-winning journalist, columnist for the *Washington Post* and author of *Gujarat Files* (2016).

Amitabha Bagchi lives in New Delhi and is the author of four novels, *Above Average*, *The Householder*, *This Place* and *Half the Night Is Gone*, which won the DSC Prize for South Asian Literature 2019.

Gautam Bhatia is a lawyer and the author of *The Transformative Constitution: A Radical Biography in Nine Acts* (2019) and *Offend, Shock or Disturb: Free Speech Under the Indian Constitution* (2018).

A Note on the Contributors

Amit Chaudhuri is a novelist, poet, editor and musician and a Fellow of the Royal Society of Literature in the UK.

Priyanka Dubey is the author of *No Nation for Women: Reportage on Rape from India, the World's Largest Democracy*, and has reported extensively on social justice across India.

Yashica Dutt is the author of *Coming Out as Dalit*, a memoir that is also the narrative of Dalits, and lives in New York City.

Deepa Ganesh is a translator whose translations include *Hunt Bangle Chameleon: Selected Short Stories of UR Ananthamurthy*, and several memoirs from Kannada into English; she is the author of *A Life in Three Octaves: The Musical Journey of Gangubai Hangal*.

Dr Menaka Guruswamy is a senior advocate at the Supreme Court of India and is the co-editor of *Founding Moments in Constitutionalism* (2019).

Raghu Karnad is the 2019 winner of Yale's Windham-Campbell Prize for non-fiction, the author of *Farthest Field: An Indian Story of the Second World War* and part of the founding team of *The Wire*.

Akhil Katyal is a poet and teacher; his books include *Like Blood on the Bitten Tongue*, *How Many Countries Does the Indus Cross* and *Night Charge Extra*.

A Note on the Contributors

T.M. Krishna is a Carnatic vocalist, writer and public intellectual; his books include *Sebastian and Sons: A Brief History of Mrdangam Makers*, which won the 2020 TATA Literature Live! Book of the Year Award – Non-Fiction, *Reshaping Art* and *A Southern Music: The Karnatik Story*.

Aanchal Malhotra is an oral historian, writer and artist; she is the author of *Remnants of a Separation: A History of the Partition through Material Memory*.

Pratap Bhanu Mehta is an academician, former vice chancellor of Ashoka University and one of India's most widely read columnists; his books include *Navigating the Labyrinth: Perspectives on India's Higher Education* and *The Burden of Democracy*.

Suketu Mehta is the author of *Maximum City: Bombay Lost and Found* and *This Land Is Our Land: An Immigrant's Manifesto*, and teaches journalism at New York University.

Perumal Murugan is a novelist, poet and short-story writer, whose books have been translated from Tamil into a score of Indian and other languages; his works include *One Part Woman*, *The Goat Thief*, *Pyre* and *Poonachi*.

A Note on the Contributors

Karthika Naïr is a poet, librettist and dance producer whose works include *Until the Lions: Echoes from the Mahabharata* and the script of Akram Khan's dance solo *DESH*.

Snigdha Poonam is a journalist and writer; her first book, *Dreamers*, won the 2018 Crossword book award for non-fiction.

Gyan Prakash is a historian and the author of *Mumbai Fables* (2010), *Bonded Histories: Genealogies of Labor Servitude in Colonial India* (1990) and *Another Reason: Science and the Imagination of Modern India* (1999).

N. Kalyan Raman is a Chennai-based writer and translator; his translations from Tamil into English include works by Devibharathi, Vaasanthi, Perumal Murugan, Poomani and Ashokamitran.

Vivek Shanbhag is a novelist, playwright, short-story writer and editor who writes in Kannada; his novel *Ghachar Ghochar* was translated into English in 2017.

Aatish Taseer is a British-American writer and journalist; his books include *The Temple-Goers* and *The Twice-Born: Life and Death on the Ganges*.

Romila Thapar is an Indian historian and the author and editor of over twenty books, including *Early India: From*

A Note on the Contributors

Origins to AD 1300 (2002) and *The Past As Present: Forging Contemporary Identities Through History* (2014).

Salil Tripathi is a writer based in New York and chairs PEN International's Writers in Prison committee; his books include *The Colonel Who Would Not Repent: The Bangladesh War and Its Unquiet Legacy* and *Detours: Songs of the Open Road*.

Annie Zaidi is a playwright, poet, novelist and short-story writer; her novel *Prelude to a Riot* won the 2020 TATA Literature Live! Book of the Year Award – Fiction.

THE APP FOR INDIAN READERS

Fresh, original books tailored for mobile and for India. Starting at ₹10.

juggernaut.in

1

CRAFTED FOR MOBILE READING

Thought you would never read a book on mobile? Let us prove you wrong.

juggernaut.in

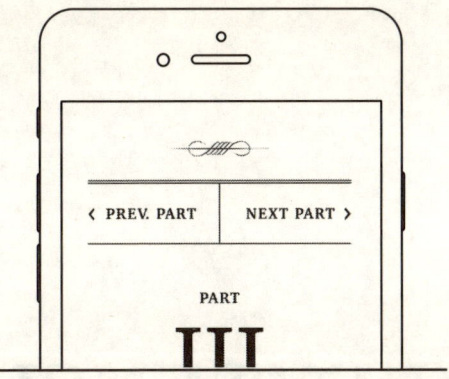

Beautiful Typography

The quality of print transferred to your mobile. Forget ugly PDFs.

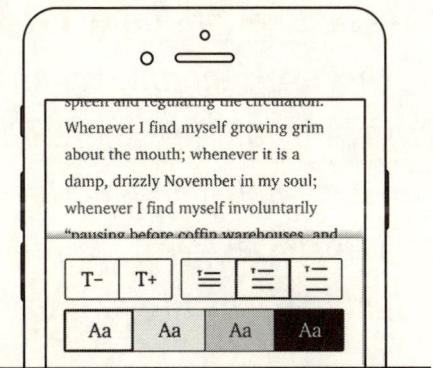

Customizable Reading

Read in the font size, spacing and background of your liking.

juggernaut.in

AN EXTENSIVE LIBRARY

Including fresh, new, original Juggernaut books from the likes of Sunny Leone, Praveen Swami, Husain Haqqani, Umera Ahmed, Rujuta Diwekar and lots more. Plus, books from partner publishers and loads of free classics. Whichever genre you like, there's a book waiting for you.

juggernaut.in

juggernaut.in

3

DON'T JUST READ; INTERACT

We're changing the reading experience from passive to active.

juggernaut.in

Ask authors questions

Get all your answers from the horse's mouth. Juggernaut authors actually reply to every question they can.

Rate and review

Let everyone know of your favourite reads or critique the finer points of a book – you will be heard in a community of like-minded readers.

Gift books to friends

For a book-lover, there's no nicer gift than a book personally picked. You can even do it anonymously if you like.

Enjoy new book formats

Discover serials released in parts over time, picture books including comics, and story-bundles at discounted rates. And coming soon, audiobooks.

juggernaut.in

4

LOWEST PRICES & ONE-TAP BUYING

Books start at ₹10 with regular discounts and free previews.

juggernaut.in

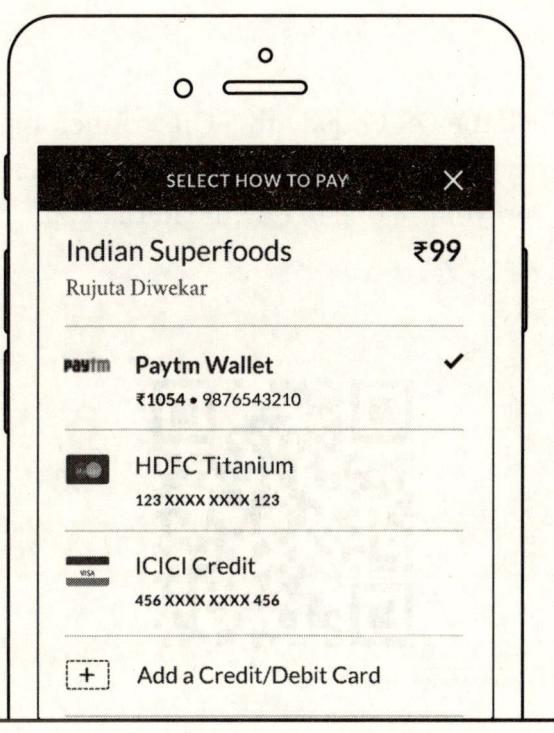

Paytm Wallet, Cards & Apple Payments

On Android, just add a Paytm Wallet once and buy any book with one tap. On iOS, pay with one tap with your iTunes-linked debit/credit card.

Click the QR Code with a QR scanner app or type the link into the Internet browser on your phone to download the app.

For our complete catalogue, visit www.juggernaut.in
To submit your book, send a synopsis and two sample chapters to books@juggernaut.in
For all other queries, write to contact@juggernaut.in